Covington Hang

A Novel of the Civil War

Lee Cooper

Covington Hang
A Novel of the Civil War

Copyright © 2025 Lee Cooper

Deucecoop Press

Paperback ISBN 979-8-9920545-0-7

Printed in the United States of America

For Bill, in fields of stone, against the wind

In Memory Of

Alta Mae Covington Smith, my maternal grandmother,
who was proud of anything I accomplished
Georgia Carder, my sister, who thought I was a good writer
Sally Hilderman, my sister, who simply believed in me

1

The Cave

Eliza Ann

THERE IS NO path. The way is marked by marble outcroppings that glitter in the sun, the shape and shade of certain chestnuts and chinquapins. It follows the slopes and hollows of the land as it rises into blue ridges, behind our farm. I'm not good at much, but I do have a sense of direction.

Hiking up to the cave is our reward at laying-by time, after the fields and gardens have been planted and hoed and the corn is growing higher than the weeds. I know most girls my age wouldn't think of it as a reward or adventure. I'm fourteen, the youngest girl in our family, and taller than all of my sisters. I still wear my hair in a single braid. I have been told I ought to pay attention to other things than reading books or going into the woods for the fun of it.

It is the summer of the War, and eleven states have seceded from the Union. No one knows what this will bring. We get real news from our neighbor, Mr. Monroe, when he travels to Canton. The rest from rumors that don't make sense. We do know that the school has closed, and my four older brothers may have to join the Confederate Army.

I learned the woods from my brother Ananias. He's eighteen, the middle one of our eleven. To us youngest ones, he's our leader and best brother. Because of him, we know where to find patches of wild strawberries, bee trees, and groves of sassafras. Because of him we generally get along.

Mary Jane and I carry the dinner baskets. We packed them with ham biscuits, green onions, boiled eggs, butter cakes, and peaches. She is sixteen and small, my closest sister.

Tom is seventeen and follows Ananias like a shadow, not saying much and toting more than his share. The twins, Luke and Lafe, are twelve and trail behind us, hitting at trees with sticks they pretend are swords, racing ahead to jump out and scare me and Mary Jane, running back to pick up the blankets they've dropped.

Our last resting place before the steep, rocky slope up to the cave is at the bent oak of a Cherokee way-marker. They were driven from this land before my family and most of our neighbors moved here, but folks still call it Cherokee Georgia.

We drop our baskets, drink from water jugs, sit on rocks, and admire the view south, past the farm hidden in its valley, to land that flattens beyond the thin ribbon of the Etowah River. None of us have been there, but we know that Atlanta and most of Georgia are on the other side of the river.

The cave is a relief from the heat and the climb. Cool air moves across its walls. We set to cleaning out blown leaves and the bones of small animals. The twins gather wood, and Tom lays a fire near the entrance. Mary Jane and I unload the baskets for a cold supper. With dusk coming on, Ananias lights the fire, red hair shining in the glow, the angles of his face lit up. He doesn't touch his food.

I bite into a butter cake. Across the fire, Ananias stares into the flames. It's his way of avoiding talk. He must know I'll start asking questions if he doesn't talk. I always do and sometimes get so caught up in the complications that I forget where I started. But I really do want to know the answers.

"Are you worried about what we'll do if the War comes to Georgia?" I ask.

He looks up at me.

"That is not the most companionable thing to talk about while sitting by a fire," he says.

"But it's what I want to know about."

"Depends on how the Confederate Army fights. If what they say is true about whipping the Federals with cornstalks and getting it over before harvest, they don't have much time."

"Do you wish you could go?"

"I do," Luke pitches in.

"You're too young, and Pap wouldn't let you go anyways," Ananias says.

Luke can't keep a secret and would be the last one any of us would tell of plans and dreams. Tom probably knows what Ananias is thinking, and he would keep it to himself.

"You think he'd let any of us?" Lafe asks.

"No. You all know why, and I don't want to talk about it," Ananias answers.

He gathers up his blanket and walks away from the cave, the fire, and me, the sister who cares most. I look around at the rest. Tom lifts his hands and shakes his head. Mary Jane starts cleaning up the food.

"Why doesn't he want to talk about it?" Luke asks.

"It might be too much for him to take on right now," Tom says.

***

The dying coals blink like small red stars. Ananias hasn't come back into the cave. I listen for the even breathing of Mary Jane and the twins. Tom is snoring. I pull my blanket over my back and creep into the darkness outside. Small birds and animals rustle and settle in the underbrush. *Hoo, hoo-hoo*, an owl's call spooky in the night. White with stars, the sky opens above me. The Great Bear tips like a milk dipper pouring out more stars. The Little Bear has the North Star at the tip of its tail, as sure a way-marker as the Cherokee tree. Cassiopeia the Queen, Pegasus the Winged Horse, Corona Borealis the Northern Crown, I love saying their exotic names. Ananias has shown me where to look for the constellations, summer and winter, taught me their names and how they move across the sky. When I was afraid of the dark, he told me they would be my companions in the night. A shooting star streaks bright.

"You see that?" he asks.

I can just make him out in the starlight, his back against the side of the cave, knees hugged to his chest.

"You didn't answer my question," I say.

"Because you won't like the answer."

"You're not going to join up are you?"

"I am. Before the War comes to Georgia."

I sit down next to him and lean my shoulder against his.

"What about Pap?" I ask.

"I know he thinks this war is wrong. I do, too."

"Then why would you want to go?"

"Because it's the biggest thing to happen in our lives, and I want to see it for myself. There's places I'll never get to if I stay on the farm, towns bigger than Jasper. Virginia has those sea-faring ships we read about. I might see one of those whales. It would be my own way, different than David, away from Howell."

How can I convince him not to do this? If the War hadn't caused the school to close he probably wouldn't. My favorite brother, the only one who takes my book-learning seriously, how can he think it would be good to fight in a war that split the Union?

I believe the lesson Pap uses, the fable of the farmer whose sons are quarrelling. He hands each of them a bundle of sticks to break. When they can't, he gives them the sticks to break one by one. He tells them if they stay together their enemies can't injure them, but if they're divided among themselves they will be no stronger than a single stick. The moral is Strength in Unity. I think the same of our family. If Ananias goes to war, or any of my brothers, our family will be divided, with less sticks to keep the bundle strong, just like Pap said the seceding states have done to the Union.

"What about Howell and David? Or Tom? What if they want to go?" I ask.

"That would be theirs to decide. I've had a hard enough time reckoning this out for myself."

"Tom would follow what you do. I know you two have a plan."

"Tom's too young, for now. And I don't want to talk yet about any plan."

"When are you going to tell Pap?"

"When I get my thoughts in order. So he'll understand."

I pull my blanket tighter around me. No one stands up to Pap. If the boys go against him, it will be worse than a bundle with missing sticks. Our family would crack and fall apart, like the shards of a broken crock.

2

Homecoming

October 1861, Covington Farm,
Pickens County, Georgia

Eliza Ann

SWEEPING THE PORCHES and the passage between them is one of my chores. It isn't hard. I can daydream and move the broom at the same time.

A man walks over the top of the lane with a girl. He raises his hat and chases away the hissing, honking geese. They return, snaking out their long necks, flapping wide gray wings.

He hollers out, "Eliza Ann, come get the geese off me!"

It's David. We've been expecting him home from harvest work in Gordon County. But who's that with him?

I jump off the porch and run up the lane, waving the broom at the geese. The unsmiling girl stares at me. I must look like a wild woman. She wears a purple dress, a red and green plaid wool cape, and a straw hat.

"Eliza Ann, meet Lydia," David says. "My wife."

"You're married?" I squeak out the words.

"Last week in Calhoun."

I smile at my new sister-in-law. She has curly black hair and golden brown eyes. I say, in what I think is a friendly way, "Glad to meet you, Lydia. What's your family name?"

"Covington."

"I mean before you married David."

"Any name I had before that is not one I want and none of your never mind."

This is not a good start. If she acts like this with the rest of the family, it's going to be a long winter. I follow them down the lane. The whole family comes out, Mam and my sisters on the porch, Pap and the boys from the barn.

"Hey, you all, meet my wife," David says, putting his arm around her. "This is Lydia."

Mam recovers first and walks down the steps, smiling and holding out both hands. She takes Lydia's hand and says, "Welcome to the family. We had no idea David intended to marry. We never know what he'll have done when he comes home, but this is the best surprise. Let's get you settled. Supper's on. You've come just in time to help with hog-killing."

Everyone else is speechless.

I latch the gate. Cedar wood-smoke rises from both chimneys of our double-log house. The front porch runs the full length of it, big enough for the whole family to sit out in fair weather. I sit down on the bottom step and stretch out my legs. Might as well let the excitement die down. In all my worrying about how the War would change our family, adding to it is not something I've reckoned on.

***

"I met her at a dance, and she wouldn't come home with me until I married her," David says, waving a ladle and taking another helping of rabbit stew. "So I bought her a new dress and took her to the Justice of the Peace."

I sneak a sideways look at Lydia who has not said more than "pleased to meet you" to Mam and Pap and answered my sister Rebecca with "no, I don't know how to sew" in a tone that makes me think she doesn't want to and won't. She eats with her head down, arm curled around the bowl, gulping down the stew. Clearly, she has some edges to her.

"There's a new call for volunteers," David says. "I saw it before we left Calhoun."

We all sit up straighter.

"From where?" Pap asks.

If he listens to anyone, it's David. I look over at Ananias. He hasn't talked anymore about wanting to go. Maybe what David has to say will convince him to stay.

"Five infantry regiments from the north counties. Five thousand men. There's fifty dollars in bounty pay for volunteers. Mister Young owns the biggest store in Calhoun and plans to raise a company. With the armies in winter camp, I told him I'd join up come spring. Maybe bring my brothers."

I'm sick to my stomach. Pap opens and closes his mouth, dumbfounded.

"What ages would they be taking?" Ananias asks.

"Anyone over eighteen," David answers.

"Why not wait for another company to form here?"

"I admire Mr. Young. People listen to him. He's not a rash man."

"Stop!" Pap shouts and smacks the flat of his hand on the table he made, along with every other piece of furniture in the house, from the oaks in our woods.

"This war is not about any right but the one to hold slaves. The planters who want it don't give a whit about this family or this farm. Have you listened to anything I've said?

"In the end, you won't have a say," David says. "If we don't sign up as volunteers, we'll be conscripted. I'd rather take the bounty money and go with a good man."

"You'd do it for the money?"

"It's not as shameful as being arrested by conscription men and sent to an outfit that doesn't want you."

"I won't have it. Just because some storekeeper in Gordon County wants to be an officer is no reason why I should send my sons to fight for a false cause."

"I want to know what Ananias and Tom are thinking," David says.

"I'll sign up when you do," Ananias says.

"Why?" Pap asks, his body shaking in anger.

"I want to know for myself what war is about, how I will do in it, my own way."

"So you'd go to a war that's wrong to prove you're a man?"

"Something like that."

"What about you?" Pap turns to Tom.

"I'll go with Ananias."

Pap glares around the table. I shrink lower, hoping he doesn't think I know anything about this. He'd never ask us girls what we think.

"Everything I believe in goes with the Union and its flag," he says. "I stood overnight in the cold to see it was kept flying over Jasper. If you all go in the Confederate cause, I can no longer call you my sons."

"You can't disown all of us," David says, almost cheerfully.

That's David's way, everything with the wink of a blue eye and a grin. He can talk most of us into anything. Lydia must be a challenge for him.

"You'll have no one left but the twins to work the farm," he says. "Besides, you taught us to make up our own minds."

"Young men do foolish things," Pap says. "This is one of them."

"Would you have gone as a young man?" Ananias asks.

Pap hesitates. "I would've been proud to fight the British to form this country. I can't see the pride in splitting it over slavery."

"I don't either," Ananias says. "But hiding out when everyone else goes is shameful, and I won't be taken as a conscript. How will you feel if you send us off in anger and we die in battle?"

Pap scrapes his chair back. "My heart will die. You know nothing of war."

***

The tension between Pap and my brothers has us eating meals in silence. Pap spends time in the barn, hammering wood. David and Lydia stay closed up in the back sleeping room. Ananias goes to the woods alone. Tom never has much to say, and now he says even less.

I take any chance to be out on the porch, this time to scrape muddy shoes. The north wind blows the smell of manure scattered in our fields. Dry corn stalks, withered pea vines, and broken pumpkins litter the patchwork of fields tilting up and down our hilly land. Mounded in dirt-covered piles, Irish potatoes and sweet potatoes are drying before the digging in for winter storage. In the garden, winter collards, kraut-cabbage, and turnips wait for harvesting.

The geese strut up the lane, eating burr weeds along the fence. They are not the most agreeable creatures, but I do admire how they pair up for life and watch over their families. Pap will not keep dogs. He says geese are better at scaring off intruders and don't have to be tied up or fed much. The ruckus they raise is often our first warning of visitors, human or animal. Like they're doing now, honking about something.

Ansell Bowen appears over the top of the lane, riding a bony mare. His wrists and hands stick out from ragged shirt cuffs. Despite his shabby appearance, he is known for getting the best of a deal, no matter what it takes. He and Pap have a running feud over a piece of land.

I set the shoes on the step and stand up straight. There has to be something good I can make of being tall for a girl.

"Your pap to home?" he asks, stopping at the closed gate.

The look of him is hateful. The only good Bowens are slow-witted Kize and the brothers closest to him, Ike and Joe, who, in the face of Pap's loud disapproval, have never given up on courting my older sisters, Rebecca and Charlotte.

"Not close by," I answer, thinking it might make him leave.

"I heard your brother's home from Gordon County."

"You come all the way here to tell us that?" The sassiness of it slips out.

"I come to tell your pap how his standing with the Unionists will be remembered. If your brothers hide out, I'll point the Militia your way. Just a friendly warning."

"That would be the first friendly thing you've said. Didn't know you cared so much about our family."

"Tell your brothers to watch out. My boy Luther told me about you. Says you think you're right smart."

"He's too dumb to know."

We both reel back from my retort. I've never talked back to an adult before.

"Watch out for your own self." He turns and rides up the lane.

The thought bothers me, of Luther doing more than hounding me at school, snickering during my recitations, following me to the privy. I'd always stood up for myself, knowing Ananias and our teacher, Mr. Woodall, would back me up. Without them, I'd be alone in the face of Luther's nastiness.

3

Hog-Killing

Eliza Ann

"ELIZA ANN! IT'S time for you to be up," Rebecca calls from the stairs. "We've got hogs to kill."

I pull the pillow over my head. Rebecca has the need to tell me when I should be up and working, what I ought to be doing, and why what I am doing isn't good enough.

All of my sisters are different. Louise so quiet and capable, pale and freckled. Rebecca, dark and outspoken with her high standards. Charlotte, a wispy strawberry blonde, shy and tender-hearted. She mothers every young and growing thing from budded flowers and downy chicks to me and Mary Jane, her youngest sisters. Mary Jane could be a twin to Tom except she's the shortest in the family. From Pap we have light hair, blue eyes, and stocky builds. Dark hair, brown eyes, and lankiness come from Mam. In each of us, it's all mixed up. Our temperaments are too.

I drag myself downstairs into the noise of my oldest brother Howell and his wife Callie arriving with their two small girls. They have a farm over in Dawson County, but our whole family works together for hog-killing.

"Try this for your nerves," Louise says and hands me a steaming mug. "Jane gave me the receipt."

I never say no to her. She's my oldest sister. I take a sip, tasting mint, sugar, chamomile, and the bite of Moody Simpson's whiskey.

"Are you sure this will help?"

"If it don't kill you first. Just drink it and don't eat much."

That makes me smile. No one has ever died from trying one of Jane Graham's receipts but it isn't out of the question.

"Just because you can't eat her cooking doesn't mean her receipts are bad," Louise says. "Seems you could kindly use some extra help today."

She's right. Hog-killing is the time of feasting and plenty, when everyone looks forward to fresh meat. I dread it. The first time I saw Pap slide a knife down the belly of a dead hog, hind legs spread by a hickory gambrel, guts spilling into a wash tub, I retched and gagged all the way to the back of the smoke house and vomited next to a pool of hog blood. I've done the same every year since. Thinking about it makes my stomach turn.

I'm not particularly tender-hearted about other dead animals, just partial to hogs and sickened by the way they're treated in the killing—knocked on the head, throat slit, legs spread, belly sliced. It isn't wrong to favor an animal. All of us indulge

Cassiopeia the sow, queen of the barnyard. Tom thinks mules are smarter than people. Mam coddles General Cornwallis, if a rooster could ever be coddled. And Mary Jane has secret names for the barn cats.

Feeling strangely calm, and a little tipsy, I carry the slop buckets out to Cassiopeia and the young boars Pap has saved out to sell. In the other pen, the gilts fattened for butchering rush the gate. I've fed them from the time they were weaners, scampering around my feet, rolling over to have their bellies scratched, turning for me to tickle their ears, fetching the corn cobs I toss. Ananias and Tom walk up to kill the first one. I turn away.

***

It's a cold and windy day, perfect weather for hog-killing. I'm standing across the wash boiler from Mary Jane as I have always started out, Rebecca eyeing me for when Charlotte will have to take over my job. Tied at the head and legs, throat-slit and bled out, the dead hog bobs in the boiling water. I twist my end of the rope, rolling the hog back and forth until its hair loosens. Ananias and Tom pull it onto the butchering boards. Louise pours hot water over it. Rebecca, Charlotte, and Callie grab and scrape the hair off every inch of hide from the hocks to the ears. Lydia joins in, knowing exactly what to do. Just what I need. One more older sister competent enough to lord it over me, even if she can't sew.

Howell and David stretch the hind legs apart with a gambrel and hang the hog from a porch beam. Pap raises his knife and slides it down the hog's belly. Bile rises in my throat. I think hard of how Louise wants to help me, what Lydia might think of me.

I swallow it down and will it not to come back up. It doesn't. Must be the whiskey numbing me. I look up and see the whole family staring, waiting for me to be sick before they go back to stoking the fire, cutting off the head and hocks, and making ready for the next dead hog.

"You did it," Mary Jane says, nudging me. "Well, at least you didn't do it."

Rebecca looks disappointed when I pick up my end of the rope. Five more hogs to take a hammer to the head, bleed out, roll in hot water, and slit open.

At the end of the day my arms ache, and I'm soaked to the skin. Mary Jane and I scour the plank table of the hair, bits of hide, and flesh that stick to it.

"You lasted the whole day," she says. "I was glad having you with me instead of Charlotte. You're stronger."

"It was because of Louise. And Jane's receipt. Too bad it won't last."

"Look around at what you helped do!"

Six carcasses hang from the porch roof. Six heads stare up from a tub. Hocks stick out of a pail. Intestines, kidneys, sweetbreads, and brains wobble in bowls and basins. The twins are kicking blown-up bladders for Howell's little girls to chase after. The smell coming from the house is the frying of fresh livers seasoned with red pepper. Everything I've missed out on in past years. It's childish to wish it didn't have to come from hogs.

***

We've been up since before first light tending to flesh, bone, and fat. It means ribs for roasting, hocks for dumplings, tenderloin, fresh meat to give to neighbors who return the favor after their own hog-killings. There's bones for jelly, head meat for souse. Hams, shoulders, and side-meat middlings for salting, smoking over hickory coals, and left hanging to cure. Fried sausage patties to be jarred and sealed in grease. Cracklings packed in fine white lard for flavoring corn bread and pudding. All of it women's work.

A kettle of backbones and cabbage simmers at the back of the fire. Chopped brains sizzle in hot butter for Ananias's favorite dish. One thing he and Pap have in common.

Ananias sits down, and I hand him a plate of brains and eggs fresh from the pan. Pap smiles at him over his own plate.

"Nothing like it, is there?" he asks.

"Makes all the work worth it," Ananias answers.

I look around the table at my brothers, eating biscuits and apple butter, brains and eggs. It looks like a good start to the day.

"So, schoolboy," Howell says. "I hear you're going to war."

So much for a good day. I'm not sure if Howell really wants to talk or is angling for a rise out of Ananias, something he's been doing ever since I can remember. It's lately that he's started calling him "schoolboy."

"You interested in going too?" Ananias asks.

I can tell by the red spot on his forehead how close he is to anger. If Howell notices, he's not saying.

"Not really. I've got a farm to tend, a wife, babies to raise."

"Would you go with conscription?"

Howell passes his hand over his dark beard and around to the back of his neck, a familiar gesture of discomfort. He's named for Mam's side of the family and takes after them in dark hair and eyes.

"I'd volunteer before that," he says. "Seems strange though, being Unionists joining the Confederate Army just to avoid conscription."

"There's bound to be some who hide out," David says. "Others like us are waiting."

Pap keeps his head down, eating. Ananias does too, probably relieved that it's David and Howell talking.

"How can we join what we don't think is right?" Howell asks.

"That's the worst of it," David says. "We almost have to. Even Joe Brown held back the Militia hoping the War would end before he had to send Georgia boys to fight in Virginia. If we stay home long enough it might end."

"Wishful thinking," Pap says, raising his head. "It will not end before spring, and the worst of it will not be what you think. Then there's these two," he motions at Ananias and Tom, "want to go for the adventure. Never thought I'd raise fools for sons."

"What would you have us do?" David asks.

"Hide out or go north."

"Be found out and hanged? Never allowed to come home? What do you say, Ananias?"

Ananias leans into the table and closes his eyes. I know he's pulling his thoughts together before speaking. He looks at Pap.

"I know it doesn't fit with Unionism or opposing slavery, or hardly even makes sense. I'm only nineteen, but this is what I've reckoned out. We live on the wrong side of this war. But the Confederate government's going to conscript us or punish us for hiding out. We aren't the only ones with no cause to fight against the Federals but don't want to fight for them. Our friends are facing the same thing. I know I'm young and foolish, but there is a war, and I don't want to run or hide from it."

The earnestness on his face hurts my heart. He's the best looking of my brothers and doesn't even know it.

But now I know. I'm going to lose all four of my older brothers to war.

4

In the Woods

Ananias

AT FIRST LIGHT, the air is cold and still, the skies clear. I take the musket, cartridge bag and cap pouch from hooks above the door. Ham biscuits from the food safe go into my haversack along with a game bag, matches, tin cup, and my hunting knife. I like to keep my necessaries in order.

Doves call to each other in the trees. When I walk into the woods alone, in quiet places where only the wind breaks the silence, I find my own way. Sometimes I walk animal paths, sometimes those marked by the Cherokee. It's how I found the cave.

I don't intend to hunt for much today. The winter woods are quiet, fallen leaves crisp. The deer could hear me a mile away. I walk west and come out behind the Meeting House.

Before Mr. Woodall came from Ohio and started the school here, I had not imagined doing anything but farming and hunting these hills and mountains. He brought us the world. I want to learn what there is to know about it and the men who made it, why men go to war, what war is like. It seems that all of history happens around wars. What I told Eliza Ann is true. This is the biggest thing that will happen in my life, and I want to see it.

There are no locks on the Meeting House doors. I sit on the back bench where I recited lessons with Ike and Joe Bowen, Chadwick and Jeremiah Buchanan, Jimmy Chastain, and Levi McFarlin. The Buchanans had more schooling, and I learned from listening to them.

Benches arranged in neat rows, lectern in place on the pulpit, it looks like a Meeting House again. The blackboard marked with lessons is gone. The table once stacked with Readers, Spellers, and Arithmetics is empty. When the War started, Mr. Woodall went back to Ohio. There will be no schooling until it's over.

I turn to the crossroads. At Fourth Creek I stop to take a drink of water under the oak that spreads across and shades the road. How many others with their lives on the change have rested under this tree—new settlers looking for farmland, the Cherokee rounded up and forced to leave? From here the Federal Road climbs west and north and then descends in sharp, steep turns, dropping west to Harnageville where the marble quarries have been cut into the earth. The Tates' plantation is there. They hold the most slaves in the county.

I can recite every one of Pap's arguments for Union, against Secession, about the uselessness of war and the evils of slavery. I know the boys, like Chadwick and Levi, who bragged about answering the call and went with the first Georgia companies. I don't know how I will get along with men who believe in this war—slaveholders, plantation owners, and those who wish they were.

Moody Simpson's cart rattles down the road, full of the whiskey jugs he trades for corn or, if he doesn't like the customer, cash money. His cabin and still are farther up the creek. Way back when Pap first let me hunt on my own, Moody found me in the woods, lost. He never made fun of me, showed me how to back track by the lay of the land, the places of certain trees and rocks. He's told me stories of his Cherokee people, how his family hid from The Removal and stayed. I seldom know when he's in the woods, but he knows when I am.

"This isn't where I'd expect to find you on a day like this," he says.

"I pretended to go hunting. I needed to get away."

"You and your brothers up against it with your pap?"

"Up against it would be easy. He talks to us only when he has to. The whole family's upset."

"This war will take all of us. Don't matter if we agree with it or not."

"Are you going?"

"With the company forming out of Dawsonville. I'm hoping Howell will go that way too. Might as well go with men I know than wait to be conscripted. Reverend Childs has signed up to be Chaplain."

If anyone can get along with Howell, it's Moody. Reverend Childs rides circuit and serves our Meeting on Fourth Sundays.

"You'll be in good hands," I say.

***

I shoot and dress out two rabbits. The afternoon clouds up, and the smell of rain comes on the wind. The first hard drops fall. I set the musket against a tree, muzzle down, and stuff the rabbits into my game bag. Caught out like this, I usually hole up under cedars and wait for the storm to pass or morning to come, but I'm close enough to the Wilders' farm to make a run for it.

Hail bounces against my hat as I turn up the slick lane. Wilders' hounds whimper from under the porch.

"Come in to supper," Jacob calls from the passage.

I hang the game bag on a hook and shake the wet off my hat. The supper fire lights their keeping room. The house smells of baked pumpkin and small boys.

The family sitting around the table is as familiar as my own, Jacob and his wife Tabitha, their two small sons, his mother Lucy. His sister Genny and brother Noah are the same age as Mary Jane and the twins. Lucy passes me a steaming bowl of squirrel stew and dumplings. Noah brings me a mug of hard cider. There's pumpkin pudding waiting for dessert.

After supper, Jacob builds up the fire. We stretch our legs to it and talk about what my brothers and I intend to do.

"David wouldn't lead you wrong," he says.

"Will you sign up?"

"If I have to. But if the War comes to Georgia, I'll come home to defend my farm."

"I think that's what Pap will ask of us, once he sees us going."

Genny is sitting on a low stool beside the fireplace. Her knitting needles click and flash in the firelight. Her hands are small and fine-boned. Gold from the fire reflects on her face and hair. She looks up at me with eyes the blue of forget-me-nots and smiles.

My heart lurches and hammers, my breath catches in my throat. I look down at my hands and wonder how a smile could make my body do this. Years of seeing her playing with Mary Jane and Eliza Ann, singing at Sunday Meetings, reciting in school have never produced this sensation. I want her to keep smiling at me, want to touch her hair and hands.

Jacob is still talking, but I can hardly make it out. Something about how Pap will come around. How he wishes his own father was still alive.

"Are you all right with leaving your family?" I ask, pretending I haven't just been poleaxed by a smile.

"I'm not," he replies. "Noah is too young to handle this place. My hope is the War will be over before I have to do anything about it."

I lie awake in the night on a pallet near the fireplace trying to figure out why now, why Genny. I know what this is but won't say it. I leave before first light, go so noiselessly out the door, the hounds never wake. I remember to take the rabbits, so it will not be a lie that I was hunting.

5

Leaving Home

Ananias

PAP HAS SET us to mending every fence. We've already cut enough firewood to last into next winter. I lift the last chestnut rail for David to rock into place.

"You think he's trying to work us to death?" I ask.

"No more than any other year. He'd have us plowing if the fields weren't so wet," David answers and leans on the rail.

"What else can he come up with?"

"Building a new hog pen. Starting after dinner."

"I'm going to help the Wilders after dinner."

"You've been there a lot lately. Genny have anything to do with it?"

"How'd you know?"

I don't know where these questions are going or what I'm doing, but David has experience.

"Jacob doesn't need that much help, and when the girls mention Genny you act like you've been shot."

"That's the way I feel. Watching her work, hearing her voice, I don't know what's happening to me."

"Sounds like you're courting."

I shrug, pretending it isn't that important. But it is. And I ask the next question.

"How do you tell them?"

"That you love them?" He smiles. "You have to talk to them. Then you have to believe that you love them. Then you have to say it."

"Love?"

"Love. Get used to saying it out loud. Then when you're alone with her, take her hands in yours, look into her eyes, and say, I love you. Works every time."

"For what?"

"Kissing."

My face is hot. I haven't thought that far ahead.

"It's like kissing Mam on the cheek," he says. "Only you aim for the lips."

"What if I can't?"

"Someone else will."

***

Pap sits alone near the fire. Until this I have never done anything that would make him so angry. I sit on the floor next to his chair.

"I'd like to have things right with us before I go," I say.

He leans toward the fire, covers his face with his hands.

"They'll never be right again," he says. "My sons are going to fight for the wrong cause."

"I won't be fighting for a cause. I'll fight to keep the War from coming to Georgia."

"If it does, will you leave the Army and defend the farm?"

"If I can." Love, war, I have no idea how any of it works.

"We'll see how right it will be then," he says.

Eliza Ann is sitting at the table, pretending to read in the candlelight. There's nothing left for me to do or say. The front porch at night is a good place to think. I sit on the top step. The front windows of the house glow pale gold from candlelight and firelight. Stars fill the moonless sky. Down from Orion, the cluster of Seven Sisters blinks out when I look at it straight on.

I hear her come out into the passage.

"Look up," I say. "You see the Seven Sisters? Moody told me the Cherokee call them Pigs in Heaven."

"I'll think of that next hog-killing," she says. "I can't count more than six."

"The seventh is so far away it takes a special glass."

"Mr. Woodall told you that. Aren't you going to miss studying the things we learn in the Readers?"

"Not enough to keep me home. Not without a school."

"What about Genny?"

Seems like the seven sisters of our household, counting sisters-in-law, know more than I do about me and Genny.

"That would be my business," I answer.

31

"Do you love her?"

"It won't stop me from leaving. Neither will you."

"Who'll lead us to the cave?"

"You know all the ways to get there."

"It won't be the same without you and Tom."

"Nothing in our life is going to be the same. It's time for you to know what you can do. Time for me too."

"I'll miss you most."

"I know. I wish I could make this easier. For Pap, for you. After I go, look up at the stars. I'll be watching them too."

"What kind of comfort is that? Looking up at stars, not knowing where you are, so far away no special glass would be enough to find you."

"Small comfort, I guess. But they'll always be there."

"And you won't." She stands up and goes back into the house.

I look back up at the stars, wondering what the circumstances will be if I see them in war.

***

Even if I can't talk to Genny in private, I want the memory of her smiling eyes. The Wilders leave us time alone on the porch.

She stands straight and still, hands behind her back.

"I have something for you," she says.

She brings one hand forward, in her palm a yellow silk drawstring bag embroidered with tiny blue forget-me-nots.

"They're the color of your eyes," I say, taking it, tracing the flowers with a fingertip.

"I don't know that you'll have a use for it," she says. "It might not suit a soldier."

"I'll think of you." I put the bag in my shirt pocket.

Someone else will. David's words keep my courage up. I take her hands and look into the blue of her eyes.

"I love you, Genny."

I lean down and aim my lips for hers. What will happen next? The pressure of her lips kissing me back. My heart lurches like it did that first time she looked up at me. My hands move on their own to her waist and pull her closer. I want to move my hands to other places, kiss her longer. And not stop.

"It takes my breath," she says, pulling away.

"Can I kiss you again?"

"Yes."

***

Sitting on my bed, I go through my haversack to make sure I have what will be needed—candle, comb, hard soap, piece of towel, razor, in addition to hunting knife, matches, tin cup, the food Louise has packed. I've rolled extra socks, drawers, and shirts into the quilt Rebecca remade for me. I wear a wool vest over my heavy shirt, wool trousers, long drawers, two pairs of socks for the cold walk, felt slouch hat, wool jacket. Genny's silk bag next to my heart. I think I am ready.

Outside on the porch, David holds Lydia, her head pressed into his shoulder. Mam has had to explain to both of them that Lydia's odder-than-usual behavior, breaking down sobbing, too sick to her stomach to eat, is because she'll be adding to the family.

All the rest except Pap wait at the bottom of the steps. Tom was supposed to be coming with us. Mam has decided differently. She wants oldest to look after youngest. So, I am going with David to Gordon County. Tom, when he turns eighteen in a few weeks, will go with Howell in Dawson County. We won't be in the same Company. She thinks dividing us up will help us survive.

Eliza Ann hands me a bundle of turkey-red flannel folded over itself in thirds and tied with a yellow ribbon.

"Mary Jane and I made it for you," she says. "It's called a housewife. It has what you'll need to mend your clothes."

I unfold it open to three pockets made from one of the girls' old orange and navy plaid dresses. Two needles pierce the thick flap, and the pockets hold small rolls of thread, buttons, pins, and Eliza Ann's silver thimble.

I roll the thimble in my fingers. "This was your birthday present."

"You'll need it to poke through heavy cloth. Rebecca says I'm too clumsy for one that nice. I can always use Mary Jane's."

"I'll bring it home to you before your next birthday."

She's grown tall enough to hug me around the chest. Mary Jane gives a whimper and hugs me at the waist. They hold on.

"If you two start to cry I won't be able to leave," I say.

"If that will keep you here, I'll weep until my eyes fall out," Eliza Ann says.

I almost laugh at that. She's not one to cry much. Louise, Rebecca, and Charlotte are the sisters with tears in their eyes. I untangle myself from these two and turn to Mam.

She places her hands on either side of my face and looks into my eyes. I hold myself still for what might come next, so I won't break down.

"*For he shall give his angels charge over thee, to keep thee in all thy ways. They shall bear thee up in their hands....* Come home to us, son."

34

I look back into her brown eyes, put my hands on each of hers and make a promise I have no reason to believe I can't keep. "I will."

Pap is nowhere to be seen.

6

Camp McDonald

March 1862, Big Shanty, Georgia

Ananias

ATTENTION! RIGHT FACE!

Beside me, Eli Rutledge turns left, and Lewis Knell, on my left, turns right. With both of them facing me, I'm not sure which way to turn. So I stand as I am, facing front. We aren't the only ones stuck this way.

"Ridiculous!" our Drill Instructor screams. "If you don't know which way to turn, you won't march in the right direction."

He walks down the crooked ranks, realigning oddly turned men.

"Do you know your right from your left?" he asks Eli.

"Mostly," Eli replies.

"You'd better make it always. The men in the Rank guide Right, on you."

"And you?" he asks me.

"I couldn't decide."

"You don't get to decide," he says. "If you can't form a proper File from Ranks, you will march in this formation until you do. Do you know why you men are at the end of the Rank?"

"Because we're tall," I say.

"It's not because you're smart," he says. "We will repeat this until everyone is in correct alignment, every time. *Attention!*"

I stiffen to Attention. This is going to take forever. In addition to directions for facing, there are requirements for how to stand with my heels, toes, shoulders, elbows, even the palms of my hands, just so, and which way to turn my face and position my chin. When in doubt, I don't move. This too is often wrong. If one man does it wrong, we all have to start over. The Drill Instructor calls it the *School of the Soldier*, but it's not like school. There are no books.

Right Face! All three of us turn right and form the File, next to Rufe McDowell, David, and Posey Huff.

Squad, forward! Common Time! March!

I start with my left foot, one of the few things I do correctly. Lewis starts with his right and steps on my heel. Our File stumbles forward. All of this facing and turning and marching is called Drill. After a week of not getting much better at it, I agree with Posey. It should be called Trial. I try to follow what Pap told us when we learned something new at home: watch, listen, think, and remember. In the noise and confusion of drums and commands, thinking is the hardest.

***

It rains every day. Camp is never quiet, even in the night. The rapping and beating of drums start at daylight, Reveille, followed by the coughing and hacking of men rising in white canvas tents holding the stink of wet wool, sweat, and farts. I am up before my messmates and head for the Sinks at the edge of camp. With no walls, seats, or ceilings, they are not privies. Filled with bones, carcasses, rotten food, and human waste, the smell makes me gag. I hold my breath while I relieve myself.

Back at the tent, waiting for Breakfast Call, I look out at endless rows of Company streets. The one hundred men in our Company number more than the friends and neighbors I know in all of Pickens County, and everything except going to the Sinks is ordered by the rhythm of drumbeats and done as a group.

We shuffle in line through the cook tent.

"What do you think they're going to poison us with this time?" Rufe asks. "Fried pork? Bloody or black?"

"That depends on the cook," I answer.

"Then there's the bread. Burnt crust and gooey middle. My little sister can do better than that."

Rufe reminds me of Mam's rooster, puffing up and crowing out to the morning when none of the other animals care whether it's daylight or dark.

"The coffee tastes good," Eli says. A quiet man, he was a hired hand on a large farm north of Calhoun.

"It's the only thing that does," Lewis says. "I'd just like to see a difference between potatoes and peas." He comes from a small farm like ours.

I follow Hugh Owens, who keeps to himself and speaks only to answer direct questions and Roll Call.

"I'll bet they give us the same for dinner," Posey says, poking a fork into beef boiled into tough shreds and Irish potatoes stewed to mush.

The least likely soldier, Posey is a Calhoun Academy scholar and son of a lawyer. He's never slept on the ground, built a fire, or walked farther than the length of town. I know from my own family how each person has a talent to be called on. Inept at most of what we're learning, it's hard to reckon what Posey's will be.

When we arrived here with our Company, The Calhoun Blues, the only thing we had in common was our height, all of us over six feet. Captain Young put us together at the right end of the Ranks and assigned us to the same mess. According to him we will be Comrades in Battle until the end of the War. Aside from David, I have no reason to consider these men as comrades and no way of knowing how they, or I, will act in battle.

At Roll Call we stand at Attention and answer to our last names. Captain Young and Sergeant Williams explain and shout commands for actions with confusing names. Sorting it all out is much more interesting than mending fences and planting corn. Everything happens in Details—Sentry, Picket, and Fatigue, which describes our condition after picking up trash and digging new sinks, but that's called Policing. Supplies come from the Quarter-Master, wages from the Pay-Master. Posey says there really is a book for the *School of the Soldier* with all the commands, instructions, and duties written out. I'd like to study that.

There are sergeants and corporals in charge of everything. For now, most of them know as little as we do. We're privates. We don't question, and we salute everyone. Every part of my life in the Georgia Infantry is decided by someone else. So much for going my own way. I make one decision every day. To get better at it.

***

Our File stumbles forward, men switching feet until most are marching in step, following an Arms Instructor to a corner of the Parade Grounds. Across the way a band is playing *The Bonnie Blue Flag*. It has a catchy tune. Anyone in my family would be humming along. No singing in the ranks.

Strapped and belted across my chest and back, I wear what the Army calls accoutrements—a cedar canteen with a cork stopper, a canvas haversack, leather cartridge box, cap pouch, and sword scabbard, the last three empty. They bump and twist every time I move. The first time I put them on it felt like I was about to be tangled up and strangled.

We've been told we'll be training in the *Manual of Arms*, the commands for loading and firing muskets. I know how to load and fire a musket. The others probably do too, except Posey. How much ceremony can be attached to such a common action?

An Ordnance Sergeant hands out long wooden poles topped with double-edged blades that have two side blades.

"What the hell is this?" Rufe asks, fingering a blade.

"It looks like a clover leaf with sharp edges," Posey says, sticking a bleeding finger in his mouth.

"Privates, these are Georgia Pikes," the Arms Instructor announces.

"To use against the Federals?" Rufe asks.

"If necessary. Governor Brown designed them himself."

"This ain't no more than a stick with blades," Rufe says.

"These are your Arms until the Army issues you others."

"If Joe Brown's sending us off to fight the Federals with sticks, he must think they'll laugh themselves to death. I'd as soon fight with my own hands and arms."

Rufe jabs his pike at Eli, who reflexively jabs back. Swinging back at Eli, Rufe waves his pike over Posey's head. Posey ducks and runs. Rufe chases after him and almost everyone breaks ranks with him, chasing each other around the Parade Ground, waving and jabbing their pikes. The Instructor shrieks and spins, grabbing at men to get them into line. They laugh and run in bigger circles. I don't move. Neither does Eli.

"They're sure making a mess of this," he says.

"You're the one who started it, poking back at Rufe. Why didn't you break ranks too?" I ask.

"I might get distracted by a fool but I don't follow one. What about you?"

"There was no command."

"Company! Halt!" Sergeant Williams roars. He has Rufe by one arm and Posey by the collar. "Every one of you is on the Black List, and none of you better complain. I could have you bucked, gagged, and hung by your thumbs for breaking Ranks. You're lucky it's not the firing squad. Reform the Line! Now!"

Sergeant Williams always commands our attention. He's a veteran of the Mexican War, and the Company voted him in as First Sergeant. I stand at Attention, knees locked, shoulders squared.

The Arms Instructor picks up his pike and shouts the commands—*Shoulder Arms, Support Arms, Present Arms, Order Arms*—as he performs quick, precise maneuvers, shoulder to shoulder, in front of his face, back to a shoulder, moving his hands from the middle of the shaft to the butt, dropping the right hand, the left hand. If I did that hunting, the game would get away.

We go at it long past the time for Drill to end, maneuvering Joe Brown pikes and pretending they're muskets, before an audience of Sergeant Williams.

What had I expected? There has to be more to war than this.

7

Sunday Meeting

Eliza Ann

NOT ONE WHIFF of air moves in the Meeting House. It's so hot it hurts to breathe. Sweat drips down the inside of my half-corset. I want to loosen it and lift my petticoat, but I'm sitting on the front bench next to Mrs. Buchanan. I've envied my sisters their half-corsets and double-pink calico petticoats, until now. At Rebecca's insistence, my hair is done up in an affair of loops and braids that she says is called a *she-none*. It makes me feel silly, pretending to be some way I'm not. Escaping hairs stick to the back of my neck. Swiping at them would also not be proper. I'm up front because today is my turn to read a chapter of Scriptures.

The congregation isn't as big as it used to be, missing the men and boys gone to war, empty of neighbors who quarreled bitterly over Secession or Union. The circuit preachers are gone too, but those of us who want the sameness of holding Meeting still gather on Fourth Sundays to have prayers, hymns, and Scripture readings.

Mr. Buchanan is the storekeeper, and he enjoys running Sunday Meeting. He's taking his time with announcements, telling where the men and boys are serving, even though we all know it's his chance to brag on his son Chadwick, who signed up and went to war before any of the others.

What I know of war comes from lessons in the Reader, *The Splendor of War* and *The Horrors of War*. There doesn't seem to be much splendor in *mangled carcasses of the fallen…writhing agonies…piteous moan of the dying…desolated families*. The only people I know of who died were either old or babies. None in my family. I've never seen anyone die.

I don't want to imagine my brothers suffering like the soldiers in the lessons. *Without one companion to close his eyes. No sister…to weep over them…no gentle hand…to ease the dying posture, or bind up the wounds…left…amidst the trampling of horses.* It seemed just as terrible if men survived battle, *confined to a scanty or unwholesome diet, exposed in sickly climates, harassed with tiresome marches and perpetual alarms.* Why would they go through it?

Mr. Woodall showed us where the places we read about were in his Atlas, wrote on the blackboard how to pronounce the names. We'd sat on these same benches, different classes reciting at the same time, older students like Ananias helping younger ones. I miss memorizing and reciting, spending whole days learning new words, ideas, the capitals of states, the countries of Europe. Now, Mary Jane and I are working our way through the advanced Readers alone.

Mrs. Buchanan nudges me. The room is silent. Mr. Buchanan motions for me to come forward. Flustered, caught daydreaming, I stand and walk to the lectern. His large, ornate Bible is open to the page. I place a finger at the first line and follow it down the page. I've practiced reading this out loud to Mary Jane so many times I could almost recite it by heart. She could, too. I enjoy this chapter of *The Acts* with its *rushing mighty wind* and *cloven tongues like as of fire*. I come to the names I still can't fit my tongue around and read them faster, hoping it will distract from my not knowing how to pronounce them. I wish I could speak in other tongues, like the Cretes and Arabians speaking *in our tongues the wonderful works of God*.

I finish reading and walk back to the bench. Mam and Pap smile at me. Jeremiah Buchanan, sitting on the other side of his mother, smiles at me too. That makes me so nervous I twist my hands into my skirt, bunching it up, exposing my petticoat. More hairs have come loose from my she-none. After a long prayer from Mr. Buchanan for the soldiers and their heroic sacrifices, Mrs. Buchanan leads the closing hymn, *Am I a soldier of the cross, A follow'r of the Lamb*?

Mary Jane's clear soprano rises into the still air. Pap's bass follows. Without looking I can identify the individual voices of my whole family. Summer evenings on the porch, winter nights beside the hearth, walking anywhere, whenever the mood or a memory strikes, someone starts a song and the rest of us join in.

I find Mam and Mary Jane at the edge of the women gathered in the Meeting House yard. Friends and neighbors greet each other despite their differences, avoiding talk that could split them apart even more. Most are talking about the hideouts, men who haven't signed up or some who did and deserted from the Confederate Army. Rumors have them hiding in the hills above Dawsonville, raiding gardens and fields, stealing livestock and supplies.

"You didn't pronounce those names correctly," a voice says next to me.

It's the new girl, a niece to the Halfords who own the gristmill at Yellow Creek, not far from Howell's farm. She has come from South Carolina to live with them. I know her name is Harriet, but I haven't met her yet. Small and sturdy, she wears a white silk shawl over a gray taffeta dress. Her petticoat is creamy white over a hoop. A white ruffled cap perches on top of fine dark hair pulled into a she-none fancier than mine. The top of her head does not come up to my shoulder. Her dark brown eyes spark. Head cocked and arms akimbo, she looks like an angry little chickadee.

"It's pronounced EE-luhm-ites, not El-a-MY-ties," she says. "And sigh-REE-nee, not KY-reen."

"Is mispronouncing a sin?" I ask, hoping to make a joke of it.

"Only if you care about words and how they sound."

I do care about words but won't admit that to her. With Ananias gone, I had no one to ask about the names I couldn't pronounce. I feel stupid and awkward in comparison to this smart, tidy girl.

"How would you know?" I ask.

"Because I learned them at the Charleston Female Institute," she replies.

"Maybe next time you could give the reading."

"It would not be worth my while, to cast pearls before swine."

"Your pearls might be worth trampling to pieces. I've read *Matthew*. For all I care you can go back to South Carolina and pronounce all the fancy words you want."

And once again I've let my mouth go first. My face is hot, and I'm tongue-tied as she turns and sweeps across the yard, gathers her skirt, hoop, and petticoat, and steps into her uncle's carriage. They're new to Meeting, the one near them being all Secessionists. I hope they don't attend regularly so I won't have to see Harriet often, or even ever again. But I would like to know someone who can pronounce words like this.

"She's not as smart as she'd have you think she is," Mary Jane says from behind me.

"Why do you say that?" I ask. Mary Jane never says unkind things.

"She's trying to prove herself in a new place. And you're smarter than you think you are. You went over that reading so many times, and none of us knew how to say those names. Don't let her bother you. She's probably jealous about how well you read the rest of it. Just like Mr. Woodall taught us."

Leave it to Mary Jane to stick up for me even when I'm wrong.

8

Crows

July 1862

Eliza Ann

TWO CROWS LAND on the gate and stare into the garden.

"I could watch them all day," Lydia says. "How pretty they fly, black silk and velvet, drifting down to a rail, always looking for something to eat."

"At least the corn isn't ripe, and Pap won't come charging out to shoot them," I say.

We are resting on the porch steps. Lydia is the only one who shares my silly pleasure in watching crows, how they strut across a field in their wide-legged, cocky way, tilting their heads like they're paying attention.

"When I hear them calling in the trees I imagine them talking," she says.

"Sometimes I think they're arguing. Or having a serious conversation," I reply.

"Or being silly." She laughs. "Like us. I go on about the strangest things nowadays."

The change in Lydia is a relief. For a time she wouldn't speak to anyone but David and Mam. She really couldn't sew and didn't care to learn how, but she willingly took on milking and churning, killing chickens, and emptying night jars.

Mam and Louise noticed her condition just before David left. Lydia hadn't understood what was happening to her. I am grateful for how her manner has softened as her body changes.

"What's it like knowing a baby's inside you?" I ask.

The only women I know to birth babies are Jane Graham, Tabitha Wilder, and Howell's Callie. It was something not talked about, at least when men were around. Their bellies grew bigger and stuck out from their skirts, and then one day Mam, Louise, Rebecca, and Charlotte would go to them for their lying-in and come home talking about the new baby.

"Other than making me sick to my stomach and growing so my skirt waist doesn't fit, it kindly seems to mind its own business."

"Do you wonder what it'll be?"

"Sometimes I think it's a boy we'll name after your pap. Other times I want a girl named after your mam. I know she waits the first year to name a baby, but I don't see waiting that long. Just think, when you have babies they'll be cousins to mine. We'll have so many babies we'll run out of names for them."

"There's no one else you'd name it after?"

"I've been on my own so long, this is the only family I want. Once he knew about my condition, all David talked about was how he'll come home from the War and we'll raise a big family and farm this land with your pap. I love having such hopes and dreams. Don't you?"

"I don't have anyone to think of that way, not like my sisters."

"I can't understand why your pap won't let the Bowen brothers court Rebecca and Charlotte. Wouldn't even let them say goodbye when they went to war."

"It's an old feud between him and their pap."

"That raggedy man? Who'd care enough to feud with him?"

"He accused Pap of cheating him out of buying the back acreage and took it to the court in Jasper. Pap won and they've been at each other ever since."

"I want everyone to feel like I do with David. I saw that Buchanan boy smile at you in Meeting. Do you have feelings for him?"

I haven't paid much attention to feelings for boys. Mary Jane has Levi McFarlin who fell for her on the very first day there was a school. Charlotte and Rebecca, mainly Rebecca, talk about Ike and Joe Bowen whenever Pap isn't around. As for Jeremiah, I liked listening to him recite at school, so confident in his voice, *"Once more unto the breach, dear friends, once more…"* Once he asked me what I thought of a poem, about a raven. I didn't know of any poems about ravens. I don't think I have feelings for him in Lydia's way. I mostly feel embarrassed about not knowing things.

"I wish I had as much book learning as he does," I answer.

"That's not a feeling. Don't you like how he looks or talks? David made me laugh the minute I met him. Then he made me mad. I hope my baby looks like him."

I do too. And I'm grateful to have Lydia as another sister.

***

I glance at the Readers on the shelf with the Bible and the Speller. Sunday afternoons leave some time with no chores until supper preparations. I could sneak outside to read just a little and be back to help with supper before anyone knows.

I finish the clean-up from dinner and put away the crockery and tinware. Mam and my sisters are on the porch, sewing and resting. I should go out with them and practice my patchwork. The patches of cloth I try to sew together end up rumpled and bunched, filled with more knots than stitches. I've worked them over until my fingers bleed and I have no hope for ever doing it well. If left to my skills, my husband and children will wear rags, or all go naked. Lydia and I have joked about this too. Rebecca tells me patchwork is no different than embroidery, which I do better with, but it's not. Embroidery doesn't have to keep two pieces together. And there's the hoop holding it tight.

I pull the advanced Reader from the shelf and go out the back of the passage. The copper wash-kettle tilts against the smoke-house, upended black iron pots litter the yard, and clothes-ropes hang from a porch post, ready for wash day tomorrow.

I cut behind the privy and the smokehouse so no one can see me, pass the spring house in its grove of cedars, and head uphill to the shady peace of the orchard. It smells of cider apples and cropped grass. I sit propped against the trunk of the widest apple tree, ready to be taken away.

Just by opening the book I visit Iceland, Alexandria, the Alps, the Pacific Ocean, places I know in my mind. I turn the pages, remembering the lessons on punctuation, the electric fluid of lightning, and the Rule to avoid thinking about me and concentrate my mind on the lesson. Doing just that catches me up in a contest of tigers. I am in India, under attack by beasts that growl and roar with heart-piercing howls.

"So this is where you snuck away," Rebecca's voice breaks in. "Wasting your time reading when there's supper to start."

I drop the book, coming back through clouds of story.

"I told them you'd be off daydreaming," she says. "Might as well throw out those books for all the good they'll do you mopping floors and slopping hogs. If you paid as much attention how to do things around here as you do books, you might be worth something. Louise is waiting on you."

I stare after her flouncing down the hill. I pick up the book, knowing better than to finish the tale. But I will, given another chance. I don't know how to convince Rebecca that I'm worth something, but I'll do that too.

9

Harvest

August 1862

Eliza Ann

THE WEIGHT OF the pick-sack cuts into my shoulder. Grit and chaff stick to my fingers, and my bare feet burn in the hot dirt. I check on the sun, high and white in the cloudless sky and wish it was time for Rebecca to ring the dinner bell.

Being in the fields is a change from the stuffy house, especially early in the morning when the air is fresh from the night. There's a rhythm to pulling field peas, and it's satisfying to see the progress we make, even though my hands are cramping and my back aches. I wipe my sweaty face with my apron and bend to yank another vine from the tangled row. Mary Jane works the row beside me, just as sweaty as I am, but she doesn't take to this like I do. I would rather be outdoors. Rebecca can't criticize me here, and Pap is easier going, now that my brothers have gone.

"I never thought I'd need daughters working the fields," he says, coming up the row with two buckets. "I planted so much hoping the boys would be home."

"I don't mind it," I say, wishing those buckets were full of water.

"Charlotte's toting water to the garden," he says, handing the buckets to us. "Leave your sacks and go help her. That'll keep your mind off the heat. You've done good work."

We step across the rows downhill to where the branch runs through the narrow woods of hickories, dogwoods, and blackberry bushes that shield the farm from the road. The water is cool on my feet and ankles, and the current tugs at my skirt. I stoop to fill a bucket. I want to lie down in it, clothes and all.

"Don't you wish we could get wet all over?" I ask Mary Jane.

"Rebecca would say it's unladylike," she replies as she wades in. "But it'd feel so good."

I plop down in the middle of the branch. My skirt and apron billow in the water. I lie back, roll over, and splash water at her. She cries out, throws up her hands, bucket and all, and falls backwards into the water.

"I've wanted to do that all morning," Charlotte says, coming through the trees. She wades in and fills her bucket.

I can't resist scooping a bucketful of water at her. She shrieks and dumps hers over my head. Mary Jane sneaks up behind her and pulls her down into the water. We splash and throw water at each other, laughing and squealing until we run out of breath, bonnets drooping over our eyes, wet skirts clinging to our legs.

"This is not getting water to the garden," Charlotte says.

We climb out onto the bank, relaxed and giggling, and wring out our skirts, aprons, bonnets, and hair.

I fill my bucket and follow the muddy trail of my sisters' skirts dragging in the dust. Charlotte looks toward the house and screams, "Oh, no! Hogs in the garden!" She throws down her bucket and runs.

I drop my bucket, run past her, and round the fence corner into the garden. I grab the first small hog by the hind legs, a rooted-up turnip dangling from its snout, and swing it out the open gate. I haul the next one from a row of kraut cabbage and drop it over the fence.

"Shoo hog! Shoo hog! Get out of here!" we shout, flapping wet aprons and herding more out the gate. Cassiopeia, settled between rows of mustard and collard, is in no hurry to leave. We shove against her flanks until she heaves herself up and allows Mary Jane to herd her into the yard. During the day, the hogs wander around the woods and yard as much as the chickens and geese, eating anything that doesn't eat them first.

Charlotte pushes an onion back into the ground. We all think of the garden as hers. She's the one who plants and tends blue-spiked catmint, red bee balm, white feverfew, lavender, yellow tansy, and pink English thyme. It's her flower garden. The herbs growing near the fences have survived, but the vegetables we depend on into the winter are scattered across the rows.

"Who left the gate open?" Charlotte asks.

Rebecca, coming out to ring the dinner bell, answers, "I did the last picking. My hands were full. I must not have pulled it tight."

I can't believe she can act that careless about it. If it had been me not closing the gate, she'd never let up on how I did wrong.

"How'd you get so wet?" she asks, obviously trying to change the subject.

"It's a hot day," Charlotte answers, looking a little like a drooping flower as she turns from one ruined row to another. "We'll just kindly have to gather up and eat the ones that won't grow back. I'll tote more water for the rest, and we'll see what lives or dies."

"I'll help," I say and pick up a trailing tomato vine. I don't know which plants need deep rooting, which ones shallow, whether they'll grow back or not. I've never paid much attention, just planting, thinning, and picking what Charlotte tells me to do. That's what most of my chores are, doing what one of my sisters says needs to be done. Ananias was right. I'm old enough. I ought to know what I can do on my own. I'm also grateful to Charlotte for not telling how we got wet and who started the water fight.

***

I like being up early on Sundays, before the birds start their day songs, putting the coffee on, helping Louise. She directs most of the work of the house. Being alone with her gives me time to think about how I can help her and Charlotte more and not just escape the house to work in the fields.

I pour fresh-roasted coffee beans into the grinder and turn the handle. Lard sputters in the spider while Louise pats dough into corncakes. The stew pot at the back of the fire is full of simmering apples.

"Buchanan told me coffee's scarce because of the blockade," she says.

I measure coffee and water into the boiler and set it on the fire. Coffee, sugar, spices, saleratus, salt, needles, pins, all the goods we buy at Buchanan's store are scarce. Whoever would have known that Federals blockading the Mississippi River would affect us so in Georgia? How could a day begin without the smell of coffee?

"I visited Jane yesterday," Louise says. "They're falling behind. With Alex gone to war she can't get the work done. Alfred does his best, certainly better than the twins could, but he's so young. It's too much for a lone woman and children."

"I can't imagine her not doing everything to perfection," I say. "Except for cooking."

Jane Graham is Louise's oldest friend. She has a quilting frame, and all the neighborhood quilts are finished on it. Some of my earliest memories are of Jane's house, sitting on the floor by Mam, sometimes hiding under the quilt on the frame, listening to women's voices while they sew together, the house always smelling of roses. I look out the window at Charlotte's Cloth of Gold rose twining up around a porch post. It was a start from one of Jane's.

"She'd be the last to ask for it, but I was thinking maybe you could kindly stay with her a week or so and help out, get her caught up in the house while she and Alfred bring in their corn."

That doesn't make sense, me helping her with house chores when I'm the worst at ours.

"What good would I be?" I ask. "Anyone else could do it better."

"She's always liked you best. I thought that might make it easier for her to take help. The coffee's boiling over."

I grab a potholder and reach for the boiler, realizing that Louise and Mam have already decided and arranged this, without considering what I might want.

10

Skirmish

Ananias

DUST CAKES IN the creases of my skin, blisters weep into my sweaty socks, and the brim of my hat droops over my eyes. I push it up. There's nothing to see but soldiers in gray, ahead and behind, disappearing into dust clouds raised by their own tramping feet. I shift my rifle and keep moving, tired and stumbling.

If it isn't dust, it's mud, as the weather changes, sometimes hourly, from scorching heat to heavy rain. None of that seems to matter to whoever is in charge of this grumbling column of soldiers snaking through the hills of eastern Tennessee. Infrequent orders to halt allow no time to rest, only enough to relieve myself off the roadside, drink the warm water from my canteen, and gnaw on the side-meat and corn bread that pass for rations. Men drop out of the column and straggle along the way.

Marching back and forth on the same roads up and down the Cumberland for five months is not my idea of going to war. Not that I'd had much of an idea of that in the first place. What I wanted then seems foolish now. I'm not close to seeing sailing ships or whales. Sergeant Williams has told us once we get into battle we'll see the elephant. Elephants are in circuses and I've only read about them. The way he said it makes me think it will be a disappointment. So far, I've seen the rail stations of Chattanooga and Knoxville and stood in one Battle Line, ready for a fight that never came.

Company! Halt!

David and I shuffle to a stop.

Company! Fall Out! Sleep on Arms!

By now I'm used to laying my quilt and blanket out in hard dirt, tall grass, whatever fills the field by the roadside. Sleep On Arms is one of the stranger Army commands. At first I thought it meant sleeping on my stomach with both arms under me. Now I know to lie down and keep one hand on my rifle.

I look up into the sky. The constellations are still moving in their paths, the Great Bear, Queen Cassiopeia on her throne. Waiting for sleep to come, I watch them on clear nights and go home in my thoughts. They'll be harvesting now, eating garden greens, stewed chicken, fresh peaches. I don't dare think about Genny.

***

This morning's march goes over hills and ravines, through fields overgrown in briars and small cedars. It ends at a belt of woods.

Company! Form the Line!

I look around. There's no sign of why we should form a Battle Line, no warning of nearby Federals. I move into Rank like we learned in Drill, elbow to elbow with Eli and Lewis, David close behind me. We wait for the next command.

The roar comes like a cyclone. I cover my head and duck to the ground, too scared to run. Pieces of iron and lead fly overhead like hail. This isn't a storm. My mouth goes dry, my bowels loosen, my butt squeezes up. A log, there. Crawl behind it, squeeze tight against it. Trees blast apart. A whistling overhead. Bullets. I cover my ears, rattled. Must make my body small, block out the noise, hide. Why is someone shouting? Where is David?

"Get up and form the Line, you cowards!"

I look up. It's Sergeant Williams, waving his arms. That could be a command, but I'm not standing up. I'll crouch. David, Eli, and Rufe come out from behind the same tree, Posey and Lewis from behind other logs. I have dropped my rifle. I pick it up and scuttle into the Line with them, look around for others. Not one of us has remained standing in the face of fire.

"Quick Time! March!"

That comes back to me. Step up the pace. Touch elbows. Keep my rifle tight to my shoulder.

We are walking over bodies. Men broken in two, tossed like rag dolls, bent and twisted, leaking blood, blood-covered, blown apart. A color-bearer's limp body props up the Third Tennessee's flag. He looks to be no older than the twins. I'm crying. He raises a hand. I hesitate, holding up the Line, see his guts spilling out. Gag back the contents of mine.

Company! Halt!

We stop on the edge of a sandy road, breathing hard. In the field behind us, men shriek and wail in pain. Litter details wander the field, sorting wounded from dead, carrying stretchers of moaning men, leaving motionless men where they fell.

Musketry pops, ceases, pops again, too far down the Line to see.

"Boys, this was just a skirmish," Sergeant Williams announces. "Wait'll you see a real battle."

Pap was right. I know nothing of war.

***

Evening in camp, I can't get the skirmish out of my mind. The color bearer raising his hand. Men dying in terrible ways. I hadn't reckoned on this. Death coming out of nowhere.

Posey and I have been studying the book, *Hardee's Rifle and Light Infantry Tactics*. There's more words to the title. It's a little book in small print so full of details it ought to tell the difference between a battle and a skirmish, but we haven't found it. The book is for officers. Posey talked one of them into selling it to him.

The whole Brigade is camped in a valley, hazy with the smoke of mess fires. David says we should look for Tom and Howell. We don't know how their Regiment came out of the skirmish. Eli always listens with interest whenever we talk about the family, so I invite him along. We walk the road through the valley, asking and looking. The Fifty-Second's colors are the last we see, Tom and Howell's mess in the rear section of Company I's street.

"You couldn't be farther away from us if you tried," David says. "Were you in the fighting?"

"We went forward and fired," Howell replies. "Couldn't see a thing. Heard the Third Tennessee had the best of it."

"Looked to us like they had the worst of it," I say, thinking of the bodies, my panic under fire. "Weren't you scared when it came on?"

"Nah. We didn't have a chance to think about it. What's the matter? It scared you?" Howell asks in a whine.

Same old Howell. Never misses a chance. I know he's showing off for his mess, and Eli.

"I bet you didn't even fire," he says.

"We had no command to. How about you?" I ask Tom.

"They were running by the time we got into it," he answers. "I fired with the rest. More hungry than scared. We've been on short rations."

Always slight and catlike, Tom looks thinner.

We sit around their mess fire. More than anything I want to be certain that Tom is all right. In the fading light, big guns rumble and flash in a duel of long-range artillery, like the thunder and lightning of distant storms.

"Reminds me how we'd sit on the porch of an evening and watch lightning in the hills," I say.

"And wait for the air to cool and the twins to settle down," Tom says.

"How many brothers are you?" the man next to Howell asks.

"Six," Howell replies. "If you count the twins as two."

The man starts singing, "*We are a band of brothers, native to this soil...*"

David and Howell sing along. Tom and I join in. We have come to like this song better than *Dixie*, even though Pap would hate the parts about property and Southern rights. At the end,

Howell, in his smooth baritone, starts *Aura Lee*. The words bring me Genny's blue eyes and golden hair. I feel tears forming and shield my eyes. David's hand comes to rest on my shoulder. Howell's voice subsides into silence and dying embers.

I thought going into battle would be how we drilled for it. Marching in a straight line, following our Captain and Colors, stopping to fire our rifles as commanded. Now I think we might have seen the elephant.

11

Lessons

Eliza Ann

I NOTICE THE CHANGE as soon as I walk onto the Grahams' place. The weeds are as high as the corn, choking out the potatoes and pumpkins.

"We're trying not to give up on the fields," Jane says.

Her wide expressive mouth settles into a grim line. Small and wiry, her big ears stick out under thin brown hair skinned back into a tight bun.

Alfred is harvesting corn in the near field. Cynthia is trying to pick beans in the garden while three-year-old Carrie helps.

"It's hard enough keeping the garden and animals alive," Jane says. "The way I've let the house go is shameful. Go on in and see what I mean."

I walk up the porch steps and into her keeping room. It's a shock to see sooty windows and dirty floors in what has always been an immaculate house. Jugs of wilted rose blossoms line the windowsills. Velvet petals have fallen into rose-shaped piles. Dishes and food scraps clutter the grimy surface of the table. The house reeks of spoiled food and unwashed clothes. Of course Jane is embarrassed to have anyone see it this way. Alex Graham has been proud of his well-kept farm and his intelligent wife.

I put my satchel in Jane's sleeping room, find the broom, and start sweeping up rose petals.

***

I tidy Jane's sleeping room and pull the sheet and quilt to the foot of the bed for airing. The house is clean, and dinner is cooking. These last days have been a drudgery with only eleven-year-old Cynthia for help. Keeping Carrie from getting into everything, I feel like one of those eight-armed octopuses I've read about. Here on my own, I've faced how much work it takes to keep a house clean and neat, a family fed. Rumpled beds, bawling cow milked late, undercooked and overcooked meals, these things never happen at home.

A light-stand next to the bed holds a stack of Lady's Books. I lean against the bed and thumb through embroidery patterns, directions for fashioning hair bracelets, and pages for cutting out paper dolls and their paper clothes. Each issue carries stories, poems, household instructions, songs, and cooking receipts. I'll be going home tomorrow and want one last look at all they hold.

After dinner we sit with sewing baskets in the shade of the porch. I take in a breath and smell roses. They bloom in every color on bushes and climbing vines. With all the other work, Jane has managed to keep them watered.

Remaking one of her old dresses for Cynthia, she allows that simple mending is a good way to rest on the Sabbath. Alfred helps Carrie hop up and down the steps. Cynthia is knitting small cotton stockings. I wrestle with a torn seam on Alfred's good shirt, the cloth going one way, the needle another, poking my finger. I suck the blood so it won't stain the shirt.

"Why don't you read to us from one of the Lady's Books?" Jane suggests.

I know just the one, with a story about young people on a picnic far away from Georgia, the War, the farm. It's a silly story, but near the end I look up to see all of them simply listening, watching me read.

"They must miss you at home," Jane says. "You're a big help."

"They don't miss me. They sent me because they don't need me."

"I don't believe your mam feels that way. I know Louise doesn't. She's always telling me how smart you are, how fast you learn."

"Rebecca says all I'm good for is sticking my nose in a book and daydreaming. But I like reading and learning new things. It makes me think."

"There's room enough in this world for all types. You read well and gave us something to take our minds off all the work and the War. I'll miss having you here."

***

In the last of the evening light, Alfred asleep, Cynthia putting Carrie to bed, I take a Lady's Book to the porch steps. Jane comes out with a candle lantern.

"Some would say it's a waste of candles. Don't stay up too late and ruin your eyes."

All the riches of life before the War are spread out on the pages. The receipts are as interesting as stories, one for preserving Pine-Apple, a fruit with a rough outside. I imagine thick-skinned apples growing on pine trees. I turn the page to *Wedding Breakfast for Forty, In January* and study the table setting, the placement of flower vases, the array of fancy breads, breakfast cakes, savory pie, wine jelly, pigeons in jelly, calf's foot jelly. Why so many jellies? There are placings for food I have never eaten, oysters and terrapins, and ones I've never heard of, lobster salad and pate de foie gras.

"Be still." Jane's voice comes low from the doorway.

In the quiet night, something rustles in the garden. I turn and see the musket in Jane's shaking hands. The noise stops.

"I know you're out there," Jane calls. "Take what you need, and we'll leave you alone."

Suspended in the silence, me on the step, her in the doorway, whoever is in the garden, nothing moves.

"Let's go in the house," she says. "We'll give him a chance to leave. There's worse things than losing a few vegetables to a hungry man."

I close the book and take up the lantern.

"How do you know it's a man?" I ask.

"An animal would've scared off. He's probably one of those hideouts."

"You going to shoot me if I move?" a disembodied male voice asks.

Chill bumps raise on my skin.

"If I have to," Jane replies and awkwardly raises the musket.

He appears from the dark garden and walks into the light of the porch, wearing a gray uniform. The greens he's been picking stick out of his haversack. He walks up the steps past me and takes the musket from Jane.

"You don't know how to shoot this, do you?" he asks.

She shakes her head.

"You'd better learn. An empty threat is more dangerous to yourself."

"I think given a chance, a gentleman will do the decent thing."

"Then you're lucky with this one. Women alone need to be careful."

He turns to me.

"Do you know how to shoot this?"

My heart pounds and my breath sticks in my throat. Words would stick there too if I could form them. I shake my head.

"You should. Never know when you'll run into a man worse than me."

He leans the musket against the porch wall and walks back into the darkness, turning to say, "I thank you for the pickings."

Jane slumps down next to me on the step.

"I never dreamed something like that would happen," she says. "We need to tell your pap. Everyone needs to know."

"Are you going to do like he said?"

"Learn to shoot?"

"Don't you think so? If this is what the War brings us, we need to be ready."

"We'll see what your pap says."

***

"It's not fitting for a female to shoot a musket," Pap says. "Alfred's a good enough shot to watch over Jane."

"But he was asleep," I say. "And what about us when you're gone to Halford's Mill or Jasper?"

He can't say it would be the twins. When he and Ananias tried to teach them, their tomfoolery drove him to sputtering frustration. Ananias kept at it until they were mostly competent, but they've gone hunting and come home with nothing.

"There's more to shooting than you realize," he says.

Of course I don't know the first thing about shooting. Girls don't hunt. But I won't sit so helpless again. Not when I could have taken Jane's musket and threatened that hideout. Other men will be easy targets if they don't believe a girl could shoot.

***

I stare at Pap's rifled-musket above the door, trying to see how it works. He traded in his old muzzle-loader for it when talk of secession turned to talk of war. Ananias said it's more accurate, but I couldn't follow the reasoning. I finger the cartridge and cap bags hanging below it. I do this when Pap is gone. This morning, he and the twins harnessed Abe and Shad to the wagon, carrying the first of the corn harvest to Halford's Mill.

Mam comes from behind me, lifts the musket off the hooks, and hands it to me. The heft and length of it feel awkward.

"It's loaded," she says.

Her brown eyes spark with light like they do when she is amused or angry. She is smiling.

"I believe a girl should know how to shoot. I learned as a girl when our place was wilderness, and you didn't know what would come at the door."

She takes paper cartridges and copper pieces from the bags and carries them out to the porch.

"The rest of you can come out and watch, but don't a one of you tell your pap about this. Sometimes what men don't know won't hurt them."

"How come you're teaching her and not us?" Rebecca asks.

"You haven't asked. Or shown any interest. She's been fussing over this since that hideout. She's also the tallest and ought to be able to handle the size of it. And she knows the woods better than any of you. Like the man said, we don't know how other men will act. Lydia knows what I'm talking about."

Lydia takes up the block of wood that holds the front door open and sets it on the gate post.

"I learned when I was on my own," she says. "It made a difference. Long before I met David. He doesn't know. This isn't much of a target but if you knock it off you'll be doing better than most the first time."

I hold the musket with both hands, arms straight-out and stiff.

"You need to get friendlier with it," Lydia says and stands sideways to me, trying to keep her swollen belly out of the way.

She guides me in pulling the musket up to my shoulder, moving my hands to the stock and barrel, and setting my finger against the trigger.

"Look down the top of the barrel," Mam says. "See the two sights? Look through the back one to the front one. This here's the cap." She holds up one of the copper pieces. "You put it on this nipple just so. It's what sets everything off. Now, rest the stock against your cheek, take a breath, and steady yourself. If you don't hold it steady, it'll kick and scare you and you'll miss. Keep your eye on the target. Squeeze the trigger slow and easy."

The wood stock is smooth against my cheek. The cool metal of the trigger fits into the curve of my finger. I can see the wood block plain as anything through the sights. I hold on hard and squeeze as slowly as I can. The blast and smoke, roaring and sharp, fill my ears and nose. I choke and cough. Mam, Lydia, and the girls are cheering. The smoke clears. The block is on the ground.

"Not one of the boys ever did that the first time," Mam says. "If you can learn how to load as well as you took aim, I think we've found something you'll attend to."

12

Letters Home

August 1862, Rutledge, Tennessee

Ananias

A T THE END of another day's long and dusty march, I let my haversack and blanket roll fall, unbuckle and drop my accoutrements, lay my rifle on top of them, and sink to the ground, too hot to move, too tired to care.

Posey brushes the dust from his blanket, sits on it, and takes a pencil and diary from his haversack. The things he carries and pulls out at the end of a march are a wonder—writing paper, pen knife, volume of the works of William Shakespeare, Hardee's Tactics, packet of letters, housewife, and a small, thin-handled brush for cleaning his teeth. Our family uses shaved twigs for that.

I've never written or received a letter and do not have a book of my own. At home we read from the Bible. When school ended Mr. Woodall gave us a set of Readers. I took charge of them, but they're as much Eliza Ann's as mine

Posey still isn't good at Army skills like shooting and camping, but he has other talents, like getting ahold of Hardee's book. He keeps track of the rumors spreading along the Regimental grapevine. He notices who comes and goes at the headquarters tents and listens to young staff officers brag about what they know. Sometimes he knows we'll be sent out on the march before Sergeant Williams does.

In camp for the night, our mess box arrives, and it's my turn to cook. I slice side-meat into the spider and set it in the flames, pour peas and water into the kettle and set it aside.

"I think that has to boil," David says.

"Do you remember anything about how Louise made gravy?" I ask.

"It takes some flour in the grease."

I move the skillet to one side, set the kettle in the flames, and spoon flour over the side-meat. I remember Louise at the table, chopping and stirring, kneeling at the hearth to tend a skillet, dishing up savory stew, sweet pudding, soft bread. I knew how good it all tasted, not how it was prepared.

Remembering distracts me from cooking. The meat is burnt on the outside and raw in the middle. Lumps of flour clot the gravy, the peas are hard, and no one complains. If a man criticizes the cooking, he will fix the next meal. My messmates salt their food and chew in silence. I hope anyone will turn out to be a better cook than me.

Around the evening fire, we have our own entertainments. Eli whittles, fashioning rings, chess pieces, canteen stoppers, buttons, anything a soldier pays him to make. Posey writes in his diary and reads aloud sections of Hardee's *Tactics*. Lewis slumps on his side, weak from the constant marching, his jaw harp dangling from his accoutrements belt. Rufe is at the next mess, losing his money in a poker game. Hugh didn't last, disappearing after we received our bounty pay at Camp McDonald. We think he went home to Gordon County, but we don't know.

I stare into the coals. It's good to sit with David and talk about how the twins will get along with the mules, how long Pap will put up with their crooked rows, what Tom and Howell are doing in the Fifty-Second. It's different for me, not having Tom around. The only other time was school. He didn't last a week with the noise of recitations and the confusion of letters and words. As for Howell, he's teased and bullied me since I was a little boy. If that served any purpose, it helped me learn how to keep my temper.

After Tattoo comes the three drum taps to Extinguish Lights. I scatter the coals with a stick. Sleep comes hard in the noise of camp, men coughing and snoring, the click and rattle of guards patrolling their posts. Every clear evening I mark where the sun sets so I'll know which way is south, home.

***

We come to know each other over campfires. Tonight I take the low harmony to David's tenor on *Home Sweet Home*. Posey sings the melody. Lewis plays along on his jaw harp. Eli does not join in.

"If you all get along as well as you sing together, that's something to admire in a family," he says and picks up a good-sized wood chip, turning it from side to side.

"Not all of us sing so well," David says. "My Lydia sounds like a wailing barn cat."

"Does she feel bad about it?" Eli asks, cutting into the chip.

"Nope. She says somebody has to be the listener."

"I feel that way too."

"Some of us do better at getting along with others," I say, thinking of Howell's derision, Rebecca's scorn for Eliza Ann.

I watch Eli's long fingers working knife and wood, a skill no one in our family has taken up. Pap does all the woodworking.

"Seems like you all take care for each other," Eli says.

"I still don't understand why Mam sent Tom with Howell instead of me. I watched over him from the time we were little."

"What would you do if he was beside you in the Battle Line?" he asks, keeping his eyes on small details he works with the knife point.

"Be worried sick that harm would come to him."

"Maybe your mam wanted you to take care for yourself. Seems like Tom's doing fine. He survived the fight."

"He's quiet, like Mary Jane. They think of others first."

"You're proud of all the younger ones."

"I'm not sure being proud counts with the twins. They've been their own world since they were babies. We all helped raise them. Eliza Ann, yes, she's the smartest of us all. Her mind goes off in notions none of us can follow. When she comes into her own, she'll be something."

Talking about them makes me miss them even more.

"When the War's over you can come and listen to all of us sing," David says.

"I'd like that," Eli says. "Maybe you could give this to your wife when you get home."

He hands David a small wooden cat.

I smile at the gentle joke and gift, knowing Lydia would like it too. Eli is a little like Tom, paying attention to things that would pass another's notice, offering friendship in his steady way. He never speaks of having any family. Maybe we can take him home with us.

***

Posey is the only one who receives anything in Mail Call—weekly letters from his mother, today a package. He opens it and takes out ginger cakes, a jar of strawberry preserves packed in straw, six pairs of socks, a quire of writing paper, and two pencils. It makes me homesick for what my own family would do, if they only knew how.

"I can't keep all this for myself," Posey says and passes the ginger cakes around. "The preserves will keep in the mess box. Anybody need socks?"

"I could use a pair," Eli says, munching on a ginger cake. "But I doubt they're big enough."

"Her letter says the Ladies Committee made them. It looks like there's several sizes. I know she didn't make them. Our house-keeper did all the knitting."

He passes the largest pair to Eli.

"These'll do," Eli says. "I thank you, and your mother."

Rufe and Lewis take a pair each and give the rest to me.

"I've still got spares," I say and hand them back, knowing Rufe and Lewis are marching with no socks.

"Me too," David says, "But I'm grateful for the thought of it."

Posey rereads his letter, sharpens a pencil with his pen knife, and places a sheet of paper on the back of his cartridge box.

"What do you write on them papers?" Rufe asks.

"Where we are, what we do," Posey replies. "How I miss them."

"I suppose a man's family would like that," Rufe says.

I feel the same about my family, but letter writing is another thing we've never had a reason to do, and it wasn't something Mr. Woodall taught us.

"I'd write for anyone who couldn't," Posey says.

"No one at home could read it," Rufe says. He stands and leaves the fire.

"I'd write my own, if you'd help me," I say. "How do you start it?"

"At the top of the page write where you are, the date, and the salutation."

"Exactly where are we? And what's a salutation?"

"We're near Rutledge in Tennessee. Write Dear Family."

Posey gives me a sheet of paper and a pencil. I use my cartridge box for a hard surface like he does.

***

It has taken me three evenings to write the letter, in the lingering light between Supper and Tattoo. I think first of what I don't want to tell them, the misery of Drill, Fatigue, and Guard Mount in the rain, how fearful it was to form a Battle Line, mouth dry, chest tight, even when it was only a skirmish, how we've been without our supply wagons, no tents or mess boxes, sleeping in brush and bark shelters that leak in the rain and blow apart in the wind, that the Army uses the word *foraging* to describe stealing greens, corn, chickens, and pigs from the poor farms in the valleys of eastern Tennessee.

I want to tell them how rosebays bloom in red and pink among dark pines, and chestnuts and hickories leaf out and turn color, like they do at home. Probably only Eliza Ann will appreciate that. I want Pap to know how Sergeant Williams watches out for us, that all the marching has turned into something, guarding the gaps in the mountains, blocking the Federals from coming through Tennessee and moving on to Georgia.

Writing in my smallest script, I am surprised at how it makes me feel closer to everyone at home. I fold the paper into the envelope Posey gives me, back the envelope as he tells me with "Covingtons, Buchanan's Store, Pickens County, Georgia" and wonder how they will ever receive it.

13

New Life

Eliza Ann

"I'M USELESS AT this," Lydia says, holding up a diaper with a lop-sided hem.

"Then you're second worst to me," I say.

"Only because you took on something with so many colors and shapes. I think it's beautiful."

"The edges are crooked, the seams don't match, and nobody sees that it's crows."

I'm making a cradle quilt. I picked the pattern of triangles and squares for the name, Flying Crows. My squares don't look exactly like the sample in the Lady's Book, but I like the colors, dark green, blue, and lavender from remnants Jane gave me, and I've tried to do it right.

"I see crows," Lydia says. "And the colors of the farm in summer. It will make my baby feel warm and loved. What do you think it would look like if I'd sewn it? I would call it Talking Crows."

"It's turning out more like Laughing Crows."

Laughing and teasing, Lydia's ability to make fun of herself makes me feel not so bad about my own shortcomings. Until lately, now that she's gotten so big, we've practiced shooting when Pap is away from the farm. The last time she set up old eggs for targets. When I finally hit one, she said, "Now you can hit anything." I almost believe it.

She places both hands on her hips and arches her back.

"My back hurts something awful, and I have to go to the privy all the time. Lucy Wilder says I'm close to lying-in. I don't know what that means."

"It's when the baby's about to be born. I used to think it was like laying-by time, but it isn't. I've never been at one, but all the women go to take care of the mother and baby. Mam says it's how they give her their love and wisdom."

"Whatever it is, I want you with me. You make me forget how hard it is to have David gone, how strange I feel about birthing a baby. I wish I was better at things so I can be a good mother."

***

"I'm a little scared, aren't you?" Lydia asks.

We are sitting on the porch, waiting for whatever is going to happen next. She giggles.

"Here's the two of us never having a baby, acting like it happens every day."

"Just tell me what you want me to do," I say, hoping I can make up with love what I lack in experience.

"Would it be wrong if I got up and walked?"

"If it is, Rebecca will tell us."

I haul Lydia up from the chair and walk her up and down the passage until she is winded and shaking, testy with everyone, including me.

"What's got into me?" she asks. "I don't know what I'll do next."

"I'd say have a baby."

She laughs. "A big baby from the way it feels. I keep getting cramps."

"That's the next sign," Mam says, taking linens into Lydia's room. "We'll send the twins for Lucy. Get some tea going for her, blackberry root."

I carry steaming tea into her room. Louise follows me with a basin of hot water, Mary Jane with clean cloths. Mam pulls Lydia's night shift up, wets a cloth, and places it on her belly. The stretched skin of her enormous bulge moves. Propped against pillows, Lydia presses her hands along it, trying to smooth it. She's pulled off her drawers and cocked her legs. I know a baby comes out the private parts but can't see how there's room.

"Please sit with me. You too, Mary Jane. If I have the two of you, I won't fret so much."

We sit into the evening, Lydia clenching our hands, crying out softly when she cramps, holding her breath, rubbing at the bulge of baby.

"I want to stand up."

We stand her up. She leans her head onto my shoulder, rocking herself. Mary Jane stands behind her, gently rubbing her back. We help her back into bed and back up out of bed whenever she asks.

Night has fallen by the time Lucy arrives with the twins, each carrying a big basket.

"Why isn't this baby coming?" Lydia wails. "Callie and Tabitha said theirs came fast."

"The first one takes longer sometimes," Lucy answers.

She ties on a clean white apron and places her hands on Lydia's bulge.

"I think this is the baby's head. It's not turned the right way," she says, pushing at it.

"Why does it hurt so much?" Lydia cries out, rigid with fear.

"It's the pain of birthing," Mam says. "Every mother goes through it, but you'll forget once you hold your baby in your arms."

Lucy presses and pushes, trying to turn the baby's head.

"What's wrong with it?" Lydia is wet with sweat. "Why did David leave me like this?" She rolls away from Lucy and hugs her arms around herself, wailing, "I don't want to do this anymore. I can't. I want David."

"We need the doctor," Lucy says.

Pap saddles Abe for the ride to Harnageville. The doctor there treats the marble quarry workers and their families.

Waiting in the long night, I take my turns heating water, rinsing out cloths, and sitting with Lydia. Propped against the pillows, she moans and writhes, clenches her jaw, pushes her heels into the mattress. I feel helpless in the face of her pain and fear.

"Don't fight it," Mam says, smoothing Lydia's dark curls back from her face.

"Let's get something to calm her," Lucy says. "I have laudanum but don't want to use it before the doctor comes."

"Currant wine," Louise says and goes to the kitchen.

When not helping, I pace the passage. I remember the nights I heard anguished sounds coming from David and Lydia, the bed thrashing and bumping against the wall, as it does now with only Lydia in it. I've overheard Callie and Tabitha talking about the pleasures of the marriage bed. It didn't sound like something I'd want to do, not if it leads to this.

The front of the house is quiet, the twins oblivious in sleep upstairs. Hoof beats in the lane announce Pap and the doctor. He wears a black suit and white shirt and wipes his hands on his trousers as he carries a saddle bag up the steps. I lead him down the passage. He smells of horse sweat.

Mary Jane and I huddle together in the kitchen. Lydia screams. Pap comes running. The doctor comes out of her room, cleaning a bloody hand with a wet cloth.

"The baby was turned and the mother is small," he says to Pap. "I gave her laudanum to calm her. She's healthy and should come along fine. Mrs. Wilder is capable enough to see to the rest of it."

"I thank you," Pap says. "What will you take in payment?"

"What do you have?"

"We've just harvested potatoes."

"That will do."

Pap goes to the barn and returns with a sack of potatoes.

The doctor unties his horse from the gate, and Pap helps him strap the potatoes onto it. He rides off as first light touches the horizon.

"You girls try to get some sleep," Pap says. "These things take time."

I lie in bed next to Mary Jane, remembering the story of Ananias's birth, how long it took, how his name was chosen, the only time Mam named a baby before its first birthday. The twins' birth took all of Mam's strength. As for mine, she always smiles and says, "You were my easiest baby."

Louise is shaking me. "The baby's coming."

***

Lucy takes hold of a small head emerging wet and waxy. Lydia screams, and a baby slides into Lucy's hands, all white filmy skin, tiny arms and hands curled against its chest. A long slimy cord snakes from baby to Lydia. My stomach turns.

"It's a boy," Lucy says, gathering him up in a towel.

Lydia closes her eyes and smiles.

Lucy ties and cuts the cord. Louise wipes him clean, swaddles him in flannel and lays him on Lydia's chest. Rebecca wraps the bloody mass of afterbirth in a cloth and sets it in the basin. Charlotte wipes Lydia's bloody legs and binds her belly. Seeing them do what they know, without having to be asked, I will never forget this.

"Go get some sleep," Mam says. "Everyone's tired."

"Lydia wanted me with her," I say. "I could sit and hold her hand. I'd be here when she wakes up."

"There's nothing to do for her until she wakes. We all need rest. Louise will know what she needs."

***

Lydia is fretful and feverish, too listless to take the baby to her breast. Her room reeks of blood and night soil. Lucy is holding the baby.

"We need to move him to your mam's room so he doesn't take a fever too," she says. "Louise made up a sugar tit he can suckle til Tabitha gets here. You can feed him with that."

She hands him to me, a lump of a thing, bald head tucked down, tiny fists clenched. He yawns, opens his eyes, and stares up. My heart lurches. I carry him into Mam's room and do what Louise tells me, fitting the sugar tit into his mouth. He sucks at it, closes his eyes, and lies tucked up in my arms.

***

Into the next day, Lucy and Louise try to break Lydia's fever with wet cloths, close the room when she has chills, open it when she's hot. Tabitha arrives and nurses Lydia's baby along with her own.

"She doesn't know us," Mam says as Mary Jane and I hover outside the door. "Go help your sisters. We still need to keep the house going."

How can I pretend what is going on across the passage is normal? I look to do the things I think will take my mind off it—carry in firewood, haul water, wash the milk pans and churn, all the chores I've considered so tedious before. In desperation I finish the last stitches on the quilt thinking that might help. I sneak it into Lydia's room. Louise is the only one there.

"Best take that back upstairs," she says. "What happens here might ruin it."

"I just want to hold her hand. She wanted me to."

I take Lydia's hot hand and place a corner of the quilt in it. She isn't awake. Her skin is blotchy and her breathing is shallow. Only a sheet covers her. I can smell the foul discharge and see the blood staining the sheet.

I clutch the quilt to my heart and ask Louise, "Is she going to die?"

"I don't know."

How can Louise not know? She knows everything.

"Fevers usually break in the night," she says.

"Then she could be herself again in the morning?"

"It's the best we can hope for."

***

In the dim light before dawn, Mam wakes me and Mary Jane. "She's gone."

I stare at her. Lydia hasn't gone anywhere. Gone means dead. I stumble downstairs. Lydia lies in the bed, still and quiet. I lean my head into her stiff and lifeless shoulder and sob.

"I can't help her anymore. What can I do? What should I do?"

"You can learn to care for her in death," Mam says, gently pulling me upright and handing me a wet cloth. "We clean the dying away and make her presentable before the Lord."

I smooth the cloth down Lydia's body, her front creamy white as fine marble, her back bruised almost black. My tears drip onto her skin. Rebecca cuts the purple dress down the back and folds it around her. Charlotte puts a bouquet of lavender in her hands. It isn't right, the rituals of death following so close on those of birth.

I haven't noticed Lucy and Tabitha getting ready to leave. Mam hugs the baby to her and hands him to Lucy.

"We'll take care of him as long as you need," Lucy says, cupping his head in her hand.

"He's not staying with us?" I ask.

"He's best off with Tabitha," Mam replies.

"We can feed him and take care of him. I can do that right now."

I go to Lucy and try to take the baby.

"Stop this," Mam says. "You can't take care of him as well as Tabitha. It's done this way when a mother can't."

"I don't care. Lydia would want him with us."

I'm desperate. Why can't we keep this tiny wonder here in his home?

"Can't we name him? He needs a name for us to know him by. She wanted to name a boy after Pap. She told me."

"David will see to his name. When he comes home."

Why can't Mam break with her tradition just this once?

"I don't understand," I said.

"That's true. You don't. These things are not for you to decide."

"Can I get the quilt? Wait til I get it. Can I at least send him off in that?"

"That would be fitting."

I run upstairs and grab up the cradle quilt, bury my face in it, hoping to fill it with love. I wrap it around him and watch Lucy carry him up the lane.

We sit with Lydia through the night. All I can think of is laughing crows, her crooked hems, how I'll never laugh with her again. My tears are hot. I clench my jaw to keep from bawling.

***

In the Meeting House graveyard I stand to the side, among the markers. Most are boards, upright, tilted, or fallen. The graves of prominent families have marble headstones. A crow calls from the woods. Another answers. A tree creaks. Mr. Buchanan steps forward.

"One generation passeth away, and another generation cometh: but the earth abideth for ever. The sun also ariseth, and the sun goeth down,…The thing that hath been, it is that which shall be; …and there is no new thing under the sun."

I take no comfort in the familiar cadence of his voice, the words. Lydia was too young to be of a generation passing away. Am I to believe this is nothing new? If God is so wise and understanding, why would he take Lydia so terribly and leave a baby motherless? I turn away, my heart like marble, closed to God's will for allowing this.

14

Invasion

September 1862, Eastern Tennessee, Kentucky

Ananias

A FORTRESS OF ROCKS and cliffs, Cumberland Gap looms above our camp north of Tazewell. On clear mornings I can see the Federals on the mountainside loading and firing the big guns that lob shells down at us. Our Regiment is at rest after a month of marching back and forth in the east end of Powell's Valley.

This morning the Gap thunders with explosions. Flames and smoke rise from the Federal positions. At Roll Call, Captain Young tells us why.

"The enemy is almost surrounded and unable to be resupplied. Their evacuation is expected, and we will pursue them into Kentucky."

I don't know what that pursuit will bring, but I do want to see Kentucky. The air smells of dry leaves and the coming of cold, like early September does at home. Today is my twentieth birthday. I've always liked to use the day as a measure of how tall I've grown or how much I've learned in a year. The events of the past year are beyond measure, and I know the Army doesn't care how old I am, only that I'm old enough to fight.

I fall in beside David. "Happy Birthday, little brother," he says quietly, as our Company joins the long column marching north on the Tennessee Road.

We pass through the town of Cumberland Gap, a small settlement of log buildings. At the edge of town, a creek tumbles beside an iron furnace. The road turns to switchbacks. The once forested mountain has been stripped of trees, cleared for lines of artillery fire and cut for firewood. We march up into desolation. Piles of supplies smolder, ammunition dumps burn the earth black.

At the top, I look out at Kentucky, a state that belongs to the Union. Rough mountains rise above narrow valleys, and autumn colors the trees too distant for use by the armies. Federal supplies litter the roadside—overcoats, tin plates, books. I pick up a tin canteen and replace my ragged blanket with an almost new wool one.

At the first rest, Posey unbuckles an abandoned leather knapsack and picks through the contents.

"They carry the same as us. And more. Anybody want playing cards?"

"I'll take them," David says.

"Hard crackers and tinned sardines," Posey says, putting them aside. "We'll keep these in the ration box."

He opens an envelope and pulls out cards with portraits pasted to them. "Oh my. We should burn these."

"Let's see," Rufe says.

Posey hands him the cards. He fans them out, fancy girls exposing their breasts and bare bottoms, ruffled skirts raised above the hair and gaps of private parts, legs cocked up and open.

I haven't seen a naked girl since my sisters were toddlers, don't have words for what I see here. Imagining Genny's breasts under my hand, her legs like these, the sensations that rise shame me. How any man could feel about a woman the way I do Genny and want to ogle bawdy cards of fancy girls is no way to think of love.

"Posey's right," I say. "Nothing good can come from those."

"I bet we can get a quarter a piece for them," Eli says.

"We?" Rufe asks. "What does we have to do with it?"

"Like the crackers and sardines, we'd all gain from it," Eli says.

"Let him have them," I say. "He needs the money."

Rufe is always asking to borrow against his pay, running out of water and rations, trading off Fatigue duty, getting out of what he's too lazy to do.

"Do what you want," Rufe says and tosses the cards to Eli.

***

In the warm mornings, the front of the column and every marching foot that follows raise the ever-present dust cloud. We breathe it in, swallow it. The heat rises with the sun, through barren lands, dry creeks and rivers. In long stretches, the only water comes from shrunken, muddy ponds. I fill both canteens when given the chance and swallow whatever comes with the water. My clothes are stiff with sweat and dust, and every part of my body stinks.

We march into the night. Exhausted men fall out by the roadside, beg for water, and straggle behind. I manage to do little more than stay upright, afraid if I fall behind I'll be lost. Dust coats my messmates so thoroughly I can hardly tell one from another. I close my eyes, my thoughts jumbled with wanting to arrive at any destination, clean myself, drink fresh water, and eat food not full of dust.

The column stalls. Lewis faints to the ground. I open his canteen and revive him with a handful of dirty water.

"I'm finished," he says.

"If you straggle, General Barton'll have you shot," I say, grabbing him under the arms and trying to pull him upright.

"I don't care," he says, resisting the pull.

"We do," Posey says. "I'll carry your rifle."

"Just let me rest," Lewis says.

The column restarts. Eli, Rufe, and David fall in.

"It's not right to leave him," I say.

"We can't stay with him," Posey says. "We'd be shot for straggling too."

"I'll catch up," Lewis says. "You go on."

I pour water into his canteen from mine.

"I hope this helps a little," I say.

We leave him by the roadside and march on without rest, rations, or sleep. Officers ride through on horseback. When ammunition wagons and artillery units force us off the road, I sleep where I stand.

Orders come to turn around and march back in the direction we just came from. I watch for Lewis, in case he's trying to catch up. We turn west, away from the hope of dawn. We stop when day breaks, near the town of London, and fall out to cook rations. David starts a fire and fries all of our side-meat in the spider.

"I'm tired of eating it raw," he says.

Lewis is not among the stragglers dragging into camp. Rumors pass up and down the roadside—a captain of one company and a lieutenant in another resigned in frustration and went home, the retreating Federals escaped into Ohio, General Barton is drunk again.

"Barton gets drunk as a fool and we go thirsty," Rufe says.

Burnett, from the next mess, shuffles in and walks up to me.

"I saw Knell turn back," he says and hands me Lewis's jaw harp.

I think of Lewis twanging out the rhythm while others sing, turn the small harp over, and finger the bent end of the steel tongue.

"Why did he send it back?" I ask Burnett.

"He told me he was grateful you were the one to help him."

I fit it against my mouth and push the tongue. The noise I make doesn't sound like his playing, and the spring cuts my lip. What to do with this gift I can't use? Take it home to the twins as a souvenir of war.

***

We camp near a river crossing in fields of waist-high grass. This part of Kentucky is a land of plenty with fat cattle and sleek horses grazing in rich pasture land. The roads, called turnpikes, are lined with stone walls that run past houses of painted boards and glass-paned windows.

Clean from a bath in the river, I pick through every inch of the seams in my drawers, socks, shirt and trousers for lice. I hang the clothes from my bayonet to dry and lie down in the trampled grass. It's almost as soft as I remember my bed at home. I pull my hat over my eyes and smell cut grass, feel the sun on my chest.

"I don't know why you all bother to wash up," Rufe says. "It'll be dust all over again tomorrow."

"It can't hurt to start fresh," I say.

I hope this is a fresh start, a change from the barren lands. Tonight we have full rations of Irish potatoes, coffee, salt, and syrup. Someone found a supply of pumpkins. Firewood details sawed up fence rails for mess fires. Potatoes and a pumpkin roast in the coals of ours.

The smell of pumpkin takes me to the night I fell in love with Genny. I carry her small silk bag against my heart. It doesn't have anything in it, except maybe hope, if you can carry that in a silk bag.

***

Camped on the high banks of the Kentucky River near Frankfort, Orders come to clean arms, accoutrements, and clothing. Rumors on the grapevine warn of a large enemy force west in Louisville, but cleaning clothing is not a part of battle preparations.

"General Bragg ordered this," Rufe says. "I heard it at headquarters. There's a governor going to be in-awe-garated. What's that mean?"

"Inaugurated," I say. "Swearing into office, like mustering in."

"Whatever they're doing to him, once they do it, General Bragg's going to start conscripting Kentucky men."

"They haven't been joining up all along?"

"Colonel says they like keeping their cattle and horses more than joining us."

From what I've seen, Kentuckians have something worth protecting. The surrounding fields are thick with corn and wheat. The cattle are bigger than ours in Pickens County, and we have no match for the horses. But why should Kentucky land and livestock be worth so much that Georgia boys have to come and fight for it? I can't do a thing about Kentucky men who won't join the fight, but the next time there are apple orchards and walnut trees ripe for the picking, or fields of potatoes and cabbages by the roadside, I'm going to forage as others do, without believing it's stealing. If we're defending them, they can feed us.

***

In the crowd of soldiers lining the road into Frankfort, I stretch to see our Brigade's General Barton. Reportedly not drunk and disgraceful since coming over the mountain called Big Hill, he parades on horseback with the rest of the generals in full-dress uniforms thick with gold frogging.

Regimental bands are playing *Dixie*, off time and out of tune. Above the music and cheering, the boom of artillery fire starts up in the west. We all turn to the sound but see nothing in the skies. Confusion spreads through the crowd as the inauguration begins. No one can say who is shooting. The ceremony for the new governor ends unceremoniously. Generals hustle away to rejoin their brigades. Our Company forms up and falls in with the column marching away.

We march through Frankfort and on to the Lexington Pike, Versailles, and Lawrenceburg. No one knows why. Big guns thunder in the south.

Company! Form the Line!

Broken-down corn stalks rustle under our shuffling feet as we form the Battle Line in a field. We don't know who is coming or from where. My mouth is dry and my throat tightens, but I have my bowels under control. I am more nervous than afraid, standing here while the noise of battle carries on somewhere else. How will I act when battle comes to me again? After all the drill in going forward, rifles ready, kneeling, aiming, firing, will I remember or go blank with fear, like I did at Tazewell? Caissons rattle and creak on the road behind us. The rumble of heavy wagons crosses the fields. Commanded to Face Right, we turn and march away.

Played-out, bone-tired, fed-up, and confused, we end up in the old camp near Danville. We have marched all day At The Ready, up and down the same road, changing directions with changing orders, expecting a fight.

"You think we won the battle?" David asks.

"We didn't even see what the battle was," I answer. "And if we did win, how come we're headed out of here in the same direction we came?"

As far as I'm concerned, some regiments are fighting this war, but ours isn't one of them. We have no prospects for being Comrades in Battle, only comrades in endless marching.

***

Standing in Battle Line at the Bardstown Pike, rain soaks into my clothes, runs down my back, arms and legs, into my socks. Not allowed to get out oil cloths, we can do nothing but endure. My haversack and shoes are wet and heavy. Drums take up the Long Roll signaling the movement away from yet another battlefield on which we have not fought.

We cross a river and form another Battle Line, muddy from the knees down, watching General Kirby Smith's entire Army of Kentucky and its supply train enter the road. Droves of hogs, sheep, and beef cattle follow stage coaches, carriages, omnibuses, and hundreds of captured new wagons with "US" stenciled on the canvas. They are traveling the same route, in reverse, of what was General Smith's glorious invasion of Kentucky. In the overwhelming stink and noise of it, I realize that the supply train is more important to the Army than we are.

Our supply wagon is somewhere else. I am hungry and tired but keep turning my eyes to the empty road behind us, watching for the enemy's approach. The Brigade's cavalry trots up the road past the muddy, rutted fields.

"Looks like we're going to be Rear Guard," I say.

"So if the enemy's chasing the cavalry, we'll be hit first?" Rufe asks.

"That's the purpose of Rear Guard."

"Don't you want to get into a battle?"

I've had time to think about this, marching around, seeing how little the Army considers us. I think winning battles is the way wars are won, but from what I've seen of the General Officers who conduct the efforts of the Army of Tennessee, I'm not so sure I want a real battle.

***

We slog along a twisting road filled with mud and manure. It cuts between small farms and woods. The constant rifle-fire behind us is either our cavalry, the pursuing enemy, eastern Kentucky bushwhackers favoring the Union, or all three. Around a curve in the road, six howitzers have formed a line, pointed directly at us. I stop myself from dropping to the roadbed in fear.

"The cavalry's been holding back the enemy," Sergeant Williams announces. "We're going to block this curve to slow them down. A little artillery fire will make them think there's more of us dug in and waiting."

Work details scatter into the woods, breaking down small trees and bushes, dragging them to the road, and piling them into a blockade.

"Didn't think I'd say work beat anything, but this beats marching," Rufe says.

I toss a bush onto the pile. It's the same work as clearing a new field except I don't have an ax or saw and there's no hot dinner waiting for me in a clean house.

"Is this really going to work?" Rufe asks.

Up and down the road, the blockade covers a good mile and stretches into the woods.

"They'll have to stop and clear it," I reply. "They might think there's more of us everywhere. Like when we guarded the gaps in Tennessee."

I go back into the woods where I'd seen a small orchard, climb a tree, and fill my haversack with apples. I ignore the raggedy children watching from the porch of a broken-down cabin.

***

Over the Big Hill where General Barton was so blue-eyed drunk, we hold another Battle Line at the rear of the column. I can't remember how many we've formed in this useless invasion and retreat, but we are good at doing it quickly. What started as something proud, standing elbow to elbow, tense and waiting for the command to go forward, has ended up as nothing more than time on our feet.

The supply train takes two days to pass over the steep road. Fanned and flanking cavalry guard the rattling, motley collection of transports, cumbersome artillery, and the whistling, shouting cowboys who herd the bleating, bawling livestock. We stand in Battle Line a day longer to keep enemy artillery beyond range of the precious supplies.

At the top of the hill, I take a last look at the grassy plains of Kentucky. We are ragged and worn out. For all of our marching, what have we accomplished? We have lost Lewis, lost time, lost Kentucky. I turn for the crossing into the rough and barren lands before Cumberland Gap.

***

With no rations, no supply wagon, broken down shoes if any at all, we push stragglers ahead of us. In the last bivouac before the Gap, a supply detail approaches with jugs.

"Courtesy of Colonel Johnson," one of the men says as he pours bourbon into my cup. "He bought it for the Regiment and hopes it eases your suffering. It's the last you'll have of Kentucky."

It tastes sweeter than Moody Simpson's. Given the choice I'd rather be home drinking Moody's whiskey than all the finest bourbon Kentucky has to offer.

It snows in the night.

We trudge down the switchbacks, shin-deep in it. I follow bloody footprints.

"Are those yours?" I ask Eli.

"I guess," he replies, looking down at his bare and bleeding feet.

"You'd think they'd let us fall out and build a fire," Posey says, rubbing his red hands.

"There isn't anything left to build a fire with," David says.

"They aren't thinking about us at all," I say.

"I have a towel we can wrap around your feet," Posey says to Eli.

"You think they'll take us for stragglers if we stop?" Eli asks.

"What are they going to do? Send us back to Kentucky?" I ask.

We fall out by the roadside. Posey rips the towel in two, winds the halves around Eli's feet, and ties them in place with package string from his haversack.

"I can see the iron furnace ahead," I say. "We went into Kentucky on this road, chasing the Federals out. Now they've chased us back in."

I stare down the road. "Our own army is going to march us to death."

15

Falling Behind

Eliza Ann

THE SPRING HOUSE smells of cedar, cold water, and warm milk. I fill two buckets with water. Steam rises from crockery pans, fresh from the morning milking. *Come butter come, come butter come, baby's standing by the gate, waiting for some butter cake, come butter come.* Lydia's churning song. I never know what will call up a memory or when, what will make my throat close up, my chest tighten, tears roll down my cheeks.

Lucy tried to explain how childbed fever comes on, how seldom it happens, but I am still bewildered by how Lydia could die. That death is so final. Who else is going to die like this?

Cold air tingles the inside of my nose. I set the water buckets on the back porch and take up the axe. Splitting wood is warm and tidy work. The steady thwack of axe into wood usually calms my mind. Pap and the twins have little time to cut wood. The pile of branches and fence rails Ananias and David left will not last the winter from what I can see. It's the latest sign of falling behind.

I carry an armful of splits into the house and fill the wood box. Rebecca is ironing shirts and blouses at the table. Louise is kneeling at the hearth, stirring apple butter and turning a turkey on the spit.

"You look like you're working something over," Louise says.

"Will anything ever be the way it used to?" I ask.

"Nothing ever is, child." I didn't hear Mam come into the room. "Life is always on the change, even without a war. We live with what the times give us."

I don't care to live with the times. They aren't giving us anything but trouble.

***

The weather has turned cold, the moon is on the wane, and it's been hog-killing time. Less than what we usually do, without the work of Howell, David, Ananias, and Tom, but some things are the same—hog-killing supper of fresh livers with red pepper and salt, butchering-day breakfast of brains and eggs. Hams, shoulders, and side-meat hanging in the smokehouse over hickory coals. I made up Jane's receipt and didn't make myself sick.

Walking home from Sunday Meeting, Mary Jane and I giggle over Mr. Buchanan's pompous ways. We are almost home. I loosen my half-corset and straighten my skirt. Ahead of us, the twins are shoving each other around. Beyond them, through the trees, smoke rises in a column.

"Pap!" I shout, pointing.

He breaks into a run. We all do, right behind him.

The smoke is coming from the back of the house. I run behind the twins into the back yard. Flames cover the smokehouse. Pap and the boys grab buckets off the porch. They're always kept full when meat is smoking, fireplaces are smoldering, and candle lanterns light the dark. Lafe empties a bucket onto the leaping flames, tosses it to me, and grabs another. Luke does the same with Mary Jane.

"Fill them from the branch!" he shouts.

We run to the branch, scoop up water, run back to the fire. Rebecca is ringing the dinner bell without stopping. Charlotte comes out of the barn carrying the full barn buckets, shouting, "There's mule blankets. We can beat it with those."

The flames rise back after every dousing of water. No one can get close enough to beat them down and smother them.

"We can't save it," Pap says, out of breath, collapsing to the ground. "We need to wet down the house roof so it doesn't catch."

Mr. Monroe and Thad round the corner carrying buckets, shouting, "We heard the bell."

We run full buckets between branch and yard while the men and boys pitch water at the house roof, privy, spring house, wood piles, anything close enough for sparks to drift and catch.

In a cloud of sparks and flames, the smokehouse caves in. Shingles, planks, and meat box, all burn in the bright fire. So does our meat. Wet, smelling of smoke and burnt pork, we stand on the back porch and watch.

"How did it start?" Mr. Monroe asks.

"We saw it coming home," Pap answers.

***

My dreams are filled with blood and fire, hideouts showing up with muskets. What else will the times give us, or take away? I never wanted my life to change at all.

I wake early, start the morning fire, and go out to the privy. Kize Bowen stands up from behind the woodpile.

"Why are you here?" I ask, startled.

"Burned smokehouse."

"You did?"

"Pap. The big boys," he says and scuttles into the woods.

Kize stinks, but most of the Bowens do. At school he'd listen raptly whenever I recited. Painfully slow at learning, when he did recite, it was gibberish. His brothers and sisters ignored him except to throw lunch scraps and laugh when he scrambled to catch them.

Pap comes out and looks into the woods.

"Was that Kize Bowen?"

"He came to tell me Bowens set the fire."

"I'd reckon as much out of them. It's an old way of warning. Some poison wells, some burn barns, never showing themselves."

"What are you going to do?"

"Stay on the watch."

"You're not mad? Don't you hate the Bowens even more for this?"

"I'd like to shoot Ansell Bowen. But I won't. It'll bother him most having to wait and see what I'm going to do about it. I can wait a good long time just thinking of him wondering when. Hatred never serves a person well. Bowen's own evil will do him in."

***

The morning is cold and clear. I carry a bucket of whey to Cassiopeia and what's left of the hogs. Pap and Mr. Monroe rebuilt the smokehouse, and we killed and butchered the boars Pap intended to sell. The Monroes and Wilders gave us cuts of their own partially-smoked meat. With less hog meat, we've turned to turkey, squirrels, and rabbits. Pap and the twins don't bring home deer like Ananias did. I don't practice shooting now that Pap insists a male always be at home. I don't mind. It won't be the same without Lydia and her targets.

Two bushy bundles of cedar boughs walk around the barn. Pap comes behind them, arms full of holly, sprigs of mistletoe poking out of a haversack.

"It's Christmas Eve," one of the bushes says in Luke's voice.

So it is. I don't anticipate or feel much lately. It seems safer.

I help Mary Jane twist ropes of cedar up and around the stair rail. We line both fireplace mantles with shiny green holly and red berries. By suppertime the sharp fragrance of cedar fills the house, and mistletoe hangs in the doorways. Piled under the stairs, where I found my Christmas gifts as a little girl, are those for Howell's children—wooden blocks for Samuel, knit shawls for Emily and Lily, and a green knit cap with red knot berries for baby Daniel, born after Howell left. Callie's family is nearby, but she and Howell always came to us for Christmas dinner.

Christmas Eve supper hasn't changed—griddle cakes served on Mam's blue Queensware platter and stewed peaches, blackberry preserves, and currant jelly shimmering in glass bowls. The family around the table is the biggest change. Last Christmas we were fourteen, passing the platter and bowls, laughing and talking. I try not to cry, missing Lydia, my brothers.

***

We sit by the light of the fire. Mary Jane's sweet soprano starts, *"It came upon the midnight clear."* Tonight the twins sing louder, in cracking voices, trying to make up for the absence of their brothers. Last year Lydia was insisting that we'd enjoy her listening far more than her singing. In a family of singers I am not one of the best, so I sing harmony, where the high notes don't matter so much. It's been a family joke that our voices vary enough to form a heavenly choir. Without David, Ananias, and Tom, we are no choir.

Quiet settles on the room, and Mam recites the old story from the verses of *The Gospel According to Saint Luke.* She finishes and smiles at Pap.

"Syllabub!" he shouts. "Follow me!"

The twins jump up and hurry out to the back porch, singing *"Joy to the world..."* They lift a kettle with its mixture of the last of Moody's whiskey and the last of the sugar and nutmeg, and head for the barn. I light a candle lantern. Mary Jane and Charlotte gather up crockery cups. We parade through the back yard, singing at the top of our voices, *"A-and Hea-ven, and He-a-ven, and nature sing."* Louise keeps time, beating a ladle and long-handled spoon. Rebecca stops at the spring house for a jug of cream. Mam comes last.

The unweathered planks of the new smokehouse shine in the light of a waxing moon. In the dark barn we stand together in lantern light. The twins lower the kettle beneath April. Pap squats beside her and pulls a stream of milk into the kettle. The warm milk bubbles as it hits the whiskey. He does the same with June. The twins stir the milky mixture until it's frothy, and Pap says, "It's ready."

Rebecca pours the cream, and Pap stirs it in. He ladles syllabub into our cups before the froth subsides. When every cup is full, he raises his.

"At Christmas time, this year and every year, especially this year, Glory to God in the highest and on earth, peace, goodwill toward men."

I sip the whiskey-laced, milk-warm syllabub. I feel peaceful enough in body if not in spirit. That's from Moody's whiskey. Peace and goodwill are not present on earth, not in our country, not in our neighborhood. I leave the barn and look up to Orion and the Seven Sisters. I hope Ananias is watching them too.

16

Who Wouldn't Be a Soldier?

Alabama-Mississippi, December 1862

Ananias

CHRISTMAS EVE, THE night of peace and joy, and I am spending it crowded together with my messmates on backless benches in a rail car, rattling and lurching through the dark.

I shift on the bench and scratch at the lice in my hair. We all have them—in our hair, clothes, blankets. Scrubbing and washing doesn't get rid of them. I've tried picking them out of the seams, like Sergeant Williams showed us, but new ones grow from the nits I don't find. We never had lice at home.

"How do you Covingtons celebrate Christmas?" Posey asks from down the bench.

"Syllabub!" I shout, almost in unison with David.

"That's it?"

"If you knew Pap's syllabub, you wouldn't need anything else," I answer. "It's what we look forward to most on Christmas Eve. On Christmas Day we have gifts for Howell's little ones and a big dinner. What about yours?"

"We attend church service on Christmas Eve, have Christmas gifts in the morning, visit the neighbors, and eat a big dinner," he replies. "Our cook makes a beef steak so tender you don't need a knife. And the best light cakes. Some do it fancier and bigger, but I like the busyness of ours."

"What about you, Eli?" I ask. I'm guessing it wasn't much but want to include him.

"The last place I worked was neighbor to the biggest plantation in the area, and they celebrated large," he answers.

"How large?" Rufe asks.

"Every way you can imagine. The whole neighborhood came, over a hundred folks. Men dressed in fine suits and ladies in lacy bonnets and big silky skirts and little cloth shoes."

"What did they have to eat?"

"Ham, turkey, eels, oysters, light bread, heaps of potatoes, pickles, all sorts of jellied things, fruit cakes, nut pies. There was fiddle music and dancing and rum punch in big glass bowls and whiskey passed around. Then they set out a supper with more food and drink and gave us oranges and little bags of candies to take with us."

"What's oysters?"

"Slimy things, come from the sea in a knobby shell. Taste like a cross between raw eggs and hog balls. They're the only thing I wouldn't take for seconds."

"They let you eat with the fancy folks?"

"I wore a clean shirt, ate myself full, and had a high time. Even danced a little. From that, things happened I never expected. Best left untold. How did your folks do it?"

"Sweets," Rufe answers. "My mam and sisters pulled taffy candy, the best in the hills. The rest was like Covington's. But no syllabub."

I close my eyes and wish for Christmas at home. It's a bright memory. Christmas in the present is somewhere in Alabama, another state I've never seen. I haven't seen much of it with no windows in the rail car.

I have no better idea of why men go to war. Posey enlisted to avoid the shame of conscription. Rufe did it for the bounty money. Eli said, "It was time to leave."

Our war has been the misery of these last months in Tennessee with not enough tents, short rations, and Drill in the cold and snow. We had no soap and no way to bathe or shave. The camp was unclean, and men died from measles and dysentery. Sergeant Williams kept us alive, telling us to stew our rations, not eat them raw, wipe out our dishes, and use the Sinks at the edge of camp. Seems our reward for staying alive and well is now we're on the way to more war.

***

It's a gray Christmas dawn. Stopped at a station town surrounded by cotton fields, we're standing beside the track eating dry corn bread. Women approach from the end of the station platform serving food and drink from baskets and buckets. I hold out my cup to one carrying a ladle and bucket of cider. Those behind her give out little fried pies and pieces of taffy wrapped in paper. That should make Rufe happy. I bite into a corner of pie. Peach. It takes me to August in the orchard, branches sagging with peaches so ripe one bite fills the mouth with sweet juice, the hot day full of peach scent, Louise's crusty pies and golden jam.

"You going to stand there all day with your eyes closed or help us thank these ladies?"

Eli's voice brings me back to the field beside the tracks, the waiting train. I tip my hat to the women and climb into the car.

What we know is the Yankees have invaded Mississippi and we are being sent to defend it. I can't say when we started calling the enemy Yankees instead of Federals, or ourselves Rebels instead of Confederates. If I'm a Rebel, it's a reluctant rebel. I don't understand why Yankees would come this far south. They have no homes to defend here. The only Yankee I've known was Mr. Woodall. I have little cause to dislike them, except they're why I'm headed west, away from my home.

My thoughts turn on themselves until the only conclusion is *Who wouldn't be a soldier?* It's not a question. It's a saying soldiers have for when Army regulations and the activities of war don't make sense. You've got to pretend you don't care.

***

We arrive at Vicksburg before the New Year, stiff, tired, and hungry after a week of riding the cars. We march away from the station on a muddy road, in which direction I can't tell. I know the Mississippi River is close, west of the city. That is something I want to see for myself, how the mighty river twists and turns like it did on the map in Mr. Woodall's Atlas.

"Company! Halt! Bivouac off the road!"

Our supply wagons are somewhere else. I chew on the dry bread I have left. I'm saving the piece of taffy. I unroll my blanket, lie down, and spoon against Eli's back for warmth. David spoons against mine. We learned to keep each other warm like this in Tennessee.

Drums taking up the Long Roll wake me. It's the middle of the night. I feel around for my rifle and accoutrements in the dark.

"Fall in!" The command echoes from one Company to the next.

"Cadence step!" Corporals take up the count, and I step out in time. It's the best way to get warm.

We march until dawn and fall out into fields, lying about in fence corners. Eli and I build a fire from cedar rails. I drowse, almost warm, almost asleep, and startle upright at the crack of an artillery shell bursting overhead, crashing into a mess fire down the line. Men scream and scatter. I scramble to douse the fire.

"Where the hell did that come from?" Rufe asks.

"Must be Yankees," Posey replies.

"I'd hope so," I say.

"Why?" Rufe asks.

"Wouldn't want it to be one of ours with bad aim."

It could be the beginning of an attack. The Company forms up in the road. It's raining. I pull my haversack under my coat, tighten the lids of my cartridge and cap boxes, turn my rifle musket down, and wait. As the sky lightens, the rain stops. Artillery fire booms from up the road. The crack of musketry opens on our Right Front.

"Just like Kentucky," I say. "A battle goes on, we don't know who it is, and we don't get into it. We've been marched around so much, no wonder they call us Barton's Foot Cavalry."

"If we don't get into battle, we don't get shot," David says.

We do not move while the firing slackens then renews.

"Company! Forward! At the Quick!"

At last. We trot across a field of broken-down cotton stems, husks, and hulls. The colors of the Thirty-First Louisiana fly on our right near a mound. Its Line fires into the trees at their Front. Enemy fire flashes in return.

We stop at a ditch. Sniper fire comes at us from the other side of a small lake.

"Maintain your line! Into the trench! Load your weapons!"

I drop into the ditch and land in a puddle of cold water. It soaks through my shoes and into my socks. I step out of the puddle into mud, my feet squishy and growing numb. A flock of bullets whine and whistle overhead. This feels like a real battle.

"Get down!" Sergeant Williams shouts.

I duck and squat in the mud. My hands shake as I pull a cartridge from the box, bite off the paper, and pour powder into the barrel. The business of loading steadies my hands and my head. I raise my rifle, look down the sight to the smoke across the lake, and fire at the enemy. For the first time. Smoke fills the ditch, and I raise my head for a breath of air.

Men in dark uniforms run from a tree line toward the mound held by the Louisiana boys.

"They're moving on our Right," I say.

"Are we aiming at them?" David asks.

"No. Ahead, across the water."

I load, fire again, duck below the top of the ditch to avoid the return fire, keep loading and firing. Afternoon turns to night, rain falls harder as we trade fire with enemy sharpshooters.

With no commands to leave our position, we relieve ourselves into the puddles, sleep standing in mud, leaning against the dirt walls of the ditch.

***

At daylight, Sergeant Williams explains that our Regiment is being held in reserve to support the Louisianans. We're firing across the lake to keep the enemy occupied at this end of the Line. The battle on our Right rages all day and into the night. My ears ring and my head aches with it.

Disembodied voices rise from the ditch.

"Why are we firing into the dark?"

"Because we're told to?"

"Can you see anything?"

"Nope."

David nudges me. "Think we convinced them not to come this way?"

"I wouldn't know," I answer. "But we finally fired at the enemy."

We bivouac beneath dripping trees. My canteens are almost empty.

"Think we'll ever get hot food?" Rufe asks.

"The chance of that is as good as getting any food," I reply.

If the last night was miserable, this night is worse, the air damp and cold, my feet wet, no food, no fire to dry us out and keep us warm. I nibble on the piece of taffy. Everyone is hungry. We sleep spooned in a row on the wet ground under wet blankets, flipping over in the night, taking turns being the man on the end.

***

Morning fog settles thick in the trees and hangs to the ground. Shivering in the wet air, I kick my legs and wave my arms to get warm. It worked when I was kept out on a night, hunting.

We return to the ditch.

"This is getting us nowhere," Rufe complains, crouching in the mud and water.

"Where do you want to go?" I ask. "We've got us a battle, even if it's only an edge of it."

"I want to kill me some Yankees. See them die."

I hunker down. Rufe's complaints are endless, have no resolution, and I'm tired of answering. I don't want to watch men die.

The guns go silent.

A Quartermaster detail comes along with rations, water, and information. The enemy has requested a flag of truce to bury their dead and attend to their wounded. Our artillery and sharpshooters on the bluffs shot down the Yankees as they advanced in ranks below them. The place is called Chickasaw Bayou. A messenger on his way out of the battleground describes it.

"I got up on our fortifications and saw them take off their dead," he says. "There was so many it took them all day. Men, boys, no different than us, bodies broken, all swollen up and stiff."

Why would the Yankees send rank after rank to die like that? Why would men march in the face of certain death? Doing as commanded, I realize. Forward March. It could have happened to me anytime we formed a Battle Line in Kentucky. It still could. All of those Yankees died following orders. And I doubt the rest are giving up and going home.

"Seems like we have to kill more of them than they do us," I say.

"That's how one side convinces the other to quit," Posey says. "Kill all the young men. It's how the kings of England did it, how Napoleon did it."

That is what war is about. Killing each other. Old men, leaders and generals, start the wars and run them. Young men die in them. I've heard our officers talk about glory and courage being important to war. What is the glory in dying? Who would have the courage to take that on if they knew about it first?

Who wouldn't be a soldier?

17

Socks for Soldiers

Eliza Ann

THE LILTING LINES and rhymes are what I enjoy about poems. On cold and blustery nights like this, it's thrilling to read aloud by candle light *The Wreck of the Hesperus* and *The Inchcape Rock*. We're about as far away from seas as a place can be, and it makes me think of how Ananias wanted to see those sailing ships. We don't know where he is.

Tonight, reading is an escape from knitting socks for soldiers. It's Rebecca's idea after hearing about women forming societies to do such things. I can't come up with reasons for not doing it.

As long as Mr. Monroe's sheep keep us in wool, there'll be plenty of yarn. That's something the War hasn't taken away.

I know she won't let me carry on reciting for long, and I feel badly for the soldiers needing socks, so I shelve the Reader, take up the last sock I started, and count the stitches. When it comes to anything complicated, like turning a heel, I can't knit along while talking and laughing like my sisters do. I lose my place and have to pull apart my uneven rows and start over, with kinky yarn. That makes the socks look even worse. Without Lydia to laugh with me about it makes me feel even worse. I miss her every day.

"I heard the Bowens have exemptions for tanner, blacksmith, and Militia officers," Rebecca says. "I wish Ike and Joe had waited."

She'll use any excuse to mention them, despite knowing what their brothers did to us.

"They bought those Militia exemptions for Elias and Frank," Pap says. "Too bad Benson and Caleb don't have a brain between them, they could've bought a constable and a justice of the peace. If they'd thought of it before Ike and Joe signed up maybe they could've had a tinker and a thief. Exemptions are for necessary work. Even though George is a poor excuse for a tanner and no one wants to let Harmon shoe their horses, those boys do jobs we need done. If they'd give exemptions for farmers we wouldn't have an army or a war."

"Ike and Joe signed up like your sons did," Mam says. "They're in as much danger and only want to be worthy of your daughters. They were not here when our smokehouse burned."

"It's not enough for Bowen to want my property so bad he'll destroy it," Pap says. "Now he wants to worm his boys into my family."

Getting Pap off his high horse is not easy, and Rebecca gives up on the Bowens. For now.

"Mrs. Halford proposed a knitting bee," she says.

"We'd have to go there and knit?" I ask.

I dread the thought of exposing how bad I am at knitting. One more thing for Harriet to criticize besides my pronunciation. We haven't spoken since then.

"Of course. I reckon with six of us we could knit more socks than any women's group. It would be like quilting at Jane's."

Not to me. Quilting bees at Jane's were times of women sewing and talking together about all the things, big and little, that mattered to them, without men around to hear, without anyone judging who was educated or ignorant.

***

When we learned of President Lincoln's proclamation to free the slaves, not everyone was as happy as Pap. He thinks it will end the War sooner.

At last Meeting I overheard Harriet carrying on to Mrs. Chastain how keeping slaves is a right and we should have known what to expect from that black Republican ape of a President Lincoln. She went on about, from what she'd seen of north Georgia, she didn't know why the Confederacy would want it, nothing but cornfields and ignorant Unionists.

She doesn't have the sense to know that talking secession to Secessionists isn't going to make a difference in what people believe. We all picked our sides a long time ago. None of our Secessionist neighbors hold slaves. Their farms are small, and they aren't wealthy. The Tates in Harnageville own the most land

and the most slaves. Others in the district own some, mostly for servants. I've never been in a house that does. It makes me wonder how a person would feel, being owned.

I wish Harriet would go back to South Carolina and live with the radicals who started the War. Maybe she'd have to be a servant girl for people who don't have any reason to care about her. I know it's mean-spirited to wish bad things for an orphan girl, but Harriet is not pitiful.

***

An itinerant Methodist preacher is conducting Meeting. I look around for the Wilders and Lydia's baby. They're sitting in front of the Halfords. The Buchanans are next to the Halfords, and Jeremiah is sitting next to Harriet. What if they have feelings for each other? Thinking of how Lydia wanted everyone to have feelings for someone, I'd come to hope he might smile at me again. He and Thad Monroe are the only boys left close to my age, if you don't count Luther Bowen, and I try not to.

Mrs. Buchanan looks pale and thin. Mr. Buchanan is almost unrecognizable. His chin hangs to his chest, and the skin of his face sags in folds. His legs splay out, and he stares at the hat in his hands. Chadwick, his pride and joy, is dead, killed at the Battle of Sharpsburg in September, his body buried where he lay on the field. The Buchanans didn't get word of it until Christmas.

The preacher begins his sermon in Proverbs. "*Rejoice not when thine enemy falleth, and let not thine heart be glad when he stumbleth. Be not a witness against thy neighbour without cause; and deceive not with thy lips. Say not, I will do so to him as he hath done to me: I will render to the man according to his work.*"

"This war has taken our fathers, sons, husbands, and brothers. We make it worse when neighbors become enemies. We are bound in this together by the sacrifices of our men. We have no cause to witness against our neighbors when they have also suffered. Our own suffering makes us no better. Neither does our lack of it. Would we ask our neighbor to suffer in our stead? Would we agree to suffer in his?"

I'm not sure who all this witnessing and suffering is directed at, but Pap lowers his head and looks into his hands.

At the end of Meeting, Mam goes to Mrs. Buchanan. They hug each other. Mr. Buchanan sits holding his hat. Mrs. Buchanan takes it up and puts it on his head. She lifts one hand from his lap and helps him stand. Jeremiah takes his father's other hand and helps lead him out. He doesn't look at me or Harriet.

***

Jane keeps a pallet on the floor of her sleeping room for my visits. These days the house smells of soap and wheat bread. I've started coming on my own, at first because I knew my help was needed and wanted, then just to talk. It relieves me, to walk in Jane's door and know I'll be listened to.

"Come sit with me a minute," she says, patting the quilt.

I climb onto the high bed.

"You've been quiet these days. Thinking something over?"

"How do you get someone to love you?"

I didn't mean to blurt it out so fast.

"Do you have someone in mind?"

"I don't know. Lydia wanted me to have feelings for Jeremiah, but he sat with Harriet at Meeting."

"Why are you interested in Jeremiah?"

"He's smart and he never laughed at my questions and he asked me about things we were learning."

"More than one person can do that in a lifetime."

"But the rest are off at war. Thad Monroe's so quiet and timid, he looks at his shoes when he talks to you. Luther Bowen is disgusting and mean. And they're both a head shorter than me."

"Most of the Bowens are disgusting, mean as snakes, and more. Don't ever get caught alone with a one of them. Everyone knows they're the ones who burned your smokehouse. And boys being shorter or taller has nothing to do with love."

"Do you think anyone will ever love me?"

"I think so." She pats my arm. "It's the War what's thrown us all off. When the boys come home, there'll be someone who thinks the world of you. That's how it starts. Then knowing when someone is worthy of your thoughts in return. And when the right boy comes along, he might be a man. His look will make your heart beat faster and he'll pay attention to only you, just for being yourself. There's no way to prepare for that but be yourself."

"How do I know who my self is?"

"That's the hard question for someone your age. Think about why we all love you. Think about what you like. Love will come to you. It does to all of us."

"Louise doesn't have anyone."

"She did. He went off with Sam Bozeman to the gold fields and never came back. Neither did Sam. No one knew why. They died or stayed. It discouraged her so, she's never looked at anyone again."

"Could that happen to me?"

"That could happen to anyone by chance. But Louise is far shyer than you."

"What if all the boys die in the War?"

"They can't kill all of us, or we them. Wars have to end or there'd be nobody left to fight them. There'll be someone for you."

I crawl under my blanket and lie awake. Who loves me? Lydia had. Mary Jane does. Rebecca surely doesn't, nor Harriett. No boys, not counting my brothers. Why would one love a girl who reads and wants to know things, wants to aim a musket at a hideout?

18

Turn the Other Cheek

March 1863

Eliza Ann

O N A COLD afternoon, Pap returns from Buchanan's store with two bags of salt tied across Abe. The State of Georgia supplies salt to soldiers' families, and his name and David's are on the Salt List. He carries smaller packages into the house.

"They had saleratus," he says. "No molasses or spices, no pins and needles. He's closing the store, and they're going to her people in Savannah. I told him how bad we feel about Chadwick's dying. We agreed how we needn't have taken offense over his boy going early, ours going later. I can't imagine having one of the boys

133

dying and us not knowing for so long we can't go and carry his body home."

I try not to sigh. The Buchanans leaving ends any hope for feelings about Jeremiah. Pap sets a paper-wrapped package on the table, and pulls an envelope from his pocket.

"I saved the best for last. We have a letter from Ananias. Buchanan's wife said Eliza Ann and Mary Jane would know how to use what's in the package."

Mam takes up the envelope like it's a piece of silk work. She hands it to me.

"Let's hear it this minute," she says.

I remove the single page and read aloud.

> 13th of August, 1862, near Rutledge Tennessee.
> Dear Family. I am taking pen in hand as our messmate Posey Huff has told me this is how to start. We are in good health and hope you are the same. David sends his love most of all to Lydia. We are in Company D of the 40th Georgia Infantry Regiment and moved to this camp after being on the march the whole summer in the Cumberland. Marching is the most of what we do. We expect Orders to leave this place at any time for another camp. I have seen enough of life in the Army to miss the good things of home. We do not always get our rations and what ones we do are not often fit to eat. We visited Howell and Tom when their Regiment camped close but now must have passes to leave camp. We were in the reserve of a skirmish at Tazewell and that is the closest we came to battle.

I think of you all many times. How are the crops coming? Do Mary Jane and Eliza Ann keep up in the Readers? I thank Rebecca and Charlotte for the fine socks they sent with us when we left. They've held up better than most. David asks to be told when Lydia is delivered. If you would send a letter we would be proud to hear our names at Mail Call. Eliza Ann could do it with a page from my copybook. Louise knows the receipt for ink. Send it to our Company and Regiment in care of Gen. Seth Barton's Brigade, Tennessee. Mr. Buchanan will know how to do the postage. I keep you in my prayers and mind my own ways as Mam and Pap taught me. I am your loving son and brother, Ananias Covington.

Why would he say I could write the letter? My handwriting is as bad as my knitting. I kept at it only because it was another thing to do with him on winter evenings. Mrs. Buchanan's package holds a wooden pen shaft, nib, packet of black ink powder, sheets of writing paper, and envelopes. Now I'll have to learn how to mix ink powder and write with a pen nib.

***

Whenever Ananias made red-oak ink, it was a messy affair. Using ink powder is easier, but it scatters when I pour it into the saucer, and bits of it stick to my fingers. It's hard to know how much water to use, and some of the ink clumps up and doesn't mix in.

I dip the pen into the ink and write small letters in black script on a page of Ananias's copybook. I haven't practiced my letters since he left. He did not say that I was not to use his copybook or quill pen, but I didn't because my writing leaves a trail of messy blots. His own steady hand flows across the pages. I do like the way this nib holds ink longer. It makes it easier to connect the letters, if there aren't clumps of powder stuck to it.

"You learned as well as he did," Mam says.

"Only because I have his to copy and this pen writes better than a quill."

After writing the alphabet of small letters, I start on the capital letters with their extra curlicues and hooks. My hand is shaky.

"I'm wasting ink."

"I think you're doing good enough to start that letter," Mam says.

"How can we ever tell them about Lydia?"

"You'll come up with the words. Pap and I will help if you falter. But I don't think you will. You've come to know so much from your reading."

I realize these are words of confidence. Mam and Pap are certain I can do this. But copying letters on a page is far different than coming up with my own words, ones that won't break David's heart.

*****

Buchanan's store is the mail station. Ananias's letter is the first we've ever received. Mine in reply will be the first we've sent. I have the letter and the coins Pap gave me for postage in a pouch. Mary Jane has come along with me.

The shelves that once held shirting cloth, ribbons, marbles, matches, sugar, and candles are empty. A few bags of salt are stacked against the back wall. Mrs. Buchanan smiles at me over the counter. There is no sign of Jeremiah.

I hand her the letter and the money.

"Do you think it will get to him?" I ask.

"It could take a while. The Confederate mail is unbearably slow. You've done the cover right and you've a good hand. I'll seal it with wax so no one else can read it until he receives it."

"I thank you. And for the pen and ink. It helped."

"I reckoned it would. We'll be leaving here soon, and your family has always been a good one. It's a shame the War has to separate us so."

She hands coins back to me. "It didn't cost as much as you have here."

I can tell it's almost all of the coins I gave her. I pour them into the pouch.

She smiles and says, "I hope your brothers come home safe."

***

The road home is empty. I can't resist turning in at the Wilders' lane.

"Let's stop and see the baby," I say. "Just for a little bit."

"We'll be late for dinner," Mary Jane says.

"It won't take long to hold him and see him smile."

The house is noisy with small boys. Tabitha's Joshua wails, his fists balled up and twisted into her skirt. She hands her baby Hannah to Mary Jane and scoops Joshua up, wiping his tears with her fingers. Genny comes into the room carrying Lydia's baby. His eyes are Lydia's golden brown. Chubby and red-cheeked, he still doesn't have much hair. Genny holds him out, wrapped in my quilt.

I hand the pouch to Mary Jane and take him in my arms. He waves his hands and smiles at me. I hold him against my chest, hiding my tears in the curve of his neck.

"What do you call him?" I ask.

"Lydia's baby. We wouldn't go against your mam," Genny says.

I study the quilt. It doesn't look as bad as I thought it did. The seams are holding up. I hand him back to Genny. I want to ask her if she misses Ananias. She and Mary Jane and I used to talk about everything, but it was the talk of little girls.

"We have to get on home," I say. "I'm glad it's you all taking care of him if we can't."

***

We hurry down the road to the turn east. Someone is standing at the edge of the woods.

"Who is that?" Mary Jane asks.

I squint at the figure with a sick feeling. Boys wear the same kind of clothes and generally look alike. This one is noticeable by the way he has his arms crossed and his head to the side.

"Luther Bowen."

"What would he want?"

"I don't think I want to know."

When we come to the place, he isn't there. I look into the woods as we pass and don't see him. We turn toward home. Just before the road crosses the branch by the Monroes, a stone whisks overhead. I turn to see Luther cocking his arm and throwing another. Small and sharp, it hits me on the cheek. I raise my hand to it and feel blood. I dodge the next one and push Mary Jane across the branch, no time to stop and take off our shoes or lift our skirts. He keeps throwing bigger stones and chasing after us.

"Stinking girls," he shouts. "Now there's no Yankee teacher around to take your side."

He throws a rock that hits Mary Jane in the arm. In desperation and anger, I reach down for a stone and throw it over his head.

"Asswipe," I shout. "You're just a lickfinger to your pap."

"Eliza Ann! Where did you hear those words?" Mary Jane asks.

I throw another rock, looking straight at his head. Lydia told me that's what you do to keep your aim. It hits him in the chest. He clenches his fists and charges at me, splashing through the branch, slipping and falling in the water.

I throw another. It hits him on the forehead.

"Leave us be!" I shout. "You couldn't hit a barn if it was right next to you."

"We'll burn yours, burn your whole farm," he shouts as he stands up, clothes sagging with streaming water. "We're not finished with you."

Shaking in anger, I pick up another and rear back my arm. Thad walks out of the Monroes' lane. He looks Luther up and down and beckons to me and Mary Jane.

"Come into the lane where you'll be safe," he says. "Go on home, Luther. You got no business here."

"Who's going to make me?"

"My pap's bringing the wagon out to the road."

Luther turns. I'm not ready to drop the rock.

"Don't throw it," Mary Jane says. "You've done enough, and your face is bleeding."

She sets down the money pouch and lifts the wet hem of her apron to dab at my cheek.

"Where did you ever hear such words, and what are we going to tell Mam and Pap?" she asks.

"I heard them from David, telling Howell about the Bowens. We'll tell Mam and Pap I tripped," I answer.

"Don't you tell anyone about this," I say to Thad.

My chest burns. I hate Luther, hate that fear makes me respond in anger, against all Mam taught us. *Turn the other cheek.* Why should I when it's bleeding?

19

The Best Rise

Ananias

WE LIVE IN holes. Dug them into the hillside in the woods of Chickasaw Bayou, a place of swamps, vine-tangled bluffs, and brush-choked ravines. Mosses trail in wisps from the limbs of oaks. Strange trees, full and thick with fat dark leaves, drip water. When it isn't raining, it's misty and foggy, the air dense, so wet and cold we don't have Drill.

From the entrance of ours, I watch big snowflakes coat the tilted, board-covered entrances of other holes. The roads are too muddy for supply wagons from Vicksburg. Rations are rancid beef, so lean and dry it's like eating sticks. The water is bad.

I have the runs, and sometimes can't make it to the Sinks in time. Other men have the same problem. The ground is fouled with our own shit. And it stinks. We stink.

"Some are threatening to throw down their rifles and go home," Eli says.

"That is tempting," I say. "But we wouldn't get far in this mess of Mississippi."

"The air's poison," Rufe says.

Most men believe that, suffering and dying from ague, bloody flux, swamp fever, lung fever. Others have cannon fever, unable to bear going into battle again. I'm not that bad off, but I am tired of the way the Army conducts this war, neglecting the health and shelter of the soldiers they need to fight it.

What I will do is answer Roll Call, see to myself, though I've stopped shaving and my hair is shaggy. I will follow what Sergeant Williams says. Help my messmates stay alive. If we can make it to spring we'll probably fight one more big battle to send the Yankees running. Then I can go home.

***

The Regiment is in an uproar. The news of President Lincoln's Proclamation to free the slaves has arrived two months after he made it. Some men don't know what it means, others, mainly the officers, are outraged over the idea of losing their slaves.

"It's what this war's been about from the beginning," Posey says. "The Secessionists said it was the only way to prevent the North from abolishing slavery. Some think this'll change the War, bring more Yankees to the fight, encourage slaves to run away."

I believe a man shouldn't own another man. Pap held to that. I'm ashamed of my reasons for joining this war. We all had our reasons and most had little to do with whether slavery was right or not.

***

Spring is coming on. We are camped below Vicksburg on the Warrenton Road with good water and plenty of firewood. Foragemasters have Details out in the fields and woods. In the evenings, when Rufe is at his poker games, Eli teaches David, Posey, and me how to play euchre. It's a fast game, and we've worn out David's deck of cards. Eli traded whittled buttons to another mess for a new deck. There's time for cleaning and mending clothes. Eliza Ann's housewife has fallen apart. I have one needle, a bit of thread, and her thimble. I carry them in Genny's silk bag. Eliza Ann has not answered my letter, if they received it. We have enough time in the evenings, so I'm going to write another. We don't know anything of home.

I spread out my blankets and put my spare clothes in a neat pile. I've used my pay on drawers, socks, and a checkered shirt from the Quartermaster. We have a new tent that keeps us dry. The canvas doesn't do much for keeping out flies and mosquitoes, but it's a small bit of privacy.

"Take a look," Posey says, holding up a new mirror.

"Didn't know my face was that thin," I say.

I'm about to shave my beard, grown in redder than my hair.

"You'll look better once Dempsey cuts your hair."

"I'll be glad to have it off my neck."

Who knew that Dempsey in the next mess has scissors and knows how to cut hair? I'm surprised how much the prospect of being shaven and shorn lifts my spirits.

***

Our Regiment's Major Raleigh Camp has made a difference. We call him our Fault-Finding General because of his devotion to cleanliness and proper procedures, but the Regiment has grown stronger with full ranks of men fit and in better health. We're learning new Duties—Picket, Sentinel, and Outpost—for safeguarding camp. Each one requires attention, and I am willing to give it. I catch on more easily to the new turns and steps of Drill, four times a day, deploying from columns to lines and back to columns at Quick Step and the Double Quick. We're stronger for the constancy of it. The complicated steps and commands keep my mind from wandering home.

"With all this Drill, you think we'll go face to face with the enemy?" Rufe asks. "Given we ever get the chance."

"That's the point of it," I answer. "Given the chance, we'll be prepared."

"Some of the boys say Colonel Johnson is the meanest in the Confederate service for drilling us all the time."

"They're holding a grudge from Chickasaw Bayou."

"A colonel is supposed to see to his men."

"He led us out of there with only four dead," Posey says. "We survived the winter. Remember how he saved out that Kentucky bourbon for us? And we didn't die of disease in Tennessee."

"Captain Young still watches out for us," David says. "Even after getting promoted to Lieutenant Colonel."

"The best ones are supposed to rise," Posey says.

"Like Corporal Posey Huff?" I ask.

"I didn't mean to include myself. Being a corporal isn't rising far."

"You like being an officer?"

"I do. I think I'm getting good at this Army life."

Posey has found his place. He keeps us informed and in order, doesn't report small infractions, and marches beside us counting cadences and calling out when to close the line. Like the song goes, we are a Band of Brothers.

I've come to know my own brother better. David has good sense about when to complain and when to keep quiet. He's taken over the cooking chores because, by his admission and our agreement, he's the best at it. It strikes me how much he and Luke are alike, curly blonde hair, wide blue eyes, the same easiness of spirit. I take things hard. David says I think too much, but paying attention to Army discipline helps me stick with it when I am so homesick for family and Genny I can hardly hold my head up.

***

We fill the Parade Ground in columns, rifles aslant, bayonets shining in the sun. General Barton's Brigade is on Dress Parade. Wearing new-issue wool uniform jackets and jeans cloth trousers, we've cleaned our rifles, polished buttons, buckles, and bayonets. We stand straight, turn briskly, and hold our Line.

The silk and bunting of Regimental and Company colors flow, snapping open in the breeze, showing off blue and red stripes, yellow stars. I'm caught up in the pageantry of flags and precision marching, being part of something orderly and grand. All we have learned is on display, and I believe it will help us when the fighting starts again. The Yankees have not given up on Mississippi.

***

In the warm evening, Eli sits alone by the coals of our supper fire, looking at something in his hands. I join him to see what is taking his attention. The bawdy cards.

"You kept them?" I ask.

"They're bound to come in handy. I'm wondering how much cash money we could get, probably more for some than others. I know men who would pay."

"I've never seen females naked like that. Have you?"

"I have."

I am thunderstruck. "More than one?" I can barely squeak it out.

"Just one."

"You loved her?"

"No."

"Who was she?"

"That plantation owner's wife. She took a liking to me at their Christmas celebration. Said I was like a tall drink of water on a hot day, kept smiling up at me and patting my arm. She sent word to me later to meet her at a slave cabin she'd fixed up. I was fool enough to do it. In the end it was why I joined the

Army. She didn't want to stop lying with me, and her husband was catching on."

"You lay with her?"

"More than once. You ever been with a woman?"

"No."

"That lady taught me things I didn't know a body could want to do."

I gulp and take a breath. "Like what?"

He stares at me. "You want the particulars?"

"Only the gist of it. I hear men bragging on what they do. I want to love Genny more when I go home. I don't know anything but how I feel."

"It starts with her wanting to love you more too," he says. "Then it moves."

David and Posey are approaching.

***

Eli and I have drawn night Picket Duty, watching for enemy boats from the bluffs above the mighty Mississippi River. I never tire of watching it. The moon shines on the water, and stillness settles over the camps in the woods and bayous behind us.

"Makes you feel kindly peaceful, doesn't it," Eli says. "I never knew there could be a river this big. Makes you feel smaller, but you don't mind it."

He comes up with such thoughts. He's not educated but feels deeply. Next to Posey, he's the last man I would think has experience with women.

"What did you mean about her wanting to love me more and then it moves?"

"You sure you want me to tell you what I know?"

"I want to do it right."

"You think of her first. Keep your hands gentle."

That makes sense. My hands had moved on their own, over the cloth of her skirt and blouse. She let me do that.

"Through her clothes?"

"Under them. You touch her skin. If she wants more, you'll know. After that, your body tells you what to do."

"What does her body tell her?" I know what my body was telling me. It still tells me on nights when all I can do is think of her.

"Some of what that lady did with me I'm ashamed to know about. I'm not going to tell you how the body parts work. You love your Genny in the way that seems right. Like I said, think of—"

The night shatters with the boom of big guns. Artillery fire rolls down toward us along the four-mile line of batteries guarding the river.

We stand open-mouthed, watching. Signal fires rise on both banks, and boats that must be the enemy's are visible against the blazing backdrop. Shells cascade and explode over the water. A boat floats past in flames. Panicked Yankee sailors jump into the water and swim toward certain capture on the shore below us. More gunboats follow. All of it happens too fast.

"Looks like our batteries can't stop them," Eli says.

"This war just took a change," I say. "For the worse."

My tender feelings for Genny are lost in the violence of gunboats running the batteries. But I will not forget what Eli told me.

***

The Yankees are marching south, on the other side of the River. If they cross it, they can attack north to Vicksburg or east to Jackson. We are preparing three days' rations and getting ready to fall in after supper. I help David at the fire, frying side-meat, making griddle cakes, packing our mess box to go on the Company wagon.

The nightly concert of cannonading opens in the north. A new bombardment rises in the south.

"They made it across," Posey reports. "Taking another shot at Vicksburg. If they take the city, it gives them the whole river."

"We whipped them at Chickasaw Bayou, we'll do it again," Rufe says. "They gave up easy."

"They died like hogs shot in a pen," I say. "And they keep coming back."

"Shouldn't have gotten into the pen in the first place."

Except for believing liver and onions at hog-killing time is good eating, I seldom agree with Rufe. He has no way to compare fact with rumor and blurts out what he hears others say. He's stubborn in the face of most things, and he relishes a fight. For that alone, I'm glad to be in the same Battle Line with him.

We march south in moonlight, cross the Big Black River at daybreak, form a Battle Line at a crossroads near a church, and fall back across the Big Black, with no fighting. I don't mind now. Marching past plantations, seeing negro slaves working enormous cotton fields, overseers standing with whips, why would I want us to win this war?

The men who fought the Yankees south at Grand Gulf swarm back through our lines, all with the same story. *If they hadn't bogged down in the ravines, they'd have overrun us. They kept coming at us, rank after rank, like waves of blue.*

"Looks like we've got ourselves a little more war to fight," Rufe says and rubs his hands together.

From what the men say of Grand Gulf, it might be too big for us to handle.

***

"*Once more unto the breach, dear friends, once more.*"

Posey is reading aloud from his volume of Shakespeare about a battle in England where men fought like a band of brothers. I remember it from the Reader.

"*Be copy now to men of grosser blood, And teach them how to war.*"

It seems a lifetime since Mr. Woodall taught me how to read and write, asked for my help teaching the younger ones, called me an aspiring scholar. Compared to Posey, the gaps in my knowledge are embarrassing, but I enjoy our conversations and listening to him read. When this war is over I want to learn more about the ideas and subjects Posey knows. I could be a teacher like Mr. Woodall. Posey says I'd be a good lawyer because I'm smart and ask questions. I want to be more than a farmer.

We wait for Orders in the rising heat of the day. Rumors tangle the grapevine. *The enemy is surrounding us. The enemy is advancing from the north. From the south. On the railroad. We'll march out at dawn, east. In the evening, south.* Rufe and I agree that none of it makes sense.

Who are we to make sense of it? Our generals have enough on their hands facing a Yankee general called Unconditional Surrender Grant, a nickname he earned from winning battles in Tennessee. I would gladly return to marching up and down the

150

ridges and mountains of the Cumberland than the ravines and bayous of Mississippi.

The rumors consolidate into one. The Yankees are on the march east of the Big Black River, and General Pemberton's Army of Vicksburg will march out to meet them.

***

Morning rain falls in torrents on the crowded camps stretching along either side of the tracks at Edwards Station. I tighten my jacket collar, pull down my hat brim, and turn my rifle muzzle down. I will never understand why our officers leave us standing in the rain, not allowed to pull out oil cloths and hunker down. I resent the Confederacy, the generals, Army life, and myself for tolerating any of it.

We're east of Vicksburg. Jackson is farther east along these tracks. Our Orders are *Leave unnecessary items and prepare to live in the field*. I'd be glad to do that once I get dry. I shift my blanket roll to a more comfortable place against the back of my neck and shake my canteens. One is half-full, the other empty. It's late in the afternoon, and I haven't eaten since breakfast. We have been standing in Column all day, prepared to march at any moment.

The first holdup came when an officer realized there weren't enough rations and ammunitions to keep us in the field and more had to be sent for. The latest is a flooded creek crossing. We are restless, waiting for supplies to arrive and floodwaters to subside.

"This is foolishness," Rufe says.

"Calling it foolishness doesn't do it justice," I say.

***

At dark we fill our canteens while waiting to cross a new bridge over the flooded creek. Once across, dense woods keep our column jammed together on the narrow road. Overlapping tree branches obscure the sliver of moon. I feel the road rise as the ache in my legs shifts. So tired, rifle sliding from my shoulder, stumbling on the road's rough surface.

The hill flattens. On the left, torches burn and officers shout, "Column Right! Keep to the Right!" I swerve to the right behind Eli, next to David, wanting only to close my eyes and lie down.

Company! Halt! Fall out, to the Right!

I stumble away from the road and drop to sandy ground.

20

Nevermore

May 1863, Halford Mill,
Dawson County, Georgia

Eliza Ann

I'VE NEVER BEEN to the Halfords' house. Pap and the boys bring the corn here for milling. Girls don't do that, yet, and we don't know them well enough to visit on our own. This is the first it's been warm enough to walk here and take Mrs. Halford up on her invitation.

She greets us with hugs and shows us through the keeping room into a room with a polished chestnut dinner table and matching chairs. A balustered staircase leads to the upstairs. I look around at the carpets, pewter oil lamps, marble-top tables, a spindle-backed rocking chair decorated in gilt and painted flowers, a sofa and wing chairs, shelves of books, leather-bound and embossed in gold. I'm afraid to touch anything.

The house is built as a whole, not two log cabins joined together like ours. The kitchen is in a separate building where a hired woman cooks for the Halfords and their mill hands. I imagine there's a hired girl to keep it all clean.

Because Ananias wrote how grateful he was for good socks, I am willing to participate, even though I still can't properly turn a heel.

"We'll sit here at the table and pile the socks in the middle," Mrs. Halford says. "I'm so grateful you came."

"Who else will be coming?" Mam asks.

"I thought we'd start with just your family."

I do not want to hear what she'll say next.

"I hope it's a chance for you to get better acquainted with Harriet."

Who at this moment comes sweeping down the stairs, petticoats swishing, hoop swaying. She is carrying books.

Mary Jane whispers, "Remember, you're smart too."

"This may seem like a strange time to do so," Harriet says as she approaches me at the table. "But I apologize for being so rude to you."

I think about how to answer in the way that I feel, without being rude in turn.

"That was last autumn," I say. "Quite a bit has happened since then."

"It took me that long to understand how folks are here."

"You didn't make friends with other Secessionists?"

"Seems the nicest people are Unionists. Aunt Marian helped convince me if I hold politics against good people I won't have any friends. And for all the manners I learned, I never took the chance to say how sorry I am over your sister-in-law's passing. I was raised to do better than that."

I have no words in reply.

"Thank you, Harriet," Mam says. "Are you going to join us knitting socks?"

"I don't know how to knit. We had slave girls to do those things."

Rebecca is already knitting away and doesn't look up. Charlotte puts down her needles and stares at Harriet. I look to Louise and Mam. They're as speechless as I am.

I'm sick to my stomach. No wonder she says what she does. Now I know someone who's owned slaves. And she's not a person I think I want to know better, but I probably will.

"Jeremiah Buchanan told me that Eliza Ann is smart and likes to read poetry, so I have some of my books here. I'll read from them while you knit, if you don't mind."

"That would be lovely, wouldn't it Eliza Ann?" Mam says.

What can I say? I look down at my knitting. Did she read to her slave girls while they did her knitting? I'm not so sure about Jeremiah thinking I'm smart, but the part about poems is true. And the books are beautiful.

"Do you have the one about a raven?" I ask.

"By Edgar Allan Poe? I don't have a copy but I committed it to memory. Shall I recite it for you?"

"Of course, child," Mrs. Halford says and turns to Mam. "She recites beautifully."

This is more than I expect or want. I bend over my knitting and prepare to listen to what is surely a poem about crows. Ravens and crows are similar, and Jeremiah asked me about the poem after I spoke about crows. It was an assignment to speak on something we knew well, part of a lesson on elocution that Mr. Woodall taught in exasperation over our mumbling drawls.

Harriet begins. I look up and stop knitting. This isn't about crows. The words are beautiful, with a rhythm and rhyme more artful and complicated than the poems I've been reading. It's about a man and his sorrow for his lost love. Lenore. Like Lydia. And then a raven steps in through his window. A talking bird, the way Lydia and I imagined crows were. Even though this one says only one word. *Nevermore.*

The poem turns angry and more sorrowful, the lover in his haunted loneliness. At the end, I'm crying, big gulping sobs shaking my body like I've never done except when Lydia died, never want to do again, especially in front of someone like Harriet. Nevermore will I see Lydia, hear her laugh, get over losing her.

I feel arms around me, hear Harriet's voice consoling me.

"I know, I know. I felt this way too when I first read it. My mother and father died, one after the other, and I miss them still. That's why I memorized it. I hoped if I said it over and over, no one would die again. Nevermore."

She is crying. It's Charlotte who comforts both of us, hugging me with one arm and patting Harriett's thin back.

"Let's get back to knitting," she says.

Good old Charlotte. I'm grateful for more than one sister.

21

Battle of Bakers Creek

May 16, 1863, Mississippi

Ananias

I am awake, staring into the dark leaves and white blossoms of a magnolia. Men are moving among the trees. David and Rufe are asleep. Smoke from a breakfast fire drifts my way. I try to roll over but am tangled in my blanket roll, accoutrements, canteens, bayonet, haversack. I didn't remove them when I dropped to the ground in the night. I get out of the mess of equipment, sit up, and face Eli.

"I can hear them," he says. "Out ahead of us. Drums and wagons."

"Not Bowen or Loring?" I ask. "Their Brigades are ahead of us."

"Too far."

"Which way are we headed?"

"South. Toward them."

He sits up and pulls out his rations.

"Might as well eat," he says and offers a chunk of beef.

I take the meat and gnaw a dry bite. He breaks off a piece of corncake. We trade coarse cake and tough meat. I drink from my canteen and pass it to him.

My mind drags, thinking of the effort it will take to stand upright and be a soldier. Dawn lights the sky pink and gold. The morning is hot. A scattered popping of rifle fire opens in the southeast. The Long Roll starts in the south and moves toward us, rousing David and Rufe.

"Jackson fell to the enemy," Posey announces, walking in from the road. "They're coming at us from the east."

"Were we expecting that?" I ask.

"Not here," he replies. "We're headed south to cut their supply lines." He sits down and takes out his rations. "The generals are meeting."

"Company!" Sergeant Williams calls out. "Prepare to fall in!"

We hustle, gulping down rations, hoisting haversacks. I strap and buckle my accoutrements into marching order, pick up my rifle, and stand at the ready.

Couriers gallop past in opposite directions. A group of officers rides up from the south.

"They're in a hurry," Rufe says.

"That's General Stevenson," Posey says. "Probably with Battle Orders."

We had fallen out in the night next to a sandy road running north and south. Brush and trees block the views east and west. The sporadic crackle of nervous picket fire in the southeast grows louder and more concentrated.

The deep, heavy boom of cannons follows.

Company! Form the Column!

We line up in the road, facing south.

Tom and Howell are somewhere behind us in the Fifty-Second with Moody Simpson and Reverend Childs. Jacob Wilder, Alex Graham, Ike and Joe Bowen are all back there too, wherever the Forty-Third stopped.

Company! About Face!

"What's going on?" Rufe asks as we turn and face north.

"Looks like we're heading back the way we came," Eli answers.

The quick fire of skirmishers opens in the northeast. My body is fully alert.

"It sounds like they're coming from that way too," I say.

We set off north at Route Step, stop, and move off the road while an artillery unit rumbles past. The firing in the northeast rolls toward us. Scattered shooting comes from directly east. Couriers on horseback race by.

Company! Form the Column! Face Left!

I turn, facing the woods. Why not the road?

Forward! At the Quick!

At the trot of Quick Time, David and I follow Rufe and Eli into the woods.

At the Double Quick!

We've never had this command except in Drill. We step it up to a run, dodging trees, stumbling over beaten-down brush. The boom of artillery and crash of musketry rolls across the column from our Right. I slow and stare north toward it, ducking my head as if that could soften the deafening noise of what sounds like whole armies firing every weapon at once.

"Close up! Don't stop!" Posey shouts.

A man ahead trips and falls. The column jumbles up, pauses, and lurches forward, downhill. My heartbeat thumps in my ears. My lungs hurt. The dry beef and corncake are about to come up. A fence blocks the bottom of the hill.

"Don't stop!" Posey shouts. "Over the fence! Close it up!"

Splinters dig into my palms. My shin scrapes against the upper rail. I jump to the ground and run. The smell of new corn rises from trampled stalks and leaves.

Another fence, a welcome obstacle, a pause to gasp for breath. Running again, across a road and into a woods of thin trees and brush. My blanket roll bounces on my back, cartridge box, canteens, and bayonet bang at my hips. Sweat runs into my shirt.

The battle to our Right storms on in thundering artillery, an unbroken roar of musketry. We run, uphill through woods, across a road, and veer toward the noise.

Company! Halt!

My heart hammers against the straps crossing my chest. My legs shake. Rifle and artillery fire come at us from our Front and Right. Thick smoke drifts downhill. I choke, cough, and take a quick drink of water, want to pour the whole canteen of it over my head.

On the Left by File! Into the Line! Form the Line!

Captain Hall walks in front of us, adjusting our Battle Line. We are on uneven ground, the clumps and dips of an old field grown up in young trees. Artillery wagons clatter on the road behind us. On our Right, unceasing fire.

In the dappled shade, a breeze clears the smoke. The hot sun is straight overhead. I catch my breath, rifle at the ready.

Attention! Fix bayonets! Load at Will!

We've done this only in Drill too. I fix the bayonet to the end of my rifle and load the first cartridge.

Dress Left! Forward! At the Quick!

I look left at Burnett, bump elbows with Eli on my right, and adjust my pace to the uneven ground. The gap between us and the next Company widens. The ground slants downhill into a ravine.

Rifle fire crashes from the trees across the ravine. Bullets buzz overhead like angry bees.

Fire at Will!

I can't see where to aim, so fire low into the rolling smoke. Rufe and David fire from behind. Eli and I reload and fire again. Smoke surrounds us.

Forward! At the Double Quick!

Eli and I run forward into oncoming smoke and bullets. The firing from the tree line pauses. Smoke obscures everyone but Eli. I load and fire, reload and fire. Bullets clip the brush in front of me, rattle into the trees overhead. Showers of leaves and small branches fall on me. The only clarity I have is pull cartridge, bite paper, pour powder, ram bullet, set cap, cock, aim, fire. My mouth is gritty with gunpowder.

Eli is stepping back. I will not lose sight of him. Bullets whip by, snap against trees, thud into bodies. Men scream in pain, howl in rage. Ranks of blue-clad men move out of the opposite trees. Backing up, I stumble on, step over and around the crumpled, torn, bloody bodies of men I know. Wounded men writhing, clutching at holes and gashes. Dead men lying motionless. No time to think of how to help.

Eli stops, so I do too. Rufe and David gone. Alone together, we stand in place, load, fire, reload, fire. Behind us on our Left, the crack and boom of artillery opens up. Hundreds of rifles fire at once in a terrific crash. Who the hell is that?

A horse gallops behind us. Colonel Young's voice shouting, "Fall back! Continue fire! Fall back! To the Right!"

We walk backwards uphill until men crowd in from our Left. Bullets fall among us. The men on our Left turn and run.

"Hold steady! Fall back! Hold steady!" Sergeant Williams shouts.

I hear the horse again, see men running up the hill.

"Up the hill! Follow me!" Colonel Young shouts and spurs his horse.

David appears out of the smoke and grabs my arm. We turn and run uphill with Eli.

At the top, Colonel Young is facing us, pointing his sword to his right. We run that way and come to Captain Hall, waving us on. The rifle fire behind us stops, replaced by the throaty cheers of Yankees.

Officers on horseback and milling clumps of men fill the woods. Men run singly and in groups. I don't recognize any of the officers waving swords and shouting commands. It doesn't seem necessary to keep running with no bullets landing around us.

"Rufe went down when we fell back," David shouts. "I tried to go back for him but the bullets were thick."

"We have to get him," I say and turn back into the crowd of men swarming toward me.

"Not with what's behind us," David says, grabbing me by my back straps.

"What if he's wounded?"

"The stretcher bearers will pick him up."

"What about Posey? Where's he?"

"He was beyond me. I don't know when he turned."

"We need to find them. We can't just leave them."

I turn back again, trying to push my way past men running at me, shoving me aside. There are too many.

An officer rides up. "This way boys! We're reforming. We'll whip 'em yet."

I look to David. Our officers are nowhere to be seen.

"He's an officer," David says. "We have to follow him."

It isn't right. Rufe has fallen behind. It isn't right to leave him. We left Lewis and never saw him again. I don't know what has happened to Posey. My arms feel leaden, my legs about to collapse.

The road is a chaos of men, horses, and wagons. The cyclonic roar of battle from what was our Left Rear fills the air. It doesn't make sense to go that way. The firing from the north stops. The fighting to the northeast goes on.

"You're here," Posey's voice comes from behind, choking with emotion. "I thought I'd lost you. Where's Rufe? Where is everyone?" Tears streak his face.

"Rufe fell. I couldn't stop for him," David says. "We were falling back."

"Where's the rest of the Company?" I ask.

"I don't know," Posey sobs. "It's all a tangle. I can't think."

"Who are we following here?" I ask, trying to help Posey gather himself.

He looks around. "Some of the colors are Lee's Alabamans."

Form up! Fall in!

"Who with? We don't know anyone," Posey says.

"Here's Burnett and Dempsey," I say.

We join them beside other men we recognize, follow the commands of officers we don't know. Two corporals come along handing out cartridge tins.

"Take one," they say. "There's not enough to take two."

I check my cartridge box. Six left.

"I'll feed mine to you," David says. "I couldn't see a thing. I fired low, but I couldn't see where they were in all the smoke."

"Does everyone have water?" Posey asks.

I reach for a canteen and drink. I watch my brother, my friends, tilting back their own canteens, faces black with gunpowder, sweat-streaked in crooked lines. David's blonde curls are matted, his hat gone.

"Follow me!" Sergeant Williams comes upon us. "I have more of the boys down the Line."

We follow him amid companies, regiments, and brigades mingled in confusion. Officers try to align ranks, but men recognize others from their own companies and break ranks to join them. Some turn and run across the road, into the trees. Some turn back in response to officers begging them to hold. Others, in full panic, burst through and keep running.

The heat and smoke are suffocating. I take off my hat and fan my face. I can't think in all the noise. David is standing with his eyes closed.

A cheer goes up as Colonel Young rides up behind us. I try to cheer, but my voice croaks and nothing more comes out, so I wave my hat and pump my rifle. With Colonel Young leading us and Sergeant Williams beside us, we can prevail.

I hear a thwap and grunt behind me and turn. Dempsey folds into himself and falls, blood streaming from his head. More bullets fall among us.

"Forward! At the Quick!" Colonel Young shouts before any of us can move to help Dempsey.

We set off, stepping over bodies curled up on their sides, flat on their backs, hunched on their stomachs, arms thrown out, fingers clutching rifles, fallen in as many ways as a man can fall.

The smoke clears. Standing in the shelter of trees are men in dark blue, four ranks thick, facing us, stretching the length of our Line and beyond. Their Line erupts in an explosion of fire. In the deathly hail of bullets, stepping back is the natural thing to do.

"Fall back!" Sergeant Williams shouts. "Steady! Don't run!"

Running men stream through our Line. An officer rides up and shouts something at Sergeant Williams. "Fall back!" he screams.

I turn and run across the road, cowardly unaware of who is with me.

Eli catches up. David is ahead of us. Everyone has run for himself.

Sergeant Williams stands until we form around him. He leads us farther into the afternoon shadows of the trees to a shallow branch where men lie on the bank and drink muddy water.

"Get your water," Sergeant Williams says. "We'll rest here."

I dunk my head in it, drink from it, fill my canteens, and join what is left of the Company sitting in the shade—Eli, David, Posey, Burnett, too few others. Rufe not found. Dempsey fallen, most likely dead.

"Is this all of us?" I ask.

"I don't know," Sergeant Williams answers. "Some might be with Major Camp. Here comes the Colonel."

Colonel Young dismounts and faces us, the skin of his hands and face dark with smoke, his eyes wet.

"The enemy has taken the day," he says.

No one speaks in contradiction.

"The Order is to fall back across the creek. You fought bravely. I would rather lead you forward in victory, but it will be my honor to march by your side in retreat. We're going back to Vicksburg."

22

Retreat

Ananias

O UR COLORS ARE gone, but our drummer still has his drum. We fall into new ranks that Colonel Young has gathered from what's left of the Regiment. The sun is lower in the west. We don't know who has been killed or captured, who ran, but at least a quarter of the men in our Company are not here. Leading the loose and ragged column, he sets a slow pace so the wounded can keep up.

Across the broken countryside of fields and woodlots, men run. A few are organized in small marching columns like ours. We pass a brush shelter where surgeons work over a man.

Beside them, piles of blood-stained uniforms, severed arms, and booted legs. I look away, sickened by the carnage. A throng of bloody men surround the shelter. Rows of silent men lie bandaged on stretchers. Others limp away, supported by friends or struggling alone. Dead horses, shattered wagons, haversacks, hats, blanket rolls, accoutrements, and rifles litter the ground.

"Why did so many throw down their arms?" I ask Sergeant Williams.

"Fear. Confusion. Overwhelming force. You can be proud you stood and fought as long as you did."

I'm not proud. In the end, I ran too.

Numb with exhaustion, I can't think about what I have seen and done this day. Engulfed in the disorganized mass of the retreating Army, I walk with Eli, Posey, and David, following the setting sun. A wagon track leads to a larger road filled with men and wagons going in no order, but in the same direction, west. At a newly-built bridge over a creek crossing, men splash through the water, racing across the creek, the crowded bridge an obstacle. The cannon fire behind us is distant.

"Where are we?" I ask Sergeant Williams.

"The bridge we crossed to get here."

We arrive at Edwards Station at dusk, the Regiments of our Brigade scattered and disorganized. No one knows what has happened to anyone.

***

The morning dawns as beautiful and bright as yesterday. The Fortieth marches out in good order on the crowded road.

It takes all of my strength and attention to keep up. The road is lined with hollow-eyed men, lying injured, sitting listless, in shock.

We cross to the west side of the Big Black River. Officers ride back and forth inquiring for the whereabouts of their regiments.

The boom of artillery rises east of the river. Men run in a frantic current. The Regiment's order falls apart when the press of running men surrounds and passes our rear companies. Near the front, I can't move. Panicked horses jolt the ambulance they pull, the fearful cries of the wounded rising from inside with each bounce of the wheels. A limber without caisson or gun careens around the ambulance, almost sideswiping us. A group of teamsters, cursing and whipping horses and mules, stampedes by, wagons tilting. It's a repeat of yesterday's rout on the battlefield.

Men behind us are shouting, "Run! Save yourselves!" The Column wavers, pulled like a vine in a whiplash. Captain Hall and Sergeant Williams, run back and forth, "Stay together! Don't run!" gathering the front and rear of the Company. Sergeants and corporals, Posey among them, spread their arms wide and keep us crowded together until our group, half of the Company, can straighten out and march forward once more.

***

The sun is low in the west when we turn onto a road angled from the main route of retreat. Ahead, soldiers crowd in front of a plantation house. Tables are set up on the deep porch. Women pass out food. Girls carry buckets through the crowd. The command to halt startles us.

"If these good ladies are offering food, there is no need for us to march on hungry and thirsty," Captain Hall announces. "Take only enough for yourself. After you've eaten, we'll reform here."

The lady smiles at me as she offers a piece of fried chicken and a warm potato. Her dress is white with a green flower pattern. The sleeves end in ruffles. The skirt bells out from her waist and floats above green cloth shoes.

"Thank you, ma'am," I say

"What a polite and handsome soldier you are. Where are your people?" she asks, smiling again.

"Georgia, ma'am."

"It's we who should be thanking you. Coming all this way from Georgia to defend our homes and rights."

Her voice flows as soft and sweet as taffy syrup. A girl close in age to Eliza Ann fills my cup with water. She wears the same kind of dress and shoes as the woman and smiles at me in the same way. Like mother and daughter. Mam and my sisters have no dresses and shoes as fancy as these.

I bite into the chicken, my jaws working the crisp skin and juicy meat. My stomach cramps. Next, the sweet yellow flesh of the potato. I cannot help but make little noises of pleasure with each alternating bite of potato and chicken. I eat standing, afraid that if I sit, I will not have the strength or the will to get up.

I finish eating, wipe my hands on the back of my shirt, and look at the home I have been thanked for defending. It's a tall house of painted boards with windows on both stories and all sides. The porch surrounds it. Negroes come and go with platters and bowls. I thought my part in this war was to keep the Mississippi River and Vicksburg from falling to the enemy, not defending such stately homes and the so-called rights of these ladies in their clean dresses and shoes, with slaves to serve them. Where are their men? Would they do the same for my family should the War go to Georgia? Still, I'm grateful to them for sharing their food.

***

The Column stops again at dark. I walk into the dusty field of flattened cotton beside the road and drop to the ground. Mosquitoes swarm up in whining clouds. I pull my hat tight around my ears, button my jacket to my throat, and lay back, one hand on my rifle, the other on my haversack. Wagons clatter and creak on the road. Men moan and cry out. Eli and David lie on either side of me. Overhead, stars form the Great Bear, the Little Bear. I stare up at them, trying to remember their meaning, trying to remember if I have been brave or not, until sometime in the dark, I sleep, as dreamless as the dead in the fields and ravines of Bakers Creek.

23

End of the Line

May 1863, Vicksburg, Mississippi

Ananias

ENEMY CAMPFIRES FLICKER like lightning bugs across the great River. Picket Duty with Eli gives me the chance to stand quiet and think. The evening peace calms my mind. It doesn't stop my confusion and shame at belonging to an army that ran. I wonder what men believe now of the glorious Confederacy.

What did it matter that we drilled and drilled at forming and reforming Battle Lines if men would not hold in the face of fire, would not obey their officers' commands? What did it matter that I faced the fire and held my ground until ordered to fall back? It surprises me that I wasn't afraid. In the chaos of men, horses, wagons, the deafening noise of hundreds of guns firing at once, it was clear that I should hold my place in the Line, load, fire, advance and repeat it until commanded otherwise. Was that bravery or foolishness?

No word of Rufe, an absence in our days, our mess down to four.

The enemy presses toward Vicksburg from the east and west and will surely come from the north and south. Our Brigade is assigned to the south end of the defensive line that curves around the city, the sector farthest away from possible attack, where our cowardice can do the least damage. We are up against the River, near the camp where we paraded in such pride and confidence.

I listen for night sounds—raccoons cracking open shells on the riverbank, foxes sniffing out rodents, owls swooping through the trees. Overhead, the Little Bear stretches high, and I feel the presence of Mam and Pap, as certain as the Pole Star, the constant guide toward home. Our drummer taps out Extinguish Lights. The fires across the River go out. They do it the same as we do.

The chuff of steam engines comes from downriver, and I peer south, make out dark shapes moving on the water.

"You hear that?" I whisper to Eli.

"It's not fish jumping," he replies.

I fire the single shot that starts the relay of warning shots up the line from this last redoubt at South Fort to the fortifications of Vicksburg. There, the big guns will speak to these boats on the river, and the guns on the boats will answer. As if guns could hold a conversation. Eliza Ann would notice that.

***

Shells screech and whistle overhead in a hail of metal shards tearing into the redoubt's dirt walls, kicking up dust and clods of earth. My head aches from the smell of sulfur. The shelling from across the River stops, and we climb out of our rifle pit to check on the Louisiana gunners manning the battery. Quick with a story and proud of staying loose in tight spots, they are free with their food, know where to forage, and brag about eating anything in style.

Throughout the barrage of shelling, they have kept a cook fire going.

"Have some crawdads," a gunner says, holding out three large, long-legged, clawed critters roasted on the tip of a bayonet.

"Looks like bugs," Eli says. "I don't care to eat bugs."

"I'm hungry enough," I say. "Especially one that big."

I pull one off and peel away the legs and hard skin. I have no remembered taste for comparing, but there's flesh to it, chewy and sweet.

"It's tasty enough," I say, "but it's not worth the work of getting at it."

"When you get a mess of these, dipped in butter and pepper sauce, it's some of the finest eating in Louisiana," the gunner says.

"Where'd you get these?"

"Sent a detail down to the bayou."

"What else do you Louisianans eat?" David asks and takes a crawdad.

"Here it's squirrel, small deer, frogs."

"I haven't seen any small deer around," I say.

"These are very small, scuttle around at night."

"The only critters scuttling around here are rats," Eli says.

"Small deer. Roasted, fricasseed, they're fresher than Army beef. Some say they taste like squirrel."

"I'll stick with bugs," Eli says and takes the last one.

Rations have been short, and we're hungry enough to eat anything now.

***

"Your brothers are missing from the Fifty-Second," Posey says. "I read the battle reports at Headquarters. When the enemy attacked our artillery, the Fifty-Second was called in from Reserve. The men who stood and fought were killed or captured. The rest ran. Some might have mixed in with Loring's Brigade. He's still somewhere east of the river crossing."

No one has been able to piece together the full story of what happened at Bakers Creek. Alex, Jacob, and the Bowens are not among the few who escaped by running early with the Forty-Third. It was obvious that the Yankee force facing us was greater, their reinforcements visibly moving in.

"What about the wounded?" I ask.

"Left behind if they couldn't run."

I can't think about it all at once. Tom and Howell are missing, but I don't know how. They could be left behind like Rufe, fallen under another body, wounded, or dead.

I am at the end of my ability to reckon out the answers. And so tired.

24

Laying By

Eliza Ann

FROM THE BOTTOM porch step, I wiggle my toes in the warm dirt and turn my face to the morning sun. Some parts of the farm are as familiar to me as people—the porch, the lane, the orchard. The corn is almost head-high, green pumpkins are forming, and the field peas have new pods. I know how they're ripening because I helped them grow. Most folks believed the boys would be home before the first harvest. We'll likely bring in the second one without them.

Sounds carry in the still day, chickens gabbling and pecking at June bugs, flies buzzing at mule dung, Pap hammering a bent hoe, the twins bickering over whose turn it is to muck out the stalls. The geese in the near field take up their noisy warning of something on the road.

Noah Wilder walks into the lane. He sees me and starts running, waving a piece of paper.

"It's from Ananias," he calls out.

The rest of the Wilders come over the rise carrying babies and bundles, Genny with Lydia's baby, the rest stretched out behind, the geese following them in a raucous parade.

"It's the Wilders," I call up to the open windows.

"Look at this big boy," Mam says, coming out.

She takes him from Genny and holds him up to her face, smiling. He smiles back at her. She laughs and jiggles him. "He's going to be an easy one."

"He is," Tabitha says. "I weaned him so as he could come back to you. Of course, we'll keep him if you don't want the bother."

"Nonsense," Mam says. "His cradle is still in my room, and I do remember how to raise a child."

A sturdy chunk of a boy, he twists his head around to look at the rest of us, then back to Genny. Mam moves him to her hip and takes the letter from Noah.

"A soldier came looking for Buchanan's store and left it with us," he says. "We didn't read it."

"Of course you wouldn't. Set yourselves down and cool off. You'll stay for dinner. Let's hear it and get this little boy settled."

He reaches for the letter, crumpling a corner. Mam uncurls his fist and hands it to me.

I open the envelope, unfold the page, and read out loud.

March the 29ᵗʰ, 1863, Warrenton, Mississippi.
Dear Family, I hope this finds you all in good health
as we are here. David sends his love to Lydia and
the baby and is anxious for Eliza Ann to write
soon and tell us about them.

My hand is shaking. I stop reading. "He didn't receive ours."
Pap stares off at the fields.
"Let's hear all of it," he says.
I read through tears, my voice quavers.

It has been some time since I could take pen in
hand. We have been in camp near Vicksburg since
February. Mississippi is a sorry State. I have never
seen rain such as we have been through, and I
would not choose to come here again except to see
the mighty River. It is wider and more glorious and
powerful than any way Mr. Woodall described it.
We arrived here after Christmas and went into
battle at Chickasaw Bayou. The Yankees charged
our works and were held back. They have tried
to take Vicksburg many times and failed. It's the
one City keeping them from control of the whole
River. I do not know how there can be so many
of them dead that they would not give up and
go home. We came away from it without injury.
You are not to worry about us as our Brigade stays
in Reserve and does not get into much of the fight-
ing. We are ready for battle should it come to us.
Howell and Tom's Regiment is camped closer to the City.

179

We are not allowed to leave camp to visit them.
For directing a letter, we are still in Col. Johnson's
40th Regiment, Barton's Brigade, Stevenson's
Division, all in the Army of Vicksburg. I'd rather
still be in the Army of Tennessee. We pray this War
will be over soon and we can come home for good.
I remain your loving son and brother, Ananias
Covington.

"We need to send another letter," I say

"If his letters take this long to get to us and ours to him, the boys'll be home before another could," Pap says. "I won't give out good cash money after bad on letters that don't arrive."

There'll be no reasoning with Pap why I want to answer, to write the necessary words again, so the boys will know, and David will come home.

***

The whole house is noisy and busy with this happy boy, sitting up and creeping. He cries, gurgles, chirps, and squeals. Mary Jane and I take turns feeding him with our fingers or a salt spoon. He gums soft peas and mashed potatoes with great satisfaction, smearing his food across his fat cheeks.

Laundering diapers and ironing little dresses is tedious. I let him entertain me with banging a tin cup on the floor, set out wooden blocks for him to pick up and throw down. This evening on the porch, I pull him up to standing, his sturdy legs pushing his feet against my lap. He squirms and wiggles. I put him down on the porch floor. He crawls toward the steps, and I grab him up into a hug before he reaches the edge. If he'd allow it, I'd cuddle him until bedtime.

I still want to name him. But, as Mam has done with all of us except Ananias, he won't be named until his first birthday. Or David comes home. There's no give in her about this. She says you don't know enough about a child's character. It's also a custom because so many babies die in their first year.

***

In the heat of the afternoon, we rest in the shade of the porch. The baby is fussy and restless and will not be comforted.

"I'll take him in for a nap," I say.

No one else has the energy. I carry him upstairs to our sleeping room and set him on the bed I share with Mary Jane under the slant of the roof at the back. Rebecca and Charlotte share the bed at the front.

A braided rug lies next to each bed, sewing baskets under them. Hooks on the wall hold our night shifts, Sunday dresses, and aprons. There's a shelf for each of us. My cloth doll slumps next to the Reader on mine. No matter how Rebecca teases me for keeping the doll, I will not give her up. I named her Annie, the name I wished I was called as a little girl. The embroidery stitches of her face have split and pulled out. She has a half smile and no eyebrows, her yellow yarn hair hangs in clumps. Cloth legs split and losing their stuffing, I have loved her thin.

Now there's a live baby doll to dress and rock to sleep, although there's more messiness involved. The feeding is not pretend, and I never had to change a diaper on Annie. I was too young when the twins were born to know anything of caring for a boy baby, or any baby at all.

I prop him up on my goose-down pillow, take the Reader, and sit next to him. I hold the book open for him to see the pages and turn to *Robert of Lincoln* with its cheerful choruses, "*Bobolink, bobolink//Spink, spank, spink… Chee, chee, chee.*" His eyes on me, he seems to be listening as I read. He reaches for the book, giggling and squealing, "yee, yee, yee."

I pull the book back from his reaching hands, and find the *The Cataract of Lodore.*

"*How does the water//Come down at Lodore?"//My little boy asked me//Thus once on a time;//And, moreover, he tasked me//To tell him in rhyme.*"

I read softly and slowly, maybe not the way the poet intended but in such a way that the rhythms and rhymes are like a lullaby.

Fighting sleepiness, twisting his head and rubbing his eyes, soon he is asleep, and because I can't leave him napping alone on my bed, I look through the exercises for reading out loud. After hearing Harriet read and recite with enough feeling to make me weep, I want to practice using pauses and emphasis. There's time in the quiet afternoon to finish reading out loud for myself the long poem with its fountains sprinkling and twinkling.

It's a sneaky thing to do, stick my nose in a book while he naps, but I imagine tired mothers doing this. I believe Lydia would have too, if she'd known how to read.

25

Mail Call

Ananias

"I WON'T DO IT," David says. "It is not an honor to be a cook. They're too lazy to soldier."

"Captain put your name in," Posey says. "You're one of the few who can actually cook."

"Not with what they're giving out. Sour meat, wormy flour, rotten potatoes, no sweetening."

"He knows you can't see to shoot," I say. "It'll beat shoveling out dirt in the hot sun."

"Standing over a cook fire comes close."

"It's in the trees. You won't be hunting shade."

"I can't back off the Order," Posey says. "It starts tomorrow."

"What if I don't go?"

"Court Martial."

"Over not cooking?"

"Over any Order now."

***

The mail arrives at evening Roll Call, the last of what came into Vicksburg before the siege.

"Covington!"

I look up. Why is Sergeant Williams calling our name?

"It's us," David shouts and thumps me on the back. "We got us a letter."

The paper is sealed in an envelope, addressed in Eliza Ann's wobbly script.

"It's a wonder," I say. "She sent it to Tennessee."

"Read it!" He pulls me to the smoky remains of the small fire we use for keeping mosquitoes away.

28th March, 1863, I read. "She wrote this to answer my first letter. They didn't received the last one."

"Read the letter!"

> *Dear Brothers, This month we received your letter*
> *of September the 24th. Pap and Mam said I should*
> *be the one to write in answer. It is my first letter,*
> *and they have helped me with what to say. We*
> *have had a terrible sorrow. Lydia was delivered*
> *of a son on September the 8th.*

"A boy!" he shouts, slapping me on the back. "I have a son. Keep reading!"

Then she took a fever and died without knowing us or naming him.

David stares at me. "She died? How could she die? That has to be wrong."

He reaches for the letter. "Show me where it says that!"

I point to the sentence. I won't read it out loud again. The words blur with tears.

"Keep reading," he whispers and sinks to the ground.

We buried her in the Meeting house yard and grieve for her every day. Mam says it is for David to name his son. Tabitha took him and cares for him with her baby girl.

My voice catches. How can I do this? How could Eliza Ann have written it? I clear my throat, swallow tears and snot.

> *The other sad news is Chadwick Buchanan dying in battle. No one else hears about their soldiers. The twins have grown tall but are no match for Abe and Shad. We miss Tom as well as both of you. When your letter arrived, Mrs. Buchanan gave us paper, pen, and ink for a reply. If you remember, I was not good at writing with a quill. We have read yours until the paper wore apart at the folds. Mam says she holds each of you in the loving places of her heart. We pray for the War to be over and you to come home. I hope you will forgive me for sending grievous news. I am sorry that we can't be together to comfort each other. I am your affectionate sister,*

*Eliza Ann Covington. P.S. Jane told me this is the
way for a girl to close a letter.*

David is bent over, arms wrapped around his head, rocking
and weeping. I don't know what to do except what he would do
for me, put a hand on his shoulder.

"I never should have left," he murmurs. "I wish I'd hid out.
Gone north."

The words won't go away. *Then she took a fever and died.* I try
to think of where in the Bible we have found words of comfort.

"I can't remember the verses for sorrow's ease," I say.

"Doesn't matter what happens to me now."

"It does to me. It will to the boy."

We sit, heads bowed, brothers alone in the night.

"*He healeth the broken in heart, and bindeth up their wounds,*"
Posey recites into the darkness. He and Eli have been here all along.
"*He telleth the number of the stars; he calleth them all by their names.
Great is our Lord, and of great power; his understanding is infinite.*"

I have not said a night prayer since Tennessee, and I can't pray
now. But Posey's words bring comfort. Like the stars, each of us
has a given name, as will David's son.

"First thing in the morning, I'll report to Cook Camp,"
David says.

***

Burnett brings our rations and hands them out.

"What's this?" I ask, turning a reddish brown hunk
in my hands.

"Pea bread," he replies. "Your brother says don't eat it."

"What are we supposed to do with it if we can't eat it?"

I try to split it in two. The crust does not give. I pound it against a rock. It breaks open on the third blow. I pull the pieces apart, and the dough stretches in thin webs. I pull the filmy webbing of bread farther apart.

"Looks like a spider's lived in it. What did they use to make this?" I ask.

"Orders came to make meal from cow peas. Flour is short."

I take a bite from the inside of the bread. The feel in my mouth is raw dough. I spit it out.

"Your brother told them it wasn't fit to eat. When he saw how the loaves came out, he threw them to the side. Commissary Sergeant ordered him to put it with the rations. He wouldn't do it until Sergeant Williams stepped in. It was a standoff."

"I imagine it was," I say, taking a drink from my cup. "The water tastes good enough."

"Some claim it makes them sick. There's more at sick call every day. The grapevine says the gunners up here eat rats. Don't know what kind of man would eat a rat."

"A hungry one. You might want to stop that rumor. You hear anything else worth telling?"

"Men are deserting through the lines."

"Any more good news?"

"Your brother's trying to get on Ration Detail. Captain wants him cooking."

"When David decides to do a thing it isn't so easy to tell him otherwise."

"We saw that."

Burnett follows the Ration Detail to the next rifle pit. I throw the hunk of what couldn't pass for bread as far as I can.

"You feeling as short-tempered as I am?" Eli asks.

"That and more. I've been short-tempered my whole life and worked to hold it in. Howell used to tease me until I got mad, then made fun of me for that. The only way I could shut him out was by not taking his bait."

"So that's why you're so even-tempered for a redhead?"

"It's what gets me through most difficulties."

"Who wouldn't be a soldier?" he says and tosses his bread after mine. The ground around the rifle pits is littered with pea bread.

26

Siege

Ananias

SWEATING, DIRTY, STINKING, and hungry, we shelter in the rifle pit and play three-handed euchre. Scratching at lice and chiggers keeps us awake in the hot nights. Rations, no matter how scant, are a relief from the roar of enemy guns hammering at the earthworks of the Siege Line. Only when the guns go quiet at dusk, is it safe to deliver them.

David arrives with the Ration Detail. He's carrying the kettle.

"How'd you get out of Cook Camp?" I ask.

"Told them I'd take my chances with Court Martial if they didn't let me see for myself how my brother is holding up. Sergeant Williams stuck up for me."

"I'm holding up all right. Sick to my stomach, almost deaf. Being under siege is something I never thought about happening in war, but I reckon we few, we happy few, can hold out if they don't kill us first. What's for rations?"

"It's not rats," he answers, ladling stewed, dried beef into my dish. "I hear some brigades have turned to killing mules."

"It'd be fresh meat," I say, pushing the shreds of beef around with my spoon. "What do you hear about how long this will go on?"

"If General Johnston doesn't tear into the Yankees from the rear and break the Siege, we're done when the food and ammunition run out. I got to deliver the rest of these. I'll be back to cooking tomorrow. Take it easy on Burnett."

He crouch-walks to the next pit on the bluff. Hands holding cups rise up from the earth, and he serves them.

"Your brother is a man," Eli says.

"He's always had a way of telling me I've done wrong, without saying it. Given what's been dealt him, I'm grateful to have him keep on me," I say.

"Must be something he learned from home."

"They'd never let us feel sorry for ourselves."

The heat breaks in dark clouds that burst into hard rain. Water pours down the sides of the pit. Everything turns to mud, too sloppy to shovel. We sleep on the edge of the pit, ready to jump in when the shelling starts.

***

Five weeks we've been living under siege. The heat has returned along with the fire of mortars, howitzers, columbiads. From daylight til dark, we hug the insides of the pit under storms of iron shot and shell. Canister and shell fragments litter the ground. Each day is the future and history of every other day. In the night, we dig our pit deeper.

The Ration Detail reports more men sick with fever in the ravine hospital. The Yankees coming from the south have dug ditches and rifle pits closer, set up new parrot guns. Yesterday morning after dense fog, their gunboats fired into our position for three hours without letup.

It's Sunday. The shelling comes from the south.

"They're taking turns," I say.

"Better than all going off at once," Eli says. "Maybe the boats observe the Sabbath."

"To keep it holy?" I ask.

"Keeps us from being shot full of holes."

"I don't know how we haven't been wounded when others have. Seems it's going to be that or taken prisoner."

Surrounded by Yankee lines to the north and east, gun boats on the river, and these new ones from the south, we have nothing to do but duck shells and dig.

***

We've made it six weeks. The Yankees are digging a new ditch, closer to us. When the shelling lets up we hear their raised voices, the clang of their shovels. A hatch of insects rises up in the moist heat of the bayous, the air dense with mist and wings. An enormous explosion rises from the Siege Line to the northwest.

***

It's week seven. The Yankees are digging more approach lines. Their sharpshooters killed four men in our ditches with head shots. The ones across the River aim at our men filling water casks. Shells are hitting close to the ravines behind us.

"Sorry about your brother," Burnett says as he holds the ration kettle.

"What about him?"

"Shell fragment caught him at the edge of Cook Camp."

I climb out of the pit and run toward the ravine. Posey catches up with me and grabs me by the arm.

"You can't leave your post," he says.

"Oh yes I can."

"Not without a pass."

I push his hands off me. Stronger arms grab me from behind. Eli.

"Won't be doing you or him any good if you fight," he says.

"I won't fight you. I need to go to my brother."

"Keep him here until I get Sergeant Williams!" Posey says.

Eli does not relax his hold.

"If I let go and you take off, someone's going to shoot you."

I give it up.

"I won't take off."

He lets go. I look back at the River. It flows on, heedless of the misery on the bluffs above it, the blood and scraps of iron, the dirt and insects, the heat.

Posey returns with a pass and hands it to Eli.

"It's for both of you," he says. "Make sure he comes back!"

***

An attendant leads us between rows of wounded men in the hospital tent.

"The surgeons finished with him a few hours ago."

Blood soaks through a bandage at David's left hip. His eyes are closed, his breathing shallow.

"Got your brother here, Covington," the attendant says.

David opens his eyes, smiles, and whispers, "I knew you'd come."

***

We crowd each other on the shaded side of the pit. I didn't think it possible to be any more louse-infested, bone thin, and greasy-haired, but we are. Our clothes are rags. The only thing we haven't had a chance to make worse is wear out our shoes. Rumors of ceasefire and surrender twist along the grapevine.

"They're discussing terms," Posey says.

"I don't care what terms they come to," I say. "I also do not care about the honor of the Confederacy, the glory of the Army of Vicksburg, or that General Pemberton's a useless fool."

"Can't argue with any of that," Eli says.

Shells roar over the pit.

"I don't believe they are participating in a ceasefire," Posey says as we cower lower.

The shelling stops late in the afternoon, and Burnett comes around with supper rations.

"Your day has come, boys," he announces. "Fresh meat."

"This isn't beef," Eli says, poking at the gray flesh. "And it's too big for small deer."

"There's only one animal left that could be cooked up fresh," I say.

"You know it," Burnett says. "You're eating mule."

"And glad to have it."

"We aim to please. How's your brother doing?"

"Living. I thank you for telling me."

"I'd have wanted it done with my own brother."

Posey has worn out his copy of Shakespeare, but I remember things he read to us. *For he today that sheds his blood with me shall be my brother.* We are all brothers here.

27

Missing

July 4, 1863, Meeting House

Eliza Ann

NO ONE CELEBRATES Independence Day now, shooting off rifles and singing songs, like *Yankee Doodle*. We haven't belonged to the United States since Secession. I miss the noise and merriment, the barefoot days when all I had to worry about was what the twins would think up next for tormenting me and Mary Jane.

It's hot and quiet. The Meeting House is full. Those who can't fit in crowd near the open windows. There are families here that don't come to Meeting anymore, some who never did. Others like Callie and the Halfords came from Dawson County.

Ansell Bowen stands against the back wall with his family. Benson and Caleb, their wives cowering behind them, Elias and Franklin standing proudly in Militia uniforms, Luther slouching next to George and Harmon, Kize half-hidden behind Moses. Mrs. Bowen sits on a bench with her youngest, Violet and Verbena, twins who have never been flower-like. I know how they hide around corners and trip other girls, how ready they are to raise their fists, just like their brothers.

Mr. Halford brought the news to us that Barton's Brigade has been in a big battle, and Vicksburg is under siege. Mr. Monroe went to Canton where lists are posted and carried back the names of the wounded and dead. He arrived home last night and sent the call out for this gathering. Standing at the front of the room, he waits for quiet, holding the lists, looking down at the floor.

"Our boys were in a battle on May the Sixteenth at Bakers Creek in Mississippi," he announces. "Between Vicksburg and Jackson. The *Cherokee Mountaineer* has printed the names of those wounded, captured, missing, or dead from the counties of Pickens, Dawson, and Cherokee. I'll read the ones from Company C of the Forty-Third Regiment and Company I of the Fifty-Second. If anyone wants to know of others, ask me afterwards and I'll look for them."

He looks toward Pap with a sadness I've not seen before.

"I'll start with Company C. Ike Bowen, captured. Joe Bowen, captured."

Rebecca crumples. Charlotte brings a hand to her mouth. The Bowens erupt in an angry outburst, Mr. Bowen shouting, "You're lying." The older boys and Luther call out too and shake their fists. Kize and Moses stand silent and wide-eyed. Mrs. Bowen bows her head and sobs into her hands. Violet and Verbena look away from their mother in embarrassment and glare at me.

Mr. Monroe holds up the paper and points to the printed names, staring at the Bowens until they settle down.

"Alex Graham, captured."

Jane, with Carrie on her lap, holds her head up, her back board-straight. She puts her arms around Alfred and Cynthia. Tears roll down her face.

"Jacob Wilder, captured."

I want to comfort the Wilders and go to Jane, but there are more names to be heard besides the thirty-seven from Pickens County.

"From Company I. The Reverend Jefferson Childs, wounded and captured."

What happens to a wounded man when he is captured? Do they take care of his wounds?

"Howell Covington, wounded and captured. Thomas Covington, missing."

Mam sits completely still, hands clasped, face frozen. Louise shifts the baby and puts her other arm around Mam. Pap straightens to his full six feet, his hands clutching the twins' shoulders. Callie gathers her children close. Mary Jane grips my hand so hard it hurts my bones. I can only stare at Mr. Monroe. *Wounded and Captured*. That is understandable, but *Missing*? He must be mistaken. That word is for when some small item can't be found. "I'm missing my thimble" or "We're missing one spoon." How can Tom, who always paid attention, following every move of his brothers, be missing?

Mr. Monroe continues with the list. There are more missing and dead. "Moody Simpson, wounded and captured."

When he finishes, Pap shoulders his way through the crowd.

"I'm sorry I didn't get home in time to tell you first," Mr. Monroe says.

"What about the Fortieth?" Pap asks. "It's in Barton's Brigade like the others."

"Your boys' Regiment isn't here. I asked at *The Mountaineer* and was told it would be in the Calhoun newspaper."

"That's the only way we'll know?"

"Unless somebody comes through and tells you or goes to Gordon County for the list."

We don't know anyone from Gordon County. We know only the name of John Phillips, the owner of the farm somewhere south of Calhoun where David worked harvests and met Lydia. I remember how Mam didn't want Ananias and David to go from Calhoun. If they hadn't gone from there, they could have been among the captured from the Forty-Third.

The walk home is sorrowful. No one wants to talk. I don't want to imagine what happened to Ananias and David, don't know if their chances were better than the others. Not knowing can be worse than knowing. We at least know that the rest are alive. Except for Tom. How could things be worse? He could be dead.

I look up toward home, half expecting to see another smoke column rising. The sky is clear, and the Bowens left together. Their farm is north of the Meeting House and ours. Maybe they won't be so mean now that they share the same loss as other families.

***

I need to go to the cave, where I'll feel closer to Ananias and Tom. Up on the mountain everything will be clearer. I know the way. Without them, our group is too small. In moments, I can almost glimpse one of them ahead of me. It's only hope.

The twins take turns carrying the musket Pap insisted we bring. They stay close, paying attention to the ways I'm choosing to go, instead of wandering off to follow a deer trail or chase wild turkeys. We climb and turn past the markers of trees and stones until the Cherokee tree. The haze of the humid day obscures the view. I can't see the Etowah River.

Ananias wanted to see new places. Now he's in Mississippi, under siege, if he hasn't been killed or captured, or gone missing. I asked Mr. Monroe what it meant, being under siege.

"One side has the other surrounded. The other side has to outlast it, fight its way out, or be taken prisoner," he answered.

"What happens to prisoners?" I asked.

"They'd be sent to prison camps in the North, like jails."

"Is that what they did to the ones captured in the battle?"

"Most likely."

David used to describe the jails of Jasper and Calhoun to excite the twins, telling them, "They shut you up in the dark and feed you moldy bread and dirty water." Were Howell and the others being treated this way? Could it happen to a whole army? As far as we know, the Siege is still going on.

The cave is a cool refuge as we clean it out and start a fire. Louise has done her best, given the shortages, and sent us off with a basket of boiled eggs, tomatoes, and griddle cakes.

Some things don't change. The call of an owl in the warm night, the dark sky now clear, the constellations in their places.

I startle at the streak of a shooting star. I do not believe in omens and haints, but this gives me chill bumps.

What if I never see my brothers again? Never hear Ananias's soft drawl, his careful words, telling me how I need to know what I can do. I know more than when he left, more than I could have imagined—how to shoot a musket, that by helping Jane I can do the work of running a house, earning her calm attention in return. I've done field work like a boy and not minded it. Sewed a quilt. Waited out the agony of Lydia's lying-in, grieved the loss of her, still missing her every day. Learned how to care for her baby. I tolerate Harriet when she carries on about the Southern cause. I've learned better when to hold my tongue.

I want to be worthy of all of it. I feel as if I've tilted over an edge, never again to be the girl who trusted that life would never change. I wonder if Ananias has learned enough about war.

The stars keep shining, the constellations move in their paths, and the night hunters are out.

28

White Flags

July 3-4, 1863, South Fort,
Vicksburg, Mississippi

Ananias

TOMORROW IS THE anniversary of the Independence of the United States, whose soldiers are enemies to us. I sit on the straw-scattered ground of the hospital tent and watch my brother breathe. Straw and a blanket keep him off the blood-soaked dirt. The sides of the tent are rolled up to allow the movement of air. In the closeness of the ravine, heat stifles breath.

Mosquitoes and black flies swarm. I wave my hat over David's face and adjust the haversack that pillows his head.

There's little enough in it to make a pillow, so I've folded his torn and blood-stained trousers inside to soften the bumps of what's left of his possessions—tin cup, whittled cat, hunting knife.

Lice live in every seam of my clothes. The stink of my unwashed body must be something awful, but I don't notice it anymore. My hair has grown long and shaggy again. My beard feels scraggly. I'd be ashamed to have Mam see how we live. But we're still alive.

In his clearheaded moments, David knows Lydia is dead. When not quite awake, he talks to her. Now he murmurs in his sleep, "Let's name him Lydham. It's uncommon, like you." Fully awake, he talks about her. How she winked back at him when he met her, how joyfully she danced, how he can't believe she won't be there at home to sleep beside him, love him.

The night wears on. Attendants talk among themselves about the coming surrender. Eli walks down the row and drops to one knee. It's his way of settling to earth instead of sitting, always ready to get up and leave.

"White flags go up in the morning," he says.

"What's it to us here?"

"I don't know for these men," he says, looking around at the rows of wounded, "but we've orders for how to surrender."

"Do I leave him behind?"

"You have to be there to give up your Arms, then it depends on the Yankees."

Surrender will be a relief.

***

I wake to the silence of truce. Wood smoke drifts from the cook tent. The cooks bang pots and skillets onto fire grates.

Hospital food is thin broth and beans. The ration for men in the pits and ditches has been a spoonful of peas and rice with a small square of side-meat. The Louisiana gunners have run out of crawdads and small deer. Despite what they say, roasted rats do not come close to tasting as good as squirrel.

"Have they given up trying to kill us?" David's eyes are open.

"More likely we're giving up on getting killed," I reply.

I take up a rag and dip it in the pail of bloody water at the foot of David's bed.

"Rumor is we'll be prisoners," I say.

"The only time I was taken prisoner was hide and seek," David says.

As boys playing, he always let himself be easy to find, then pretended he couldn't see me or Tom in an apple tree, the twins in the corncrib. He would search the barn wondering out loud where could his brothers be hiding, giving us time to come crashing out of the branches and corncobs, running for home.

"You were the best prisoner a little brother could have," I say.

"And you were the best little brother."

I wash sweat and straw dust from his face, neck, and hands. I wipe his feet and ankles, his bare legs up to the knee of the wounded leg, and under his drawers on the other side.

Blood soaks through the bandage. One of the attendants, a wounded man too, says puss will be the sign of healing. It worries me a little that no thick liquid is coming from the wound. Clean bandages are so scarce the attendant replaces only David's under-dressing with a fresh one and rewraps it in the old bandages, dried with blood.

I prop him up to drink broth.

"This isn't beef," he says.

"Mule."

He takes another swallow and says, "Wonder what Tom would say about this."

"If he was hungry? Nothing."

"How would Louise fix it?"

"A sight better than Army cooks."

"Lydia could have done that." He winks at me and lays his head back on the haversack. "I know how I've been. I'll do better when we're prisoners."

"I have to go to the Capitulation. If they let me come back for you, I will."

"I won't be going it alone."

***

I climb out of the ravine and up the hill to the ditch line. White flags blossom from north to south, and the Fortieth raises its own white flag at the end of the line.

Attention! Company! Form the Column!

Dressed in ragged gray jackets, jeans cloth trousers faded to pale blue, shirts brown with dirt, we form Rank and File and march at Common Time onto the road where the Yankees wait in front of their line of ditches. A Yankee brass band plays *Dixie*. We've heard they do this to honor fellow warriors, and we take it so. I would rather be anywhere than the land of cotton. I want most of all to be in the land that faces the mountains, where corn grows full and golden.

The Yankee soldiers, in neat, dark-blue uniforms, stand silently, rank behind rank in such numbers anyone can see they could never have been defeated. The generals could have ended this sooner. Pride keeps our leaders from doing right by the men who suffer. We've heard that the slaves of Vicksburg have taken this for freedom and fled to the places where Yankee troops are in charge.

We file into ranks, face our enemy, and stand at Attention. A Yankee general rides forward on a chestnut horse. He is clean-shaven and young. Next to him a major raises a paper and reads in a high-pitched twang.

"On this the Fourth day of July, in the year of 1863, the City of Vicksburg and its garrison, Lieutenant General John C. Pemberton commanding, have capitulated to the United States forces, Major General Ulysses S. Grant commanding. These are the terms of surrender. *As soon as rolls can be made out, and paroles signed by officers and men, you will be allowed to march out of our lines, the officers taking with them their side-arms and clothing, and the field, staff, and cavalry officers one horse each. The rank and file will be allowed all their clothing, but no other property. If these conditions are accepted, any amount of rations you may deem necessary can be taken from the stores you now have, and also the necessary cooking utensils for them.* By order of U.S. Grant, Major General, United States Army, you are prisoners of the United States Government and will remain inside your former defensive lines until paroled."

Present Arms!

Our movements and the Yankees' are identical.

Forward!

I step forward with Eli and Posey toward our Colors.

Surrender Arms!

I stack my rifle with theirs, unbuckle my accoutrements and hang them from the bayonet. In my pockets I carry Eliza Ann's letter and silver thimble, Lewis's jaw harp, and Genny's silk bag.

We stand at Attention in the sun while each company surrenders. At the command for Parade Rest, the Yankees break ranks, open their knapsacks, and take out ration parcels. A private wearing the insignia of the 26th Indiana approaches us.

"My name's Finemore. We got rations. Come and have some."

We sit with Private Finemore's mess and eat beef and wheat bread, drink coffee with packets of sugar and thick milk from cans. It's the best and most rations we've had since before the Siege.

"You going to fight after the parole?" Finemore asks. He has snappy brown eyes and, although he seems no older than me, his dark hair is turning gray.

"I'll do what the Army orders," I answer.

"I hope we don't have to fight each other again. You Rebs are stubborn."

"You too, Yank."

We return to our former lines and are dismissed.

I go to the hospital tent. David sits propped against a tent pole.

"I know," he says, looking up. "We're going home."

29

Graybacks

Ananias

WE STOP AT the top of the lane, trousers and jackets pink with dust, hats drooping. Spread out below is home, everything and more that I have missed. The house and barn settled into the hollow of land between wooded hills and sloping fields. Shad and Abe grazing at the edge of the near field, April and June in the shade of the orchard. The sun tilting west. The windows in the house are propped open, the soft high voices of my sisters drifting out.

David leans on his cane. Eli stoops, picks up a rock, and puts it in his pocket. I walk ahead, so intent on the house I don't notice the geese until one is almost on me. Here comes the rest of the flock. I retreat to Eli and David for strength in numbers. The only weapon we have is David's cane.

Eliza Ann comes out to the alarm. She calls back to the house, leaps off the porch, and runs up the lane, flapping her apron and scattering the geese. She's grown taller, skirt hem above her ankles.

Her arms around me and David, laughing and crying, she looks over at Eli.

"Who are you?" she asks.

"Eli Rutledge."

She looks back at me.

"Eliza Ann, meet Eli," I say.

"Proud to meet you, Miss Eliza Ann," he says and holds out his hand to shake.

"I guess I'm proud to meet you too," she says and takes it.

Whooping and shouting through the gate, Mary Jane and the twins run toward us, Charlotte and Rebecca close behind. Our progress down the lane and through the yard is a jumble of hugs, tears, questions, our goal the porch where Mam stands, one hand gripping Pap's arm, the other flat against her heart. I let go of the others, walk into her embrace, and lay my cheek against her hair. A hand touches my back. I half-turn to Pap and form the words I'd almost given up thinking I would ever speak.

"I'm home."

I'd planned how I would tell them about Tom and Howell straight off. In the warm, muffled circle of their arms, smells of lavender and sweat, calloused hands stroking my head and back, my sobs choke off the words, Pap's voice, "Hush, son, you're home."

David collapses onto the first step. He stretches out the stiff leg and is surrounded. Mam and Pap go to him, sit on either side, and hold him.

"I know about Lydia," he says.

"So you do," Pap says.

Eli stands alone at the gate, straight and tall.

"Come on in," Eliza Ann says, beckoning toward the porch.

He comes through the gate and leans against the post.

"If you close the gate, you can come up on the porch," she says. "The geese might bite you, but we won't."

"I'd be tough to chew on."

"Tough or tender, if the geese get into the garden, Charlotte'll chew you up."

It makes me laugh, and I have not done that in a long time. True to form, saying whatever comes into her head, she's dug herself into a hole, threatening Eli with the geese. Innocent Charlotte, who would never chew up anyone, is staring at her along with Rebecca, too shocked to say anything, for now. Eli closes the gate and half-sits at the edge of the first step, one knee resting on the ground. He has no idea what he's getting into.

Louise comes out of the house carrying a sturdy, little boy. He rubs his eye with his fist, puts the fist in his mouth, and chews on it.

David holds up his arms, and Louise hands him the boy. He looks up into David's face, back at Louise's smiling face, reaches one hand to David's beard, and looks at Louise again. She pats his back and gently pulls his fingers away. He pats David's cheek.

"Did you name him?" David asks.

"We saved that for you," Pap says. "He's a little shy of his first birthday."

"William Richard. After Sergeant Williams, the one who kept us alive. Richard after you."

"I'm proud to share it. But it's a long name for a little boy."

"Willy, for short."

"When did you boys last eat?" Louise asks.

"Yesterday," David answers.

"There's food left from dinner."

"We counted on that."

"Tom, Howell, we don't know…," I begin.

"There was a notice in *The Mountaineer*," Pap says. "Howell wounded and captured in a battle, Tom missing. Then Callie had a letter."

"We tried to account for them. No one could tell us."

"There'll be time for the telling," Mam says and turns to Eli.

"I am Sarah Covington."

Eli stands and removes his hat. His thick hair is dirty and matted, but he stands straight and keeps his eyes on her. "Eli Rutledge, ma'am." He bobs his head.

"I'm sorry, I forgot," I say. "Eli's our messmate. He stayed to help me with David, and he's got no people, so we brought him home."

"We're proud to have you, Eli," Mam says.

"Thank you, ma'am. Sir?"

He offers his hand to Pap who stands up and takes it, then pulls Eli into a hug, same as he did with me and David.

"You helped my boys, you're as good as our own," Pap says.

Eli turns away, swiping a hand at his eyes.

Eliza Ann's cheeks are wet and snot runs out her nose. She's not alone, we're all in tears. Because we're home, because Willy has taken to David and is now squirming to get out of his lap, because

Howell and Tom are still missing—it's enough to make anyone break down bawling, and I am close to it.

She rubs the snot away with the back of her hand, wipes it on the underside of her apron, and looks up. Eli is watching her. She twists her apron between her hands, like she always has when she doesn't know what to do, and looks off at the geese eating their way along the fence. She knows she's going to get it from Charlotte and Rebecca. It'll be something to see, how she works her way out of this. I've missed her ways, missed everyone's. Sitting here in peace, belonging, it's all I want. Before I go see Genny.

"Let's get you boys cleaned up," Rebecca says. "Luke, Lafe, get a wash fire started! You boys go on down to the branch! There's clean clothes upstairs. We'll send the necessaries."

"Could I have something to drink first?" I ask.

"I bet you all would like that," she says and goes for the bucket and dipper.

"I'll get the clothes," Charlotte says, her face blushing.

"You all leave those clothes with the wash tub," Rebecca directs, waving the dipper. "There's critters crawling on your shirts."

"It's graybacks," I say. "Like us."

"Whatever you call them, we don't want them in the house."

"What's graybacks?" Eliza Ann asks. "Why are they like you?"

"Lice," I answer. "Because the jackets on our backs are gray."

"You really have lice? In your hair too?"

"Same as our clothes."

She looks down at her dress and apron and brushes her hand at them. I take the dipper from Rebecca and drink. No water has ever tasted this good.

"When can we eat?" David asks.

"When you're clean," Rebecca answers.

"We come home from war and you won't let us in the house or feed us?"

"I thought you'd want …," Rebecca falters.

"Don't worry," he says, handing Willy over to Eliza Ann. "We want to be clean worse than you want us to."

Rebecca looks to Mam.

"They'll feel better clean," Mam says. "And we don't want lice in the house."

"Then let's have at it," David says and limps to the gate.

Charlotte hands a pile of clothes and towels to Pap. Louise hands me a basket with Pap's shaving glass and razor, soap, scissors, and comb. Wrapped in a cloth are three sliced biscuits loaded with butter and blackberry jam.

***

The twins pretend to mind the fire under the wash caldron, watching us pull off our clothes and prepare to bathe as if it's something they need to learn how to do. They stare at the red scar on David's hip. Luke opens his mouth to speak. Lafe nudges him to keep quiet.

"Get your hair and beards good and wet," Pap says. "I'm going to cut and scrub those critters out. You can shave your own selves close."

I wade into the branch, lay back in the water, roll onto my stomach, and duck my head under. I could stay like this in the cool stream all afternoon, but I'm hungry.

"You boys are skinny as shorn sheep," Pap says. "We need to get some meat on you."

"Water's warm," Lafe says, pouring a bucketful into the wash tub. "Who's first?"

"Ananias got us here," David says.

I'm greedy enough to not decline, step into the tub and groan, lower myself into warm water. I soap and scrub my skin and hair with a piece of toweling, groan again as Lafe pours more warm water over me. I get out and sit for Pap to cut my tangled hair and beard close to the skin, wait while he picks out the lice and nits.

I take up the razor and shaving glass. I'm so used to how David and Eli look, I don't realize how bad it is until I see my reflection, haggard and brown. We're lucky they let us through the gate. The razor's path exposes my pale chin and cheeks. My forehead is pale too, from the mop of hair.

Clean and dry, I sort through the clothes for my old trousers and shirt, and put them on. The shirt hangs loose from my shoulders, the trousers in danger of falling off my hips.

"You can burn those rags," I say. "It's the only way to get rid of lice. We tried plenty of times to wash and pick them out and they kept coming back."

"The girls will find a way to get them clean and useful," Pap says.

"These are all the old clothes we have," Luke says.

"You two have grown," I say, recognizing they're wearing Tom's shirts.

"Eliza Ann says it's only in height," Lafe says.

"Looks to me like you've grown in responsibility too."

"They've done some of that," Pap answers and smiles. "You can quit feeding wood to that fire. We won't be sending you back to your sisters."

"What happened with the hip?" he asks David.

"A shell fragment hit me. The Yankees shelled us every day."

"Did you bleed?" Luke asks.

"More than you would want to see."

"How did it stop?" Lafe asks.

"A surgeon poked for the fragment with a probe. Bandages took up the blood."

"Did you holler?" Luke asks.

"As loud as I could."

"Then what?"

"I mended. Eli's finished with his bath. Go tell Louise we're almost ready for dinner."

I know he'd rather not talk about it. I want to forget everything.

30

A Reckoning

Ananias

HOME. COMING INTO the house, the Bible and Readers on the shelf by the window. Mam's Queensware platter in the corner cabinet. Kettles, pots, and skillets, a tidy box of kindling and splits at the hearth. That has to be Eliza Ann's doing. Pressing irons, turkey-wing fans, candle lamps, and the clock on the mantle. Mam's rocker, Pap's chair, the many-colored braid rug.

The table. Set with cold chicken, pole beans, new squash, sliced tomatoes and onions, biscuits, butter, a pitcher of cider.

"I hope this is enough," Louise says. "There wasn't time to cook up fresh but the beans and squash."

"This is a feast," I say.

We sit at the table and stare at the food, afraid it might disappear.

"We haven't had food like this since we left home," I say.

Louise passes us plates of chicken and vegetables. The taste of a fresh tomato, crisp onion, soft biscuits. I want to eat everything at once.

"What did they feed you in the Army?" Luke asks.

"Corn meal with critters crawling in it, raw side-meat with worms, and fresh mule," David answers.

He forks his food with one hand and holds Willy on his lap.

"How could you eat a mule?" Eliza Ann asks.

"You never heard of being hungry enough to eat a mule?" I ask.

"Let them eat in peace," Pap says.

I know the look on her face, too confused to ask another question, but she will.

"It's apple," Louise says, carrying a pudding from the food safe. "I had it for tomorrow. I don't think anybody'll mind you starting on it today."

Eli puts down his fork.

"Miss, I thought they were telling tales when they bragged on your cooking," he says. "Glad I was wrong."

Louise smiles and spoons pudding onto his plate. He sits stiffly, quickly moving the food to his mouth. He chews thoroughly, keeping one arm around the plate. I remember Lydia doing that. I don't think I've seen Eli eating at a table.

"You have no people?" Eliza Ann asks.

"Eliza Ann!"

She ducks her head at the sharpness in Mam's voice.

"None to count on," Eli says.

"Eliza Ann, you will apologize!"

"It's no insult, ma'am. I've been on my own so long, it doesn't matter."

"Were you born in Georgia?" Eliza Ann risks another.

"North Carolina. My pap brought us down to Georgia to raise hogs. He cared more about breeding them than raising young'ns. He'd work us 'til we got to an age, then turn us out to make our own way, root hog or die."

"Your mam did you that way too?"

"She didn't want us any more than he did."

"You won't be turned out here," Mam says.

***

The view from the porch, yellow roses twining around the posts and scenting the air, evening settling onto the land, at peace.

"I'd stand night pickets picturing this," I say. "Afraid I'd never get home."

I've taken my place on the top step between Mam's rocker and Pap's chair. Eli sits at the end of the bottom step, near Eliza Ann. She doesn't tell him it's her place. Willy sleeps in David's arms. The whole family is out here, like we used to be, sisters knitting and sewing, the twins all ears for anything we say. Except for Tom. I miss him bitterly.

"David said you're the one who got him home," Pap says. "With him wounded, how did you do it?"

"Our regiment marched across Mississippi to Corinth where the rail lines crossed. It was full of our soldiers in defeat,

Union soldiers in charge, and slaves taking their freedom. We were put in stock cars on a train to Mobile. The wounded from Vicksburg were sent there by boat. We found David at a hospital. Georgia boys were sent on another train to Atlanta to be exchanged. We weren't going to leave until we had David. We mixed in with Alabama boys so we wouldn't be found. Lots of soldiers slipped away like that, wanting to go home before exchange, like us. Once David could leave, we snuck on rail cars to Rome, everything in confusion, no one asking for papers. Eli came up with cash money and paid a wagon driver outside of Rome to carry us to Cartersville. That was the easy part. We walked the rest of the way."

I do not tell how Eli sold the bawdy cards. I do not tell them how David suffered walking, Eli and I on either side of him, half-carrying him.

"I couldn't have done it without Eli."

"And now you are home," Mam says.

I am. And that seems to be enough for Pap. I want to put off telling them what it is like to go to war. And that I have to go back.

***

I am clean. My night shirt is clean. My bed holds the warm-air smell of sun-dried sheets. The shelves above our beds are as we left them. Mine holds the fox skull and hawk's wing I found in the woods, my copy book and quill pen. Tom's his lucky mule shoe. The twins' shelves have marbles, a tortoise shell, two dried up june bugs, and two chicken feet. They used the feet for a made-up batting game with the bugs. They kept at it because it was so disgusting to the girls.

With a questioning look, Eli holds up the night shirt Rebecca gave him.

"It's a night shirt," Lafe tells him.

"For sleeping," Luke says.

"I never slept in a special shirt."

He puts it on. He also washed his feet like we did before coming upstairs. He climbs into the other side of the bed.

"I thank you for bringing me here," he says.

"There's always room for more in this family," I say.

"You miss your brother?"

"He and I slept in this bed since he was old enough to be out of the crib."

"He could have been caught up in the retreat."

The mattress across the room rustles. The twins are not asleep.

"He would have found his Regiment," I say.

"He could have been cut off behind the lines and taken prisoner."

"You think Tom's a prisoner?" Luke asks.

"The Yankees know who was taken prisoner," I answer. "They're good at keeping records."

"Will we ever know?" Lafe asks, quieter than Luke.

"Not unless Howell can tell us. If we keep talking, you won't sleep and Pap'll be at the both of us tomorrow."

"He won't be at you, and I can't sleep anyhow."

"Be still then."

In the silence, a loudly whispered argument carries across the rafters from the girls' room.

"Why did you say she'd bite like a goose?" Rebecca hisses.

"I didn't say that," Eliza Ann hisses back, higher pitched. "I said the geese might bite him, but if they got in the garden, she'd chew him up."

"Why were you talking so bold?"

"He was by himself, and we were all carrying on. He looked so alone. I just asked him to come in and close the gate."

"Will you ever learn to think before you speak?" Rebecca's voice rises.

"Leave me be. I tried to make him welcome. I'm sorry, Char. I didn't mean to embarrass you."

"I know," Charlotte says. "I didn't need to be so sensitive. You did good to ask him in."

I nudge Eli. "You'll never have a better champion than Eliza Ann."

"That wouldn't be hard to take," he says.

***

I cut a piece of butter onto the spoon bread and watch it melt, pour blackberries and cream over it, dip in the spoon, raise it to my mouth, and savor cool and warm, sweet and tart. Louise hands me a plate of sliced ham and scrambled eggs.

"Do we get to eat all this too?" Luke asks.

"You don't eat like this now?" I ask.

"Mush and milk for breakfast."

"Hush up!" Louise points an iron spoon at Luke.

"Some things are scarce, some too dear," she says. "We can't get coffee. I tried everything to substitute, but we all had headaches."

"We did that too," David says. "Then we gave it up."

He feeds Willy pieces of spoon bread with his fingers. Willy gums the food and looks up at him after each bite.

"I'd like to see her grave," David says.

"We'll go after dinner," Pap says.

"What about picking the corn?" Lafe asks.

"There's no rush," Pap answers. "With Ananias and Eli here it'll go fast."

This is what I have dreaded.

"We can't stay," I say.

"Where you going?"

"Back to the Army. We're on furlough and still on parole. We have to be exchanged."

"Show him the papers," David says, before Pap can say anything else.

"They're upstairs."

"Then go get them," Pap says.

I don't want to go through this but I go upstairs and bring mine down.

"There's one each for parole and furlough," I say. "The furloughs for me and Eli say we have twenty days to go home, then return to the Regiment. That ran out before we got here. The parole papers say we won't take up arms until exchanged, when the Yankees let some of their prisoners go and we let some of ours go. That's how armies do it."

"Read the parole paper to us," Pap says.

"Every word?"

"Every one that counts."

I unfold my parole paper and start reading.

VICKSBURG, MISSISSIPPI, July 11ᵗʰ, 1863.
TO ALL WHOM IT MAY CONCERN, KNOW
YE THAT:
I, Ananias Covington, a private of Co. D, Reg't
40ᵗʰ Georgia Vols. C.S.A., being a prisoner of War,
in the hands of the United States Forces, in virtue
of the capitulation of the City of Vicksburg and
its Garrison, by Lieut. Gen. John C. Pemberton,
C.S.A. Commanding, on the 4ᵗʰ day of July, 1863,
do in pursuance of the terms of said capitulation,
give this my solemn parole under oath.

That I will not take up arms again against the
United States, nor serve in any military police or
constabulary force in any Fort, garrison or field
work, held by the Confederate States of America,
against the United States of America, nor as guard
of prisons, depots, or stores, nor discharge any duties
usually performed by Officers or soldiers, against
the United States of America, until duly exchanged
by the proper authorities.

"Sounds to me like you can't have anything to do with the Army or the War until you're exchanged," Pap says. "That's good enough for me. You don't get exchanged."

"Then we're prisoners of war. We have to be exchanged."

"Why did they let you go if you're prisoners?"

"There were too many of us, a whole army. They hoped most of us would get home and stay home."

"What happens if you do the same?"

"Our own Army will court martial us for desertion. Then they'll shoot us. Or hang us."

"My furlough says I don't go back until I recover," David says. "I'll be here for harvest and beyond. I'm not going back."

"We could use the help," Pap says.

I'm standing here like a schoolboy after recitation, waiting to hear if I did it right. I don't know what else to say to Pap. I'd hoped we'd be farther along in the welcome home before it came to this.

"I'll do my best before I go," I say.

"Let's hope that's good enough."

My half-eaten breakfast is cold and I hate to waste it, but I leave the house. If I stay, we'll get into it more and say things we'll regret. Again. And, from the looks of the place, David will not be enough help for harvest.

***

The Wilders' hounds are as bad as our geese. Genny hushes them, smiles, and takes my hand.

"I've been waiting for you," she says.

I pull the tattered and stained silk bag from my pocket.

"This held the hope I needed for coming home."

I lead her around a corner of the house, take her other hand, and look into her eyes. She smiles up at me.

Kissing her, the sensation in my stomach the same as that first time. Kissing me, she moves her hands to my back. I want her more, want to do as Eli said. Her breasts press into my chest. I move my hands to the sides of her blouse, close enough to fit around them easily. She leans back and looks up at me.

"Someone could see us this way."

How could anything that feels this good be wrong? I want to keep the sensations on my lips, my fingertips, everywhere.

"I don't know about what happens next," I say.

"I don't either, but we have to go inside. They all want to see you."

She is all I want to see.

31

Rhymes with Eliza

August 1863

Eliza Ann

"DID YOU KNOW a surgeon probed David's hip for a shell fragment?" Luke asks from the opposite end of the table.

I fight the urge to gag. Probed means poking around. I do not want to know any more about lice, mule meat, paroles, furloughs, fragments, or probes. I keep my head down, drying dinner dishes.

"Want to know what happened next?" Luke asks.

"No."

I hang up the dish towel and leave out the back door. There's a messy pile of branches at the chopping block.

That suits my mood. I pick up the axe, lop branches for kindling, and pile them neatly. I do not want to know when or why Ananias will return to the Army. I want to do like Mam, just sit and look at him and David, gone so long, and now changed. Thinness can be fed away, shorn hair grows back, pale skin colors up with field work. David's quietness can be explained by Lydia's death, but Ananias is not so easy to read. He hesitates in acting, like this morning, not wanting to read his papers to Pap, then goes and leaves his meal unfinished.

I pick up a large piece of wood and split it. That usually calms my mind.

"That's a good pile of wood you're working." Eli's voice comes from the porch.

"It's mine to do," I say and set the axe on another split, keeping my eyes on where I will chop.

"Looks like there's enough for winter already," he says.

"Not around here."

"I'd help."

He is standing on the porch step. The trousers he's been given end above his knobby ankles. His bare feet are bigger than any of the boys'. I lean the axe against the chopping block.

"You have trouble with the size of your feet?" I ask.

He laughs and says, "You do ask strange questions."

"I'm sorry. I ask what I want to know, and it causes me trouble."

"It's no trouble. It's just not a question a man expects to be asked by a girl."

He picks up a good-sized wood chip and turns it in his hands.

"What do you expect?" I ask.

"It wouldn't be about the size of my feet. And yes, I do have trouble. The Army didn't always have shoes to fit me, and I've worn socks that are too small most of my life."

He takes out a pocket knife and whittles at the chip.

"Is Eli your full name?"

"Elijah Rutledge."

Rhymes with Eliza. I am not going to say that out loud.

"Your brother made me his friend," he says.

"David?" He's the one who never knows a stranger.

"Ananias. From the first day, when they lined us up together because we're tall. You all don't know what you have with each other."

"Lydia believed that too."

"Eliza Ann!" Rebecca calls from the passage. "Callie's here."

***

Callie and her children coming down the lane are a commotion. Emily and Lily are seven and six, Samuel four, and Daniel a few months older than Willy. When Callie walks anywhere, they scatter away from her, following butterflies to flower bushes, a turtle crossing the road, leaves blowing in the wind. She tries to keep them close, spreading out her apron like a hen gathering chicks with her wings. When she has them bunched together, they pull her by both hands.

They sit at the table eating cold spoon bread, staring at Ananias and David.

"Don't you remember us?" Ananias asks.

The girls nod. Sam shakes his head. Dan copies him.

Her hat wreathed in pokeweed blossoms, Callie pulls a letter from under the crown, and hands it to Ananias. "I thought you'd want to read it for yourself."

I know what it says, having read it over and over for the family to reckon out what happened and what might happen. He reads it out loud.

> *June 20, 1863, Marion, Mississippi. Dear Mrs. Covington, I write this letter on behalf of your husband Pvt. Howell Covington. He was brought here from the battle at Bakers Creek near Vicksburg. Pvt. Covington was taken to a hospital in the field and treated. It was behind enemy lines and took some time before he was removed to our hospital. He has suffered a grievous wounding of the spine that will take many months for recovery. Considering that, he is in good health and spirits. He asks me to tell you that you are not to worry after him but he is most concerned about his brother Thomas. Your husband fell wounded before the Yankees overran his Company and his hope is that his brother was able to retreat with the Company. He sends you his love and asks that you depend on his father and brothers for help. I am your obedient correspondent, Mrs. Patience Yancy.*

"So Howell can't tell us what happened to Tom," he says, handing the letter back to Callie.

"Ever?" Mam's voice is almost too low to be heard.

"Some men disappear in battle, their bodies never found," he answers. "If his Regiment couldn't say and the Yankees didn't report him, we have nothing else."

He's holding something back but I don't know what it is.

"Could he have been wounded like Howell?" I ask.

"We would know by now," he answers. "The only other chance is he could have been caught up in the retreat and mixed in with another regiment that didn't make it back to Vicksburg."

"Could he get word to us?"

"Probably."

"I won't mourn him 'til I know," Mam says.

I catch up with him out on the porch.

"What were you not telling Mam?"

He sighs. "Why do you always find me out when I don't want to talk about something?"

"Because I know you. Tell me."

"It's worse than David's wounding and will sicken you. I am not going to tell her of the bodies blown apart into so many pieces no one could tell who they were."

He's right. I don't want to know more. Tom is gone.

***

David kneels and rests his forehead on Lydia's marker. A woodpecker taps at a tree. A crow calls. Willy pushes himself up and totters from marker to marker. I go with him, past those naming our neighbors' dead, and steer him back to Lydia's. It's the only one we have in the graveyard.

David pulls something from his pocket and holds it cupped in his hand.

"Eli made this for you when I told him about your singing," he says. "I wish you were here to laugh about it with me."

He places a small whittled cat in front of the marker and bows his head.

I nudge Ananias and whisper, "Is he talking to Lydia?"

"He did that when he was first wounded too," he whispers back.

I don't know if it's normal for folks to talk to the dead or leave things at their graves. Mam and Pap don't seem bothered by it. To me the graveyard is a lonely place, left to the markers that have tilted and fallen, the wildflowers blown in on the wind.

"She's at peace here," David says and lifts Willy. "I will be too."

***

Eli comes down to breakfast with his haversack and hat.

"Looks like you're intending to leave us," Pap says.

"I am, Sir."

"Your papers are like theirs. You can't fight until you're exchanged."

"I've pushed my furlough far enough."

"They don't even know where you are," David says.

"I don't need a Court Martial. What about you?" Eli asks Ananias.

"I'll follow later," he replies. "They need me here."

"Why not stay a little longer and let us feed you better?" Mam asks.

"I'd like that but I need to start for Calhoun," Eli replies. "Colonel Young will have something to do with reforming the Regiment. Posey will be there too."

"Stay one more day. You can leave at first light tomorrow with food to carry. Let us do this last thing for you."

"Yes, ma'am."

"Now, take those things back upstairs and come eat your breakfast."

I put plates on the table. My body is acting in strange ways, separate from what I think is happening. When Eli comes into a room or says something, my heart shifts and beats fast. My cheeks grow hot. I like the sound of his voice and the way he talks back, defending himself with humor. I like the look of him, the height of him, and the steady expression in his hazel eyes. I have been hoping he would stay.

***

I'm up at first light, helping Louise prepare traveling meals for him, not wanting to miss his departure. I eat in silence, listening to my brothers tease him about how he'll miss out on Louise's cooking.

"When the War is over, you'll want a place," Mam says as he gathers his things to leave. "When the Army lets you go, come here. This is your home."

"Thank you for making me welcome, ma'am" he says and looks at me. "If your family wants me, I'll do my best."

On the porch he shakes hands with David and Ananias, then reaches into his pocket.

"Eliza Ann."

He holds out his hand for me to shake, leaving me with the sound of his voice, the warmth of his hand, and the pressure of something small and wooden in my palm. I pretend nothing unusual has happened. With the rest of the family, I wave until he walks over the rise.

I go out the passage and past the privy, up the hill into the orchard, my hand clutching the piece of wood. When I have cried enough to make myself feel silly, I wipe my eyes on my sleeve and examine his gift. A small wooden goose fashioned with the neck bent, the head turned to its wing. I finger the tiny feathers, the wood warm in my hand. I will keep it at the bottom of my sewing basket, so no one else will know.

32

Songs for Cowards

Eliza Ann

I SWEEP AROUND WET socks, jackets, and shawls hanging from chair backs and stair rail. The smells of stewing beans and wet wool follow me into the passage. Wind-driven rain blows through, scattering dried bean shells.

In Mam's room, Charlotte and Rebecca are carding wool. Mam sits close to the low fire burning at the front of the fireplace, hemming a winter gown for Willy.

"Don't sweep in here yet," Rebecca says.

Wool drift floats around her head. I plop down on Mam's footstool and let out a sigh.

"That's a big sigh for not having to do a piece of work," Mam says.

"It's so dreary and wet. We might as well build an ark."

"It hasn't been forty days and forty nights."

"Seems like more."

"Complaining about the weather won't change it. Start on a new patch."

I do not want to sit and sew. I would rather sweep the whole house all over again or stand in the rain and split wood. The large pile of wood stacked under the eaves is enough for several days. The way the twins keep it is not as tidy as mine, but that doesn't seem to matter to anyone else.

We keep our sewing baskets in Mam's room for the companionship of sewing together. On top of the yarn and unfinished socks in mine are pieces of cloth salvaged from the boys' lousy jeans-cloth trousers and wool jackets. Mary Jane and I, under Rebecca's direction, boiled them until the seams fell apart and the lice and nits floated dead. Mam decided I should use the cloth to sew a marriage quilt, now that I am seventeen. Rebecca, Charlotte, and Mary Jane have made theirs. I sort pieces for a square. Fitting the pattern of eight-pointed stars in small squares and triangles takes enough attention to keep my head down.

Rebecca chatters on about Ike Bowen. Charlotte doesn't have as much to say about Joe. Both brothers are home from a Yankee prison camp. They'd shown up at the gate, rail-thin and pale. With much questioning and gesturing on Pap's part and persistent answering on theirs, he allowed them to come every day after dinner until they returned to their regiment. Like Eli did. I'm the only one who seems to notice his absence, and I don't dare mention it. I reach down into the basket and touch the wooden goose.

I told Jane about it and my reactions to Eli. Her response was, "It sounds like he's decided. Now it's up to you."

To decide how I feel for him? I have so little to go on. Seeing how easy he was with my brothers, how respectful to Mam and Pap. Asking about his big feet still embarrasses me. But there is the goose.

Willy is sitting on Mam's bed, dropping marbles into a tin cup. Losing interest in that, he crawls to the edge. The high drop from bed to floor halts his progress, briefly. I catch him as he goes over the edge. He laughs and squeals as I lift him high and twirl around the room. I stand him on the floor, and he toddles toward the bright flames in the fireplace. I turn him toward the door. Every room in the house holds mischief if not danger, and he has tested most of them—crawling up the stairs and tumbling down, tipping the syrup jug onto himself, and tangling the yarn in the spinning wheel.

"*Will they miss me in the trenches, will they miss me,*" David sings from the passage, "*when the shells fly so thickly around.*" He blows into the room with fresh wind and rain and swoops down on Willy shouting, "Who's this boy? He's mine." Then swings him high and pulls him back into a tight hug.

"He my," Willy squeals, giggling and waving as David marches around the room with him, singing, "*Do they know that I've run down the hillside//To look for my hole in the ground?*"

I go across the passage, looking for Ananias. Louise is adding turnips to the kettle of beans and backbones. A bloody bag sits on the table. David and Ananias are just now home from helping the Wilders with hog-killing.

Ananias comes downstairs whistling *Listen to the Mockingbird*. The song has different words about the siege of Vicksburg, and a new title, *Listen to the Parrot Shells*. The boys brought home all sorts of peculiar words and expressions—euchre, the grapevine, skedaddle. It does not make sense to me how a colorful talking bird and a cannon could be called the same thing. It also makes no sense that my brothers can make light of men being cowards.

"What makes you so cheerful on such a wet day?" I ask.

"Nothing like a walk in the rain home to a fire and hot food," he replies.

"That's all it takes?"

"Compared to life in the Army of Tennessee, it does. Most of what we did was march and sleep in the rain."

"How'd you get dry?"

"We didn't."

"That sounds miserable."

"It was," he says cheerfully. "And that was the easy part. No one was shooting at us."

Everything comes back to the War, with someone shooting at them like they were crows in a cornfield. And then they sing songs about it.

"Can we fry up that liver with dinner?" Ananias asks.

"For you we can," Louise answers.

"No one else?" he teases.

"No one else likes liver the way you do."

"There was one in our mess relished it more than me."

"Who was that?" I ask, hoping to hear Eli's name.

Ananias stares into the fire. "Rufe. He didn't make it away from the battle."

Louise spoons lard into the spider and sets it in the coals.

"Come and slice up an onion," she says to me.

If misery could be more miserable, I am. I never know when a simple question will turn a conversation to silence. I cut an onion from the braid hanging in the corner, slice it onto a plate, and carry it to the hearth. Louise slides the onions into the sizzling lard.

"Was he your friend?" I ask.

"We weren't friendly. Most of the time we butted up against each other."

"This'll be ready soon as I put the meat in," Louise says.

I go out to ring the dinner bell. When I come back in, Ananias is still staring into the fire.

"Do you have to go back?" I ask.

Pap and the twins come in the door.

"I'm Absent Without Official Leave," Ananias says. "I should be with the Army."

Pap starts to speak. David bursts in from the passage with Willy, still singing about the coward of Vicksburg. Luke joins in, "*I'll say that I've fought them as bravely//As the best of my comrades who fell//And swear most roundly to all the others//That I never had fears of a shell.*"

Lafe twangs away at the jaw harp Ananias gave the twins. Whatever Pap intended to say is lost in the confusion.

How many soldiers did my brothers know who were cowardly braggarts like the one in the song? Would they be called cowards for staying home? They aren't the only ones. Jacob Wilder and Alex Graham, thin and sickly from dysentery and prison camp, have said they'll stay home to work their farms. Moody Simpson with one arm and Reverend Childs on one leg have been discharged and gone back to distilling whiskey and preaching the gospel. Pap calls that essential work. Others are hiding out with gangs in the mountains. Eli, Ike, and Joe are some of the few who returned to the War.

I help Louise put supper on the table. Making sense of what has happened to my brothers and our friends is more than I can do. Sweeping, sewing, setting the table, that's what I do. I want bigger things, important things that make a difference.

33

Nothing to Do with Love

Ananias

"DID I HEAR you say you should be with the Army?" Pap asks.

He's been silent through dinner. I have been dreading what he might say.

"According to them I should," I answer.

"And fight again?"

"That's what an army does. Fights. Kills all the young men."

"We gave our share of young men."

"That won't keep me from Court Martial when they catch me."

"They aren't going to catch you when they're in Tennessee."

"According to *The Mountaineer*, the last battles drove us into Georgia."

"Us? The family is us. As for the Army coming into Georgia, that's all the more reason to stay. The Yankees will come behind them, and we'll need you. I remember you saying you'd leave the Army to defend the farm."

"No need to go now," David says. "Our Army isn't doing anything but trying to stay warm and fed in winter camp. The real fighting won't start 'til spring."

"That's when I aim to go," I say.

"To go missing, be wounded, get captured, killed?" Pap asks. "What would you be worth to us then?"

"What am I worth now? A mule, a hog, an acre of new land?"

My sisters' gasps are audible. Here I am, talking back to Pap again. Nothing I have done in between has made a difference. I stayed for harvest because he needed me. And because of Genny. I don't want to return and sleep in lice-infested clothes and blankets, eat spoiled and raw food, or no food, live out in the weather with no shelter or fire. More than anything, I don't want to face endless ranks of blue-clad enemy soldiers, be scared shitless at the crash and roar of cannons and musketry. But I know I will.

"I will not have every grown son of mine maimed and lost to war."

"We're already lost to the War. We lived worse than animals. They treated us like fools. We seldom knew the why of commands and orders, just obeyed them. I came home when they told me to and I have to go back until they're done with me. And when I do go, there'll be more than one way to die. If I stay here, I'm the same as the coward in the song, and I'll face death for desertion."

"I'd take my chances with you here," Pap says. "Will you think on it?"

I can't believe he's asking me rather than telling me. That's different.

"I do that every day. Then I remember I've no business wanting to be anything but a soldier. I have to finish this. Like Eli. Ike and Joe."

"Eli is his own man. The Bowens are their pap's concern. He makes such a story of those two, you'd think they were his only sons. That's not to say they aren't good enough boys once you hear their side of it. But, I'm telling you I would have you quit. Abraham Lincoln has new generals. Grant and Sherman have driven you out of Tennessee, Kentucky, Alabama, and Mississippi. They're winning this."

Willy shrieks from the hearth. He holds up his hand and wails. He has reached for a winking orange coal. Charlotte gathers him up, murmuring, "there, there." She scoops up a hunk of lard, daubs it on his fingers, and hands him sobbing and hiccupping to David. He holds Willy's hand to his mouth and kisses each fat little finger.

"We'll let this rest," Pap says. "For now, I would have you want to stay with those who love you."

"It's not about what I want to do," I say. "And it's got nothing to do with love. If it did, I'd be marrying Genny."

I asked to marry her. She said yes. Lucy said no, her daughter's too young to be a widow. After the War, yes.

Love is being alone with Genny, loving her, her loving me. Each time we are together, we love a little harder and longer. What Eli told me is true.

34

Christmas Gift

December 1863

Eliza Ann

I T'S CHRISTMAS MORNING. The twins stomp downstairs hollering "Christmas Gift" first and loudest, waking the small children. My sisters and I have been up since before first light, putting together the makings of breakfast and dinner for seventeen.

The house smells of cedar and roasting meat. Mistletoe hangs in the doorways. Holly stalks line windows and mantles. Callie and the children have spent the night. Their excitement at finding gifts makes the house merry.

Emily and Lily cuddle cloth dolls. Sam twirls tops for Dan and Willy to chase. Pap and the twins made a Noah's Ark for Willy. They fashioned it from shaved oak, working at it in the barn. Two by two, the animals were whittled—fat hogs, sheep with carved swirls of wool, squat chickens, and sitting cats.

"How did you ever do these?" Mam asks.

"Eli showed us," Lafe replies. "He did the first ones and we copied them."

On second look, in the pairs of hogs, sheep, and chickens, one is carved with skill, the other rougher. I pick up the best-looking hog. My fingers follow the lines of a fat belly, long snout, and tiny tail, knowing that Eli's hands formed it.

"The cats were easiest," Lafe says. "Pap helped us."

"What about the geese?" Mary Jane asks.

My head jerks up. I've shown her the whittled goose. Why would she ask in front of everyone?

"Eli said live geese are hard enough to handle," Lafe answers.

So, the goose I have is one of a kind, made for me alone. I set the hog back on the ark and carry dishes to the table.

Sweet potatoes, corn custard, roasted turkey and deer meat, pumpkin pudding, the table has not been this full of good food since last Christmas. As everyone moves to their places, there is a knock at the door, and a voice calls out, "Christmas Gift!"

I drop the butter bowl. In the shriek and scramble of children surrounding Eli, I hope no one notices the thud of it hitting the table. Emily and Lily remember him, and the little boys follow them. He takes a small bag from his haversack and gives it to Emily. She opens it and pulls out pieces of hard candy. The little boys abandon Eli for Emily.

244

Ananias clasps Eli's hand. The twins thump him on the back, and David calls out from across the room, "You're just in time for the feasting."

"Come in! Be at home!" Mam says.

Eli hands her two packages.

"Coffee," she exclaims, squeezing the cloth bag. "And sugar." She holds up the blue paper cone.

"How'd you get away?" Ananias asks.

"They gave Christmas furloughs to those with a place to go. I said I had one."

"Eliza Ann, set another place," Mam says. "This Christmas feast is ready."

I put the extra place setting between Pap and Ananias.

"We ask a Christmas Blessing on this family and our Christmas visitor," Pap prays. "We pray that our Heavenly Father will watch over Howell and Tom. We thank Him for this food as we celebrate the birth of His Son."

I keep my hands in my lap and stare at my plate. I do not dare look at the far end of the table. Mary Jane finds my hand under the table and squeezes it. I glance around for who else might suspect. Everyone is eating or dishing up for someone else. If I don't start, someone will ask why. I swallow a forkful of potatoes and turkey and concentrate on chewing and swallowing. My hand shakes holding the fork. Something is wrong with my nerves.

***

On my way to the spring house, I scatter food scraps to the cackling chickens and honking geese. On the way back with a bucket of water, the geese surround me, honking for more. Eli stands at the chopping block.

"You still keeping the company of geese?" he asks.

"I have one in my sewing basket," I answer.

"It's worth keeping?"

My face is hot, my neck is cold, and I can't take in a breath. My legs don't seem to be able to keep me standing. The scrap pan falls out of my hand. Water is spilling.

He catches me by both arms and holds me upright.

"Are you faint?" he asks.

"I've never fainted. Why would I be faint?"

"I can't say."

He is holding me by the arms so close I can smell the wool of his uniform jacket, his sweat. I tilt my head up. I have never been close enough to notice the gold flecks in his hazel eyes.

"The goose is worth keeping," I answer.

He smiles. "It's all I can give you for now."

What in the world are we talking about? I step back from him.

"I need to take the water in," I say. "If the others see us, there'll be no end of teasing."

"You afraid they'll tease you?"

"You should be afraid."

I carry the water bucket through the passage and end up in Mam's room. I need to calm myself. I can't take a half-empty bucket into the kitchen so I go back out to the spring house. When I return, Ananias, Eli, and the twins are at the table starting a game of euchre.

"Your bid," Ananias says to Eli.

"I don't want to go it alone," Eli says and looks up from his cards at me.

What Jane said must be true. Now it's up to me. How safe and warm it felt, his hands holding me up, how close he was, that he sought me out, knew I was about to fall, *it's all I can give you for now.* I know how I feel, but I'm not ready for anyone else to know.

***

Our sleeping room smells of drying lavender, roses, and apples. We hang the onions and beans in the boys' room. Rebecca says they don't care what it smells like.

It's after bedtime, but Eli and Ananias are still downstairs, talking. I pull up the quilt and listen to Eli's low drawl.

"He has a nice voice, doesn't he?" Mary Jane whispers.

"He does. Why did you ask about the geese in front of everyone?" I whisper back, not wanting Rebecca to hear me.

"I was hoping he'd do them as a reminder for you. I didn't think about the others not knowing. They weren't paying attention."

I hope they weren't. My attention is with what Eli is saying.

"We were almost to Knoxville when they ordered us back to Chattanooga. We had a good position up on a mountain called Missionary Ridge. The Yankees came in under fog. We held on the Left, but when the Center gave way, we ran. They've put General Johnston over us instead of Bragg. Some say he takes better care of his men."

"How many did we lose?" Ananias asks.

"Fifteen killed. More wounded."

"How many are left?"

"There's no reserves. We need you."

"I'll be there before the fighting starts again."

"Posey was promoted to Sergeant. If you'd gone back when I did, you'd be a Corporal for certain. The Company remembers how you stood at Baker's Creek."

"I won't be an officer," Ananias says. "I won't be telling another man to forward march and die."

"There's another thing" Eli says. "We've come up with passwords for helping men trying to get home."

"Deserters?" Ananias asks.

"Men who need to go to their families. Like your neighbors. If a lone man shows up, you ask, *are you going it alone?* If he answers, *I know when to take help,* you'll know he was sent your way."

"That takes care of that," I whisper to Mary Jane. "He wants Ananias back with the Army. I'm a fool to think his being here has anything to do with me."

"Don't be so quick to give up. He hasn't left yet."

***

It's the second day in the New Year, when we clear the house of Christmas. I feed dry holly, cedar, and mistletoe to the fire in the yard. It's good to be outside with the house so full. Pap and the boys have started their winter work, repairing harnesses and ropes in the passage. In the short days of winter, work doesn't change much for girls.

Eli steps onto the back porch. We have not talked alone since Christmas Day.

"I'll be going in the morning," he says.

"Did you take care of what you came for?"

"How's that?"

"Talking Ananias into going back."

"He was one reason."

"There was another?"

I toss more mistletoe into the fire. No use for that.

"They won't give furloughs once the fighting starts. I don't know when I'll see you again."

"You didn't see much of me this time."

"You didn't want any teasing. Do you want me to see you again?"

He doesn't ask random questions. He asks when he wants an answer.

"Yes."

"It's turning into a long war. I don't know when I'll come back."

"You could write a letter."

"I couldn't."

He comes off the porch and feeds holly stalks to the fire.

"Why not?"

"Can't read or write, I'm ashamed to say."

"There's no shame in that. Can't you have that man, Posey, write for you?"

"I wouldn't care to tell him what I'd want to say."

"You could have him ask about the geese."

"I could do that."

He holds out his hand, as he has done before.

"Why do you shake hands with me?"

"The first time I came here, I put a rock in my pocket. I still have it."

"What does a rock have to do with it?"

"If you do that when you're on a new road, the first woman you shake hands with is the one you'll marry. It was a new road, and I knew I was going to meet you. Now I take your hand for the touch."

I cannot think of a thing to say or ask.

"Will you take my hand so I won't feel I'm going it alone?" he asks.

I hold out my hand. He draws me close.

"I will not stop thinking of you for one day," he says. "Will you give me a word to go back with?"

I smile at him, so close, and lean my forehead into his shoulder. I don't know what anybody would think of this behavior, but I want more than words.

"Do you want me to kiss you?" he asks.

"I think so."

His lips on mine are firm. I like the feel of that too.

"I already think of you every day," I say.

He kisses me again. I like this.

35

What Duty Demands

March 1864

Eliza Ann

LAFE SLAMS THE door open. "There's two soldiers in the lane."

"Tell Ananias!" Pap says. "Go around back! Don't run! I'll see to the soldiers."

Pap goes out the front of the passage, Lafe the back. I watch from the side of the window.

"Go upstairs," Mam says to David. "The girls' room."

"I have nothing to hide about," he says. "And it won't be under a girl's bed."

"I won't take the chance," Mam says.

David walks up the stairs and waits at the top, between the sleeping rooms.

"They're at the gate," I say, peeking out the window. "One of them is giving Pap a piece of paper. He's talking to them. They're riding off."

"They're from the Fifty-Second," Pap says, coming in with the paper. "Going to Dawson County to take in men who haven't gone back. They carried this for Ananias."

The twins rush in the door. "Can we tell him to come out?"

"Tell him there's a letter."

They head back out and follow Ananias in, corn husks sticking to his shirt.

"I won't be jumping into the corn crib again if this is all the danger," he says.

He unfolds the letter, reads it silently, then aloud.

> *February 21, 1864, Dalton, Georgia. Dear Friend, I am taking pen in hand to convince you of the need to rejoin our Company. According to Sgt. Williams, you are Absent Without Official Leave. If you do not return, you will be charged with Desertion. Sgt. Williams believes Gen. Johnston will issue an amnesty, so there is still time for you without penalty and severe punishment. With our losses at Missionary Ridge and the many who have gone home, we need all the men who will serve. Gen. Johnston's orders are to prepare to defend the Heartland. Men who fought under him say he cares about the common soldier and does not waste men's lives. We have new uniforms and shoes and plentiful rations.*

We have been drilling and training in earnest after skirmishing against General Sherman's men on the other side of the mountain. We have more purpose knowing that he will try to take us again. I do not believe that a friend can order a friend to do what duty demands. If ever there was a time that you were needed by your Comrades in Battle, it is now.
Yours sincerely, 3rd Sgt. Posey Huff
P.S. Eli sends his regards to the family.

Oh no. I told Eli to ask about the geese. Ananias looks like he's reading more but he stops, looks at me, and hands the letter to Pap.

"I'm going back," he says.

Pap turns the letter in his hands from corner to corner.

"This is the last chance?" he asks.

"The last at not facing Court Martial."

"What if the War comes to us?" Pap asks.

"There's nothing the Yankees want over here."

"What about David?"

"I can answer for myself," David says. "My furlough says until I'm healed. I can't keep up on the march with this leg."

"Let's hope the Militia is polite enough to ask for your papers," Ananias says.

"When would you leave?" Pap asks.

Ananias looks over at Mam. The knitting needles tremble in her hands.

"I'll help get the plowing started," he says.

***

253

I poke the needle through the jeans cloth patch I'm fitting onto a pair of Ananias's trousers. Good on his promise, he returned my thimble. Rebecca has pulled apart dresses Mary Jane and I outgrew for enough material to sew him a spare shirt in a red, blue, and yellow plaid. We had just enough turkey-red flannel to make new drawers.

Mary Jane and Charlotte are knitting socks. I've finished three lumpy pairs, too big for anyone's feet, save one man. Rebecca has been making fun of them ever since I put them on the table.

Ananias comes in, looks at the socks, then at me.

"I need to ask you about something," he says.

"You want to take my thimble again?"

"The first time was sacrifice enough. Let's go outside."

We've had little time to talk with all the work of spring. In any spare time, he goes to the Wilders. The porch is slick from rain. No stars, no moon. We stand under the roof.

"There was something else in the letter," he says. "I thought it might have something to do with you, so I didn't read it out loud. After Eli's regards it said, 'He asks about the geese.' Why would he do that?"

I want to hide or make up a lie. I resort to less than the whole truth and hope it will do.

"Because of how I said the geese might bite him. He whittled one and gave it to me when he left the first time."

"That's all? What about how odd you acted when he came at Christmas, dropping the butter bowl? Coming out of Mam's room with a bucket of water? And now those big socks?"

Does he know everything about me? Of course, since I was born. How could I hide something now?

"He told me when he came home with you and David he knew he was going to meet me, how if you pick up a rock on a new road, the first woman you shake hands with is the one you'll marry. That's why he shook hands with me."

"Did he ask you to marry him?"

"I don't know. He asked if I'd take his hand so he wouldn't feel like he's going it alone. He said he wouldn't stop thinking of me."

I am not going to tell about the kissing.

"What do you think of him?"

"My heart thumps and I get shaky. I like things about him."

"You're in love, Eliza Ann."

"That's what Jane says. She and Mary Jane are the only ones to know. Please don't tell the others. They'd never let me live it down, never let me forget it if he doesn't come back from the War."

"Rebecca has enough of her own to worry about, Charlotte doesn't hold grudges, and Louise would never tease you. But I won't tell. You keep your hopes and dreams. I know the man he is. He'll come back for you. In the meantime, keep practicing at those socks."

I hope he's right.

36

Them or Us

March 1864

Eliza Ann

"ACCORDING TO MY count, there should be more of these. I've never come up short before," Pap says, looking into the cartridge box.

He stores it under the bed in his and Mam's sleeping room. He hasn't made bullets since the boys left. With Ananias to help, he wants to make more.

After that first time teaching me how to shoot, Lydia and Mam took cartridges from the box to refill the cartridge bag, reckoning it would be a while before we were found out.

"Where could they have gone to?" he asks.

"We took them," Mam answers. "I did, and Lydia, so we could teach Eliza Ann how to shoot."

"Females shooting my musket. Why did you go against me?" he asks.

"Because I saw how much she wanted to after that hideout at Jane's. Even when you said she couldn't, I thought we needed it. I'm too old to shoot a musket, and Lydia's condition was too far along."

"When?"

"When you and the twins were gone. We didn't have the heart to take it up again when she died. After the fire, you or the twins were here all the time."

"What do you know about shooting a musket?"

"I learned before we married. Lydia learned like that too."

Pap puts his hand to his chin and looks down. I know I'm in for it.

"I told you then it would be a waste of cartridges, and it looks like it was," he says. "I can't believe she's any good at it."

"See for yourself."

He takes the musket down from the hooks, beckons to me, and goes out to the porch. The whole family comes behind, Ananias last, grinning.

"What can you hit?" Pap asks. "The side of the barn? The privy?"

I want to prove Mam right and him wrong. Hitting a block of wood would do that. But I want to silence his scorn.

"A rotten egg on the fence rail."

"Go get an egg," he says to Mary Jane. "Doesn't have to be rotten."

"You know how to load this?" he asks.

I nod.

"Show me."

I load the way Mam taught me. It's been more than a year since I practiced, but I've gone over it in my head since the smoke-house burned and Luther chased us.

Mary Jane sets the egg on the top rail of the gate, like Lydia did.

My hands are shaking. I smooth a hand along the stock and barrel to calm myself. I don't want to embarrass Mam. Or the memory of Lydia. Maybe I'll be lucky. I concentrate on remembering each step in order, raise the musket to my shoulder, sight in on the egg, take a breath, and fire. The egg splatters in the air.

Pap stands there, looking from me to the mess of egg and back.

"I'll be damned," he says. "That's not bad for a girl. You want to keep on with it?"

I do, but don't want to admit to it and be made fun of. Hitting the egg in front of everyone is showing off enough.

"With David here I won't be needed," I answer.

"He'd be fine holding it for a threat, but he can't see far enough to hit much of anything. I want Ananias to work with the twins on it. They waste enough cartridges as it is. I want to make sure you do it right."

"I think Lydia and I did a good enough job of teaching her," Mam says.

"You did at that. But if the time comes when she's really needed, I want her to know what Ananias can teach her."

***

"There's more to shooting than tricks," Ananias says. "Even though hitting an egg on a rail is good marksmanship. For anyone."

He turns to the twins. "It's also more than hitting a turkey sitting in a tree. If you're going to shoot, you need to be good at it."

He has inked rings around a bull's eye on a slab of wood. He sets it up in different places for us to shoot from—the back of the privy into the trees, the springhouse to the corncrib, the orchard to the barn.

He's right. There's more to it, and it's harder than I thought it would be. The light makes a difference, as well as the angles of being uphill or downhill.

"I'm wasting powder and caps," I say, after missing the target three times.

"Pap's always kept those in surplus. We've enough to make more cartridges. Try again. Think about it. You won't always have the safety of the porch."

"Did you shoot anyone?" I ask.

"We were always in a Battle Line. We all fired at once. I couldn't see a certain man to aim at and never knew if I hit anyone."

"Do you ever think about whether the men you shoot at are hurt or die?"

"I'm not saying it's easy to shoot at a man. When some do, they lose heart. Some shoot into the air. Some just keep reloading their rifle and never fire, their rifles jammed with powder and balls. But I know from the one battle that counted, it's them or us. Think of what could've happened if that hideout had come into Jane's house. If this is the hardest thing you have to do in this war, you'll be lucky."

I haven't considered that. I raise the musket and try again.

37

Rich Man's War, Poor Man's Fight

Ananias

MENDING FENCES IS what we do this time of year, waiting for the ground to dry enough for plowing. The rain is not letting up. I'm happy to be in the far fields, out of Pap's way. I walk behind David to the next section. His hip healed stiff at the joint. When we walk the fields, he hitches his leg around.

"You holding it against me that I'm staying?" he asks.

"Why would you think that?"

"Your saying that about being asked for my papers."

"That was in the heat of standing up to Pap."

"He's afraid of losing you."

"I'm afraid of failing my duty."

"Saving what we have is what we should be fighting for now."

I shrug my shoulders. "It's a rich man's war and a poor man's fight."

"Then why go back and help it go on?"

"I'm more afraid of Court Martial. Besides, the fighting won't come this far."

"What makes you so certain?"

"Posey and I studied it out at Vicksburg. All that time in the rifle pits. With the River open and Mississippi taken, Grant's Army will go for the rest of Tennessee and Alabama, then Georgia. They'll want to hit the slave holders. We're far enough off to the side of the best route to Atlanta."

Posey's words stay in my mind, "*Comrades in Battle.*" That's what I am to him and Eli. I won't abandon them.

"Pap has you and the twins," I say. "He'll have Howell when he mends and comes home."

"The twins have come a long way, but even combined they do the work of one," David says. "Howell has his own farm and family."

"Why do you think Howell made it out and Tom didn't?" It's the question that bothers me most.

"I don't know. He turned and ran sooner? Or later? How can we know?"

"Wounded in the spine means his back was to enemy fire."

"Are you going to hold that against him?"

"We stuck together, you and me, Posey and Eli."

"We ran and we lost Rufe. The same could have happened with Howell and Tom. One went down and the other didn't see it. Or did. What does it matter?"

"It matters to me what's said after a man's gone. About how he held up."

"You should know by now war doesn't work that way."

"I don't want to die an old man on a farm, remembering I was a coward."

***

This time I know where I'm going. I start out west on the Federal Road, the way David and I walked two years ago. And turn north to the Wilders.

Mist hangs and drifts in the cool morning. The hounds bark from under the porch, not bothering to come out. Jacob, Noah, and the mule are small moving figures at the far end of their cornfield. I've helped them butcher hogs, shuck corn, cut wood, and mend fences. I know how Jacob is anxious to work his land.

The little boys are first out the door, shouting, "Ananias came for Genny." Tabitha herds them back into the house.

I say goodbye to Lucy and reach for Genny's hand. At the road I turn and look again into her blue eyes. Droplets of mist cling to her hair. I smooth it with my hand.

"It's like silver on gold," I say. "I came back the last time. I'll make it home again because I love you."

She lowers her head to hide tears. I touch her chin and tilt her head up.

"Don't cry. It'll make it easier for me if you don't."

Her lips quiver into an upward curve.

"How can I help it when I'm so afraid for you?" she asks.

"Don't be afraid of what you don't know. The last time we didn't fight but three battles."

"One was enough. You're the only one to come home unharmed."

"Then I'm the lucky one."

I lead her into the woods, beneath blooming dogwoods and laurel. I move my hand along her soft cheek until it cups the back of her head. I bend my head toward hers and kiss her.

"You'll really marry me when I come home?"

"I will."

My face crumples. Tears sting my eyes. I belong with her.

"We both have to promise not to cry," she says.

I kiss her again and pull her close. After months of fumbling through each other's clothes, kissing and caressing, falling to the ground, moving against each other, we did more two days ago.

She waited for me at the Meeting House. I came with a quilt, laid it on the floor in the back corner behind the benches where I sat in school with no idea it would come to this. What we did made me feel we could die together of unspeakable happiness.

I want to feel her skin again, her body fitting with mine. I kiss her harder, move my lips to her ear. I know she likes that, know the other things she likes me to do by the noises she makes, know what I like her doing to me. My hands move to her skirt waist, unbutton it, pull her with me, want to lay her down.

She drops her hands and steps back.

"We can't keep going this way. Not here. Someone could come upon us."

"What if I stay one more night?"

"Everyone would know why. It was hard enough getting away in the day. We'll have our time for loving."

She buttons her skirt waist and pulls something from her pocket.

"I made you a new one. It can hold hope, like you said the last one did."

I finger the soft silk bag, blue with yellow flowers.

"I'll be watching for you on the road," she says. "When I know it's time for you to come home. And then we'll love each other forever."

"Just one more time," I say, kissing her softly, barely touching her lips, her skin. "Please."

She lets me pull her to the soft duff beneath the dogwoods.

38

Deserters

May 1864

Eliza Ann

DAYS OF RAIN have flooded the branch, the lane is a waterway, and the road is rutted with mud. In a normal year, the first green would be coming up, but it's been too wet for getting the crops started.

Mary Jane and I cinch our skirts up to our knees.

"I know it isn't decent," Mam says as she helps us, "but it's the only way to keep your skirts from filling with mud."

Pap tried to walk the mules through the nearby field, seeing if there was any place he might start harrowing. They wouldn't set foot in it. He's decided we'll do it by hand.

267

Luke and Lafe roll up their trouser legs, and we start out with Pap and David, barefoot, barelegged, carrying rakes and hoes. At any other time, I could make Mary Jane giggle at the sight of Pap's skinny legs, but I have to pay attention so I won't slip and fall.

"How are we going to do this?" I ask no one in particular.

"Slipping and sliding," Lafe says, picking himself up from where he's fallen.

"If you did the slipping, I'll do the sliding," Luke says. "Might as well get it over with."

He takes a running start, yells out "Woo hah!" and skids with both feet on a mud slick. He falls and slides on his rear end, turning the back of his pants red.

"The reason for rolling up your pants was to not get them full of mud," I say.

"It won't matter. You could spend a lot of trouble trying to stay clean."

Pap turns back and looks the twins up and down.

"I can't even get you into the fields before you make a mess. Get over here!"

He grabs each of them by an arm. Lafe is as tall as Pap, Luke almost. If they weren't willing, he couldn't drag them through the field like he's doing.

"We're out here because we need to eat. Now get to chopping," he says.

I look back at David and Mary Jane. It's taking all of David's strength to hitch along through the rutted field. Mary Jane is lagging so he can keep up.

A man comes out of the trees, close to the lane. It spooks me so badly I can't do anything but stare. David notices my look and turns. The man looks at us sideways as he hurries across the field toward the house.

"Hey you! What are you doing here?" David calls out.

The man turns and stops.

"Trying to get home," he answers.

"Where's home?" David asks, walking toward him.

"Hall County. I saw the house and hoped for food. Some are stealing. I ask."

"You with those hideouts or you going it alone?"

"I know when to take help."

David looks closer at his face, then turns back to me.

"Take him to the house so he doesn't scare Mam and the girls."

"They'll feed you," he says to the man. "Then be on your way. The Militia's out looking for men like you."

"They ain't looking for you?"

"I have furlough papers."

I walk ahead of the man to the house. I remember hearing Eli tell Ananias and David about passwords. I didn't know men would take them up on it.

39

Falling Back

May 1864, Dalton to Resaca, Georgia

Ananias

ELI AND I are set up in hot rocks with no shade, watching for the enemy's attack. They fill the valley below our Picket Post on Rocky Face Ridge. General Sherman's Army has come over the gap where the rail road crosses the border into Georgia. A skirmish line marches downhill past us, an attempt to draw out the enemy. It comes hustling back, pursued by sharpshooter fire. Bullets whisp overhead. A minie ball bounces from the rocks behind me and falls into my lap. I jiggle the warm lead cone, heavy in my hand, and put it in my shirt pocket.

"Keeping that for luck?" Eli asks.

"I'm going to take it home to Genny for proof," I answer.

"We've been lucky, you and me and Posey. Not a wound on us."

"I hope it holds. Some men say they'd like a friendly bullet to send them home on leave."

"Friendly or unfriendly, I've seen what bullets do to a man. I can't wish for that."

"And we both know it's only luck."

"I'm lucky to be back on Picket Post with you. They put Cobb with me before. He doesn't listen, doesn't watch, just prays and carries on about how God is keeping him safe."

"I wish it worked that way."

Night falls, and enemy campfires spread across the dark valley like stars in the Milky Way. I take the first watch while Eli sleeps.

I've seen enough of soldier life to know that it's not the adventure I thought it would be. I've seen bigger towns, even cities, but doubt I'll see Virginia and those sailing ships.

I have learned things I never considered would be useful. I can march in rain, snow, dust and darkness, sleep anywhere, roast side-meat on my bayonet, load a rifle under fire, stand under fire, stand awake at Guard Post and Picket Post. I cannot stand mosquitoes, chiggers, and lice, but live with them anyway. I have pulled my share of digging sinks and policing camp for turds and garbage, shared my canteen with thirsty men. I can take care of myself and do my part in the fight. Now I have come back, right in only one way about this war. It is the biggest event of my life. If I survive it.

I rejoined the Company before it left Winter Camp at Dalton, carrying enough socks from my sisters to outfit the whole mess, including three particularly large and nubbly pairs for Eli. Soldiers always need socks, and the rest were gratefully accepted by my new messmates. About my fellow soldiers I've learned there are many types—brave and resourceful, foolhardy and incompetent, patriotic and devoted to duty, cowardly and skilled at avoiding battle, self-seekers looking for promotion. I can't tell yet if these new men, Cobb and Green, will be as faithful and steady as Eli and Posey.

In the morning light, the valley below is so full of blue-clad soldiers, the earth itself is dark. The white canvases of their supply wagons billow like clouds moving south. How can the North keep sending so many men? Thousands of them are on the march, thousands staying behind to keep us occupied with their shelling and sharpshooting. Their supply train is so long it is still moving away from the encampment the day after it started.

Yankee batteries are moving closer to the front below the ridge. We wait all day to fire the warning signal for an attack that doesn't come. It used to bother me. Now it's less war to fight.

***

The Yankees draw us south, on opposite sides of the rail road. We form Battle Lines, they flank us, and we follow. Or we fall back, and they follow.

The cannonading of battle rises in the south. The Quartermaster's wagon rolls down our Column. Remembering the bourbon of Kentucky, I take a drink of the whiskey he poured into my cup. It burns my tongue.

"Whew, that's mean," I say and spit it out.

"You think they're trying to reward us or warn us?" Eli asks.

"I don't care. Why give us something undrinkable? Moody Simpson came home with only one arm and makes better whiskey than this."

"Reward or warning aside, seems to me we're retreating."

"They're calling it a fighting retreat," Posey says.

"We're losing ground," I say. "Our supply wagons move out ahead of us at dawn. That's retreat."

I dump the whiskey from my cup.

"If we're going to lose this War, we might as well keep marching and get it over with."

***

We fall out at a river bend above a railroad bridge and sleep on arms.

The crash of artillery wakes us.

"Up! Up!" Sergeant Williams shouts before the commands.

Form the Line! Company Forward! At the Quick!

We trot forward, spaced in double lines. Rifle fire rolls across our Front, smoke drifting as the sun rises high. This is worse than Bakers Creek, closer and heavier. Canister rakes the line ahead of us, opening gaps between men, opening bodies to gristle, flesh, and bone, tumbling them into piles. We step around them, close the gaps left by their fall. I can't help but look at them, beyond any help I can give.

Charge!

We yell ourselves into battle in as many versions of the Rebel Yell as there are men. Eli howls. I shriek until my throat is raw. It's one thing I can control, how long I yell. It helps keep panic from making me turn and run. It moves me forward to the bluff where an enemy battery is firing at us. I stumble down a steep hollow, clamber up onto a flat, and run to the base of it. Climbing, my feet skid, the dirt under me gives way. One hand gripping my rifle, I grasp at rocks and bushes and pull myself upward, not noticing the sudden silence.

At the top of the bluff, nothing, but the wheel tracks of caissons and limbers, hoof prints, horse turds. Unchallenged, we spend a hot day holding our Line.

We fall back at dusk over trampled fields where men of both sides have been mown down in swaths, slaughtered, their corpses swelling, the wounded crying out. It sickens me to leave them behind, but these are the rules of battle—hold ranks, advance and retreat in order, do not stop to plunder the dead or heed the calls of the wounded, straggling will be punished, cowards will be shot. We march back through the hollow and across the tracks to the bend in the river.

Wielding a pick axe, I help dig a shallow ditch, pile breastworks of rails and logs, protection for the morning attack that will surely come from across the tracks. The mournful cries of the wounded call from the field. There has been no truce for tending the wounded and gathering the dead. I keep digging. It distracts me from fearing the day to come, the heart-sickness of abandoning wounded men. I take into account what I know about fighting. Aim for officers on horseback, don't huddle up, close the gaps, push onward. For us at first light it will be *Charge* or *Retreat*. It doesn't matter how brave a man is.

***

We meet their attack at sunrise, firing and following their skirmish line as it falls back and back again. Ducking their whining bullets,

I can hear their shouted commands, *Fire at Will!* Deadly volleys of fire come steadier and thicker.

I reload and fire, duck to reload and fire again, move forward into the smoke-filled front. The heat of my rifle barrel burns my hand. At the tracks we come face to face with the bulk of the enemy, entrenched in battle lines so thick we could never fight our way through.

Fall back!

In a low crouch, dodging and tripping on men lying face up, arms thrown back, mangled and shattered, I run with the rest, back to the breast works we dug in the night. Loading and firing, reloading and firing with no rest or food, thirsty, sweating in the rising stink of dead bodies, we hold our Line all day. It is the hardest work I have ever done.

***

We cross the river at dawn. Posey says it's the Oostanaula. He should know, we're approaching Calhoun, his home. We do not know how many of us have died or been wounded and left behind. No one is untouched. Perforated hats, bullet creases on sleeves and trouser legs, dents in cups and canteens. I poke at the dent in my canteen, remembering the jolt to my side, the thunk of lead striking wool-covered tin. I'd had no time to pause, or think of near misses. It's hopeless to dwell on why some of us are lucky enough to live.

We pass through Calhoun in the early morning hours. Two long years ago I arrived here with David to enlist, innocent of war and bewildered by the confusion of people in a hurry, carriages and buggies, and most amazing of all, the Western and

Atlantic Rail Road along which I now march. On that day, I had never before seen a locomotive. Since then I've ridden enough rail cars to fall asleep as soon as I find a place to sit.

Marching past the shuttered stores, I remember them full, selling schoolbooks, jewelry, confectionery, harnesses and saddles. What will happen to Posey's people, the people of Calhoun and these towns along the rail road? We're told that we won the last battle, Resaca. But we didn't push Sherman's Army back north. He's following us south. It's hard to tell who wins the battles, but if this keeps up, he'll be winning the War.

40

Tired of War

Ananias

WE FIGHT EVERY day in oppressive heat, sweat-soaked
and stinking, march into the night, dig a ditch, and
fight again as the sun rises along with clouds of smoke above
the roar of artillery and rattle of rifle fire. According to our
officers, these have been engagements, affairs, demonstrations,
actions, operations, combats, skirmishes. None of us are
fooled by these words. This is battle. We sit in our ditch at
first light, waiting to see if we are winning or losing.

"If they stop fighting and we don't follow, what's that called?" Burnett asks.

"Stalemate," Posey replies.

"I thought stalemate was a draw," I say. "When nobody can move. We keep moving. South. Sometimes I think General Sherman is the one leading us."

"That's why we're not in a stalemate. Yet," Posey says. "We stand and fight, move away to follow him, find ourselves retreating before him, he flanks us."

"And it's always south," I say. "Farther into Georgia, toward Atlanta."

"Maybe when we get to Atlanta we can have some real food," Green says.

"You don't like side-meat and hard crackers?" I ask.

"I'd like a little something green. My gums are bleeding."

My gut twists. There's nothing to forage but poke weed and potato tops, and the regiments ahead of us have scoured the countryside. I'd like to have a whole jug of Moody's whiskey.

***

Past Adairsville, the people of northwest Georgia fill the roads we march along. Fleeing in masses, men, women, cattle, hogs, wagons, buggies, and carts clog the way. Small children ride, perched high on wooden trunks and stacks of chairs. One small boy, close to Willy's age, stares at me round-eyed. I wave at him, and he grins and ducks behind an older girl. Feather beds and quilts sag like sacks of meal over the wagon's sides. Cloaked women, faces hidden in the depths of poke bonnets, walk beside the wagons or ride, holding babies. Families on foot carry bulging sacks. Moving with a bulky slowness, they look like they're wearing all the clothing they own. Everyone is moving south.

Men from our Regiment are disappearing from the ranks, not answering at Roll Call.

"Where are they going?" I ask.

"Home," Posey answers. "The ones who've left so far are from around here."

"Would you have stayed behind with your family if they hadn't refugeed?"

He'd left the column at Calhoun to see his family. They'd gone to Augusta.

"I don't know," he says.

"I hear some of our men are writing their own furloughs."

"It's cause for Court Martial but I don't blame them."

I know why men want to go home. They aren't cowards. Not after what we've seen and done. They want to protect their families. I don't want Georgia farms falling into enemy hands. At least I was right in what I told Pap. Sherman's Army is not headed toward Pickens County.

***

Above the valley south of Cassville, the big guns duel in the oncoming darkness.

"It's like fighting with lightning and thunder," I say.

"Like the old gods did," Posey says.

"What old gods?" Cobb asks.

"The Greeks, the Norse," Posey replies. "It's in the myths."

"Don't matter if it's mist or rain, that's blasphemy. There's only one God."

Posey doesn't bother to explain the difference between myths and mist. We're all tired of Cobb's ignorance. I wish battles would be fought with lightning and thunder, high overhead, not touching the men below. If there is any irreverence, it is in how men die so easily under a rain of iron and lead.

This morning Colonel Young read General Johnston's Battle Orders to us. "*...you have repulsed every assault of the enemy. ... You will now turn and march to meet his advancing columns. ... I lead you to battle. ... the Almighty Father will still reward the patriots' toils and the patriots' banners.*"

I cheered with the rest but feel no patriotic duty. We have toiled mightily, and our banners are still flying, but I don't believe we'll go forward into battle. In the quiet before commands, we wait, in a rare moment of being allowed to fall out and eat rations. It's too hot for a fire, and we have no wood, but we sit in a circle.

"The grapevine says if the South can hold on long enough the North will grow tired of war," Burnett says.

"Then why does Sherman's Army keep advancing south, flanking us at every stop?" I ask. "We don't have the numbers to keep fighting back."

"We're about to go up the spout," Green says. "It's useless to deny it."

We sit there, staring into the dirt, just plain tired.

Contrary to General Johnston's fine speech, we withdraw at midnight, trailing arms to keep moonlight from glinting off bayonets and alerting the enemy. We all agree, it's a cowardly way to go. In this dark hour, all I can see ahead is more of the same stench, filth, and futile slaughter.

Across the Etowah River, more men do not answer at Roll Call, some from companies raised in our part of north Georgia. With the passwords of going it alone and taking help, I wonder how my family will be involved. David will know what to do. In the delirium of marching in the heat, I daydream of how it will be for me and Genny. I carry the memory close, how we loved each other before I left. That last time beneath the dogwoods. The first thing I'll do when I get home is marry her.

41

Visitors

Eliza Ann

A MULE-DRAWN WAGON TURNS into the lane. Behind it, uniformed men ride good horses, herding several cows.

David and I are at the bottom of the low field, resting under a hickory by the fence, taking turns dipping water from the bucket. Mary Jane and the twins are almost out of sight, working the high field.

"Those mules should be pulling Army wagons," David mutters, stepping back into the shadows of the tree line.

I prop my hoe against the fence and lean on the top rail. The wagon is filled with squealing and squawking, lumpy, wriggling bags.

Elias Bowen dismounts and unlatches the gate. Pap comes out of the barn.

The commanding officer rides through, tips his hat to Pap, and says, "Captain James Chastain, Georgia Militia. We're here to collect your tax-in-kind."

"Don't play me for a fool," Pap says. "I've known you since you were a little boy in dresses. You Militia boys are nothing but Joe Brown's pets. And that tax was collected off my corn last harvest at Halford's Mill."

"This one's for livestock. It's official procedure. Got to feed the army. We won't leave you without any animals."

I've known Jimmy Chastain since he was a chubby, unruly boy, the same age as Ananias. Now he's a fleshy, bossy young man.

Grown men scramble around our yard chasing chickens in a flurry of dust and feathers. It would be funny if it wasn't our chickens being stuffed into bags. How can they just ride down the lane and take our food like this? If I had the musket instead of a hoe I wouldn't feel so helpless. But these are my neighbors.

Advancing on Frank Bowen, neck feathers flared, spurs out, General Cornwallis resists being a tax-in-kind. Frank draws his pistol.

"Don't you shoot my rooster!" Mam shouts from the porch.

Frank swings around, waving the pistol.

"Why aren't you in the fighting with your brothers?" she calls out.

He doesn't answer, turning to help the Honeycutt brothers carry squealing piglets by the hind legs to the wagon.

"The Army's in trouble if it's taking my unweaned hogs," Pap says.

"The State of Georgia appreciates your contribution," Jimmy says. "You're lucky it's us doing this."

He turns his horse and rides past me, tipping his hat like a gentleman. Following him are men and boys I know by name, playing at war. It's one thing if our livestock is going to feed soldiers, but rumor has it the Militia keeps some for their own dinners.

Meanwhile the weeds are growing as fast as the corn. I chop my way back up a row to the top of the field, turn, and work my way down the next. David is still in the tree line. A man in a gray uniform steps out of the woods and talks to him. David listens, says something, points the man east, and watches him walk up the lane.

"We're not going to help him?" I ask.

"He's going it alone, but doesn't ask to take help."

I lower my head and chop hard at a section of goosefoot. We can't help all of them. It's too dangerous. Some could be spies. We don't dare tell our friends. No one can trust anyone, truth and lies told in ways hard to reckon.

***

Reverend Allred and a group of men came and talked with Pap this afternoon. The conversation didn't last long. After supper he asks us to stay at the table.

"I want you all to know what is happening that could put us in danger. Reverend Allred is forming a Unionist Home Guard. He came and asked me to join. I told him no."

"What's wrong with joining a Home Guard?" Luke asks.

"They're gangs looking to fight those who don't agree with them." Pap answers. "There's one bunch claiming to be a Confederate Home Guard that's been raiding Unionist farms around Jasper. A man named Ben Jordan leads them. Allred wants to lead the Unionists against him."

"How does Jordan pick out who he'll raid?" David asks.

"Our Governor set up the Home Guards to arrest deserters and draft evaders. Jordan executes them. With known Unionists he steals their animals and burns their houses."

"That would keep them busy around here."

"It could be us, our neighbors. Allred wanted me to be the example for them to join too. If it comes out the way he says, the Monroes and us would go against the Honeycutts and Chastains, fighting each other instead of making a crop."

"Do they know I'm here?"

"They want you and the twins. I said no to that too."

My sisters aren't listening as carefully as I am. He's not asking what us girls would do.

"You've always said in union we're strong," Luke says. "Would joining the Unionists do that?"

"I want my family to be strong. I don't want to lose more sons, and I'm too old to ride around the county playing soldier. Fighting each other has nothing to do with why I supported the Union."

"I don't understand who we'd be helping on either side," Lafe says. "Shouldn't we be doing things that help Ananias?"

I've had enough of listening on the side. These events affect girls too.

"What if Jordan's gang or the Militia find us out for helping deserters?" I ask.

"With Sherman close to Atlanta, the Militia will be called there," David says.

"What if the Yankee cavalry comes to Pickens County?" I ask.

"They'd be looking for Confederates."

"Would you be one they'd take?"

He does not like this question.

"I have furlough papers," he says. "Besides, the Yankees wouldn't mind me not being with the Army."

"What if Jordan's gang comes looking?"

"They'd be worse than the Yankees," Pap says.

"Worse than the Bowens?"

"Jordan's better organized and has more men. The Bowens wouldn't come at us directly."

"Would the Unionist Home Guard help us?" Lafe asks.

"They want to stop Jordan before he does more. But if they're not around when he does, no."

I want to do more than ask questions.

42

With Good Cause

Ananias

THE LETTER IS dated a month ago, addressed to *Pvts. David and Ananias Covington, 40th Georgia*, from a hospital in Newnan, Georgia. It says Private Howell Covington is a convalescent there and needs help to go home. An officer of the hospital signed it. I don't know where Newnan is.

Payroll arrived along with the mail from Atlanta. I sign my name, and the paymaster counts out twenty-two Confederate dollars, two months' pay. It won't buy much.

Our battle lines and defenses are spread thick and wide. The Yankees are attacking on the flank, edging closer to Atlanta.

How can I carry Howell home? How can a man wounded in the spine walk? *Home*. Where it's barefoot time, the fields green with new corn, the girls tending the garden. Genny waiting.

The only way is to ask for a furlough and run the long line of approvals from high officers. Requests for individual furloughs are generally refused. Sometimes captains give them. Sometimes a furlough can be bought, but the trick is in convincing the man who has it not to go himself. I don't know any such men and don't have enough money. With the whole Army packed into this place, I cannot slip away in the night behind our lines like men did on the march south. All they had to do was go east and back north through country empty of armies. I'd have to make it around Atlanta before going north, and there is the problem of finding Newnan. And there is the problem of it being Howell, who has never done any favors for me.

I read the letter to Eli.

"I can't see why I'd leave you and Posey to the War, just for him," I say.

"What if it was David? Or me or Posey?" he asks.

"I'd steal, desert, pay. But I wouldn't get far without papers."

"We could forge some."

"That would be lying."

"Of course it would. Lying for good reason."

"I grew up believing I would never be a liar."

"Why?"

"Because of how Mam named me. There are two men in the Bible named Ananias. One was a liar. The other was the man that Saul saw in his vision at Damascus. Mam named me for him because my hard birth marked the beginning of Pap's faith.

Until then he hadn't practiced any. She believed I'd grow into the same bravery and obedience as that Ananias."

"She took the chance on naming you that?"

"She said no child of hers would be a liar."

"So you've gone all this time never telling a lie?"

"Not one this big."

I know every child fibs. I did too until I was old enough to know about the other Ananias. Sometimes not lying has caused me more trouble than lying would.

"If I ask Posey about this, will you go ahead with it?" Eli asks.

That's a problem too. I don't want to leave them after all we've been through. I went against Pap to come back. But this is a chance to go home with good cause. Strange that it's Howell providing it.

Everyone wants to go home. With David unable, it's my responsibility to get Howell home. I can't be the cause of Mam losing another son, or Callie and her children losing their husband and father. Eli and Posey are more than brothers to me. And they're trying to find ways for me to leave them. I can only hope they survive the fighting until I return.

"I will," I answer.

***

"Burnett found the furlough and pass forms when he was on Sentinel Duty at Headquarters. I filled them out and forged the signatures," Posey says.

"I can't believe you'd do this."

"*We few, we happy few, we band of brothers; For he today that sheds his blood with me Shall be my brother*. I'm so tired of the fighting and bleeding and dying, if there's a chance to help you get your brother home, I'll take it."

"What if Sergeant Williams finds out?"

"He knows. He won't stand in your way."

The furlough is for sixty-days, starting June the Thirteenth. The pass allows me to travel and report to the hospital officer in Newnan. That officer will write another allowing me to carry Howell to Pickens County.

"Do you know where Newnan is?" I ask.

"No," Posey answers. "But we've got a few days to reckon that out. The fighting is moving east and north. We're being held in Reserve."

I do what I can, preparing to leave without saying goodbye. I volunteer for extra duties, keep my things in order for fast notice, memorize the faces of my friends.

***

"Sgt. Williams arranged it with the Quartermaster Sergeant for you to ride into Atlanta with the supply wagons today," Posey says. "Here's a map. Newnan's on the railroad south. Once you get your brother to Atlanta you'll need to go east as far as you can to get around the Yankees."

The map is hand-drawn. It shows the web of rail roads going into and out of Atlanta, the towns east and north, the way I will go.

"Who did this?" I ask.

"Green. He borrowed the Lieutenant's and copied it."

"Borrowed?"

"The Lieutenant didn't miss it."

I attach my accoutrements, gather my haversack and blanket roll, and pick up my rifle as I have done countless times preparing to march.

"I feel like I'm deserting."

"Deserters join the enemy. Your papers will keep anyone from questioning. Besides, we're not in the fighting for a while."

He hands me a book. I turn it over in my hands, reading the title.

"It's your new Shakespeare."

"I've read it so many times I've most of it memorized. It's the histories of the kings. In case you need something to give you courage along the way."

"I thank you. How will I ever make it up to you?"

"Carry your brother home safe. Try to get back to us."

I can't control tears when it comes to Eli. I hold out my hand to shake goodbye. He pulls me into a hug.

"You've been a better brother to me than the ones I was born with," he says. "This is for you. And the family." He holds out Confederate dollars.

"That's half your pay."

"There's nothing to spend money on around here. Your family provided for me. My turn to help them out. Give them my regards."

"You will always be welcome there. Eliza Ann is waiting for you."

"I'll count on that. Take care of Howell. Take care of yourself."

43

Atlanta

Ananias

RAIL ROADS SPOKE out in all directions from Atlanta, and I am wandering in all of them, trying to find the Central Depot. They have names. The Georgia, The Macon & Western, The Atlanta & West Point. The Western & Atlantic is the one we marched along on the other side of Sherman's Army.

Foundries, iron works, factories, and tanneries in enormous red brick and granite-block buildings line the streets, producing arms and supplies for the Confederacy. No wonder Sherman wants to take Atlanta. Afraid to ask strangers for directions, I turn up and down the busiest streets, filled with horses, buggies, carts, wagons, refugees, soldiers, and gangs of unruly boys. Hotels, houses, and academies have been turned into hospitals for the wounded of recent battles, the ones from which I have escaped injury and death, leaving my friends to it.

On a street where men sit hunched against walls, a building advertises China, Glass & Queensware above a sign for Auction & Negro Sales. I know that negro slaves are owned. But I have never thought about how they would be sold at auction like mules and cattle, from the same building as a set of dishes. The same as Mam's prized, blue Queensware platter on its own shelf in the corner cupboard.

At nightfall, gaslights illuminate the street corners. The hotels and boarding houses are full. Refugees and soldiers, with no other place to stay, sleep in tents, lean-tos, and packing crates. I find a bench against a wall, under a sign, *Soldiers' Executive Aid Association for the Relief of the Army of Tennessee.* It's a welcome center serving refreshments to soldiers passing through town. I will ask in the morning which train goes to Newnan.

I close my eyes but don't sleep. I'm afraid of being robbed. My back pay is in my socks. Eli's money, the letter from the hospital, and the forged pass and furlough paper are in the inside pocket of my jacket. I keep my rifle at hand.

It is strange to be in uniform and armed, yet able to decide on my own what to do. No one has asked to see my papers since the Quartermaster wagon crossed into Atlanta. I've read the furlough so many times I have it memorized, just in case I have to answer questions about what Posey has written in the blanks. It reads:

TO ALL WHOM IT MAY CONCERN

THE BEARER HEREOF, <u>Ananias Covington</u>, a <u>private</u> in Captain <u>Wylie's</u> Company of the <u>40th</u> Regiment of <u>Georgia Vols</u>., aged, <u>21</u> years, <u>6</u> feet <u>2</u> inches high, <u>white</u> complexion, <u>blue</u> eyes, <u>red</u> hair, born in the State of <u>North Carolina</u>, is hereby permitted to go to <u>Newnan</u> in the County of <u>Coweta</u>, State of <u>Georgia</u> and from there to <u>his home in the County of Pickens, State of Georgia, he</u> having received a FURLOUGH from the <u>13th</u> day of <u>June</u>, 1864 to the <u>12th</u> day of <u>August</u>, 1864, after which period <u>he</u> will rejoin <u>his</u> Company and Regiment in <u>the area of Atlanta, County of Fulton, State of Georgia</u> or wherever it then may be, OR BE CONSIDERED A DESERTER.

GIVEN under my hand at <u>Dallas, Georgia</u>, this <u>4th</u> day of <u>June</u>, 1864.

      Robert M. Young
    Colonel 40th Reg. Georgia Vols.

***

Ladies run this center. They serve hot coffee, sweet cider, and ginger cakes. They tell me that the Atlantic & West Point Rail Road goes to Newnan, and on the few passenger cars available south-bound, refugees with money are taken before a soldier with none. I'm trying to make my money last.

I study Green's map. The Georgia Rail Road runs east to Augusta and stops at Stone Mountain. That's where Howell and I will leave the cars to go north and back east. It's the only way to get around Sherman's Army. Getting home this time could take as long as it did from Mobile with David and Eli. All I know of Howell's injury is that it was grievous, to the spine, and has taken him a year to recover enough to go home. If I did the trip with David, I can do it with Howell. Trouble is, it'll be Howell, not David.

At the Atlanta and West Point Rail Road Depot, incoming trains from Alabama carry fresh troops for the fighting. I am waiting for the chance to ride one of those cars returning south. I avoid them until they're empty. I don't want to be caught up and found out.

Refugees fill the passenger cars and box cars on the south-bound trains. Wounded soldiers wait, helplessly sick, dirty and bloody, lying on stretchers or propped against walls.

I can't avoid the officer approaching me.

"Please step aside, Private. Show me your papers."

I salute him and pull the papers from my inside pocket. He reads the letter, then the furlough and pass, looks me over.

"How did your brother come to be in Newnan?"

"He was wounded at Bakers Creek in Mississippi, Sir. Captured by the Yankees. They sent seriously wounded prisoners to a hospital in Mississippi. I don't know how he came to be in Newnan, only what's in the letter."

"You seem to be who this says you are," he says. "How do you intend to get to Newnan with no ticket?"

"I could help with the wounded."

It came to me seeing the men left at the side of the station.

"We have an ambulance train going. In exchange for riding, would you be willing to guard the wounded in one of the cars?"

"Yes, Sir."

"It's not here yet, so stick around."

I don't know why the wounded need guarding, but the ride is free.

***

The ambulance train has a baggage-car and two passenger cars. The rest are boxcars. This car held cattle. The smell of manure mingles with the bloody, rotting stink of the wounded.

I climb in and look around at the blue uniforms of Yankee prisoners-of-war, head wounds swathed in bandages, stumps of arms and legs from amputations. One soldier, propped against a wall, is paralyzed in the legs. I am to prevent them from escaping. I don't see how they could.

I take my position standing at the door. Wooden boxes nailed to the walls hold their possessions—leather knapsacks, haversacks. Straw covers the floor. A pail of drinking water sits in one corner, a pail for waste in another. There are no mattresses or blankets, no rations.

The train jerks to a start and rolls southwest, away from the War. It jolts and shakes us from side to side, and the men complain of their suffering, cursing "the Rebs" for having no better rail roads than this. I take a good look at these dangerous men. They're better fed than Confederate soldiers, but they bleed the same. From the State of Wisconsin, westerners in Sherman's Army, they talk among themselves as I did with my friends whenever we rode the cars.

The paralyzed man is watching me.

"You going to shoot us if we try to get out?" he asks.

"Don't any of you look like you can make it to the door."

"Where you from?"

"Here in Georgia."

"Why aren't you in the fighting?"

"Got a furlough to take my brother home."

"Why don't all you Rebs give up and go home? General Sherman's got thousands more like us lining up to take Atlanta."

"This is our home. Why do you keep coming down here, fighting and dying for General Sherman?"

"We aren't fighting for him. Some of us are fighting to keep the Union, others to free the slaves. Some were conscripted. How could you break away from the Union and fight a war to keep slavery?"

I can't argue with that, unsettling as it is. I look out the door at the passing countryside, flat land, cotton plantations, piney woods so different from my home. I set my rifle on top of the row of boxes, go to the water pail, and carry it around the car, using my cup to fill the raised cups of these wounded men. Their tired eyes express relief. They thank me, like my friends would. Seeing again how we are not different enough to be enemies, I know for certain that this war is wrong. It is wrong for slaves to be owned, wrong to fight at the direction of planters and politicians who are the only ones to benefit. I will not come back to it.

***

The citizens of Newnan meet the train with buggies, carriages, and farm wagons to transport the wounded to hospitals.

The wounded Yankees are kept in the car for moving farther south to a prison hospital. I show the letter at the depot window and ask directions.

The large home has paned windows evenly spaced, a covered porch, pillars at the entry, three stories, and a little windowed room on the roof. An orderly leads me up the wide staircase and down a hall of doors. I've never been in a house this big or fancy. Carpet on the stairs and halls, painted portraits on the walls, vases of flowers on little tables.

I don't recognize Howell, seated near an open window in a cane-backed chair with wheels. Clean shaven, thin, his face drawn in pain, he wears blue cotton trousers and an unbleached cotton shirt with blue collar and cuffs.

"Here's your brother come to carry you home," the orderly says and wheels him toward me.

"So they sent the schoolboy. Where's David?"

Not much of a loving reunion between brothers.

"Home. He was wounded in the hip at Vicksburg. I'm your last chance. Unless you want me to have them send the twins."

"I guess you'll have to do."

I'd like to tip him out of the chair.

"Why're you in this chair?" I ask instead.

"It hurts to walk."

One chink in the armor of Howell.

"I'll leave you to your reunion," the orderly says. "There's a visitor's room for you to stay in until his paperwork is ready."

"How'd you get wounded was what I meant."

"The ball hit me in the back and knocked me down. I couldn't move my legs. Yankees captured the battery we were guarding and carried me to a field hospital. They didn't want to take care of us so they sent those of us still alive to a hospital east in Mississippi. I had them write a letter to Callie."

"She brought it for me to read when David and I made it home."

"How're you going to get me home?"

"Anyway I can. I got David home. What happened to Tom?"

Howell looks out the window. "One minute he was beside me. Then I was down. I never saw him again."

***

Waiting for the paperwork takes time. Helping Howell use the two canes necessary for him to walk, lurching along, takes more than time. It hurts to see a man crippled up. Even harder is putting up with his cursing and accusations that I am causing him more pain.

I walk the town. It's a break from him. In other beautiful houses patients tend gardens and each other. The whole town has been taken over for hospitals. I sit on benches and steps in front of a different one each day and talk to the men, all worried about what will happen if the Yankees take Atlanta. Sometimes I read to them from Posey's Shakespeare. I tried that with Howell, once.

"Don't bother me with that schoolboy crap," he said. "I'll tell you a story. The first hospital they had me in here, a sexton came around every day. He'd call into the wards, 'Anybody dead here? Anybody about to die?' Then he'd carry out the dead meat. That was my fight, not to be one of those about to die."

From what the wounded men on both sides tell me, they want to go home to their families, to who they were before the War, and forget it ever happened. All of us agree that when Sherman takes Atlanta, the South is doomed.

44

Guarding Home

June 1864

Eliza Ann

THE SOLDIER APPEARS after breakfast. James Newton
is tall and gaunt. A bulbous nose, bushy gray beard, and
large round head make him an awkward looking man, but he
has a kindly smile. He wears a slouch hat pinned up on one
side and a yellow neckerchief. He's from the same Company
as Tom and Howell and knows the passwords.

"I'm sorry we can't keep you here," Mam says as I help Louise
pack dinner fixings for him.

"I'm grateful for anything, ma'am."

"Were you in the battle with my sons?"

305

"At Bakers Creek. They had us in reserve to protect the Battery. The Yanks came on us with so many we never had a chance to reload. I'm ashamed to say I ran. I saw Howell fall, but it was every man for himself. I never did see Tom."

"He's a quiet boy," Mam says.

"I remember him like that. Had a way with mules. He was a good soldier."

"Where are your people?"

"Dahlonega."

"You're almost home. Good luck to you, and thank you for talking kindly of Tom. My boys can show you the safe way to get there. Eliza Ann, call the twins."

Mr. Newton puts the food packets in his haversack. There's one for the twins.

"I can show him," I say. "Mary Jane can go with me."

In the hot days, looking up at the shaded hills, I've been wanting to get into the woods, imagining how much cooler it will be.

"I doubt your pap will allow it."

"By the time the twins get here from the high field, we'd be well on the way. We can go fast and be home by supper."

I'm willing to risk Pap's anger and do my share, helping men like Mr. Newton.

Keeping to the edge of the trees, I lead the way. Summer is coming on. I can smell wild strawberries. We pass June and Shad grazing in the woods above the orchard.

Pap and David have a plan for fooling the Militia. Each morning at first light, Mary Jane and I drive the geese to the high field and leave enough dried corn to keep them there. The twins tether one mule and cow in the woods. We turn Cassiopeia and the young hogs loose to forage until hog-killing. At harvest, we'll dig storage pits for potatoes behind the spring house. We'll hide shucked corn under the beds in the upstairs sleeping rooms.

Mr. Newton walks carefully, watching the woods.

"I'm obliged to you for showing me the way," he says.

"It beats hoeing corn in the hot sun," I say.

"It beats going into battle too. I couldn't keep on marching south knowing my family needs me. We're losing this war."

I don't know what to say to this. We haven't heard the Army is retreating. Mr. Monroe read the news from *The Cherokee Mountaineer* until Sherman's soldiers burned Canton after a Home Guard gang tried to stop Yankee foragers.

The route I have taken curves around an outcropping of marble and scree. The next marker is the Cherokee tree. We round the bend and climb the long stretch through the rocks.

A tall bearded man in a gray uniform stands at the cave entrance. Another crouches just inside. They hold rifles.

My heart-beat pounds in my ears. It's hard to take in enough air to breathe. Mary Jane clutches my hand. I hear Mr. Newton stop walking behind me.

The crouching man stands up and points his rifle at us.

"Lay down your rifle!"

Mr. Newton's clatters against the rocks.

"Lookee here," the tall man says, walking toward us. "A Confederate deserter, just what we've been looking for, and two young ladies to keep us entertained, stuck up here all by our lonesome."

"You know Ben doesn't want that coming back at him," the other man says.

"He won't know. What's the use of being Home Guards if we can't take what comes our way? Come here, you. The tall one."

Mary Jane's hand loosens. I step forward, not sure what he means by entertainment. All I can do is sing and recite poetry.

"I told you, Hugh. We'd best not do this. We'll take the deserter to Ben and let the girls go."

"You take the little one," Hugh says, giving Mary Jane a shove toward the other man who moves forward to catch her as she stumbles.

"I like the tall, lanky ones, the way they wrap those long legs around me and moan," Hugh says as he grabs my arm and pulls me toward him.

He sets his rifle down carefully, and pulls my blouse out of my skirt. I feel dull-witted, can't get my mind around what is happening here.

"I like to feel what I'm doing," he says. "Real slow."

His hand pushes up my blouse and chemise, rough and scrabbling at my skin. He presses his mouth, slobbery and open, against mine. His beard scratches my nose and chin. Pulled so tight against him, I can feel his privates pressing against mine. His hand paws at my breasts. His mouth is disgusting, his thick tongue pushes my lips open. Too shocked to move or push his hand away, I can't think of anything but getting rid of his tongue in my mouth. I bite down, hard.

Aagh," he yells, spits blood, and shoves me aside, twisting my arm.

A rifle fires. Hugh falls away from me. Another shot cracks. I hear a grunt. Smoke obscures everything. I push my chemise and blouse into my skirt, peer through the thinning smoke. Mr. Newton is on his knees. He ram-rods his rifle barrel, sets the cap, aims toward the cave, and pulls the trigger.

Mary Jane screams, the other man cries out. In the fog of smoke, I don't know which way to turn. Someone is scrambling in the rocks.

"If you can shoot, pick up that rifle and do it!" Mr. Newton yells. "Don't let him get away!"

I see the man who held Mary Jane limping downhill, waving his rifle. I grab up Hugh's rifle, check for the cap, cock the trigger, and look through the sights. I can hear Ananias's words. *When it's downhill, aim low.* I aim for his legs and squeeze the trigger. He grabs at his shoulder, falls, regains his feet, and stumbles through the rocks. I stand there numb. I shot a man.

I look down at Hugh on his back, eyes and mouth open, and know he's dead. His blood puddles on the rocks, the front of his trousers wet. Mary Jane is lying on the ground in front of the cave. Blood stains the sleeve of her blouse. I drop the rifle and run to her.

Clutching his side, Mr. Newton limps to us and cradles Mary Jane in one arm. He lifts his hand from his side. Blood wells from above his belt. He pulls off his neckerchief, stuffs it into the wound, and tucks a corner of it under his belt. He rips off Mary Jane's sleeve and hands it to me. The flesh below her elbow oozes blood. I press the cloth against the swelling wound. She cries out at the touch.

"I never thought I'd hit the both of them with one shot," he says, wiping his bloody hand on his shirt. "It grazed her before hitting him. Didn't hurt either one of them that bad. I hoped your back shot would kill him."

"What do we do now?" I ask, thinking of the other man still having his rifle, everyone bleeding but me.

"We get her bandaged up and standing, and you'll walk her home."

"You're not going with us?"

"You're grown enough to do this."

"What about the other one?"

"When a man runs like that, he usually doesn't turn around. And he's not headed the way we came. Bring me that rifle."

He sits Mary Jane up, tears a strip from his shirt, and wraps it over the cloth around her arm. He fashions a sling from her bonnet.

"You're bleeding more," I say.

He looks down at his side and wads more of the neckerchief into the bleeding.

"You sure enough can shoot," he says. "Do you know how to load that?"

"I learned on my pap's."

"Load it now so I can see you do it right."

He digs into a box on his belt, pulls out a paper cartridge, and hands it to me. I load the rifle. How many times am I going to have to prove to a man that I know how to load a rifle?

"That's good. If you hear one noise, anything at all, you stop, cock, and aim," he said. "Keep this in your hand." He gives me a cap. "Don't drop it. I need to keep moving. Which way do I go for home?"

"The slope behind the cave goes down to a branch," I answer. "It leads into a bigger one. Follow that down to a bridge. It's on the Dawsonville road."

He's abandoning us. Clutching the cap, I help Mary Jane stand up, keep one arm around her, the rifle in the other, and watch him limp away.

***

A half-moon rises above the trees. The first constellations are forming. Mary Jane can't walk steadily. Both of us are hungry, our dinner haversack lost in the confusion. We stumble against each other in the twilight. I try to keep a hold on her, the rifle, and the cap digging into my palm.

"We need to rest," I say. "It'll take us longer but we're both too tired."

I lead her to a downed tree trunk and help her sit. Dusk ascends from the low places down the mountain. Birds nestle and small animals scurry before the night hunters come out. She nudges my shoulder and points to a clearing in the trees. A doe and her fawn are feeding. We sit still as the deer move uphill.

"What did you do to make that man stop pawing at you?" she asks.

"I bit his tongue."

"Eew. Weren't you scared?"

"I wanted it out of my mouth. It happened so fast I couldn't think to be scared."

"I was. Then I didn't know what was happening."

"We can't tell anyone what that man was doing to me," I say.

"How are we going to explain this?" She touches the sling.

"We'll tell that part. Just not the other. I don't want to remember it. I don't want anyone to ever ask me about it. Besides, they'll all be so upset about you being shot, they won't pay any attention to me. You have to promise."

"I promise. But I won't forget."

"I plan to."

A light bobs toward us. I stand up, lift the rifle, place the cap, and aim at the light.

"Who's there?" David's voice calls out.

"It's us," I shout.

Pap reaches us first.

"Mary Jane's hurt," I say.

"I can see that." He puts his arm around her. "What happened? Where'd you get that rifle?"

"Two Home Guards were at the cave. I think they were Ben Jordan's."

"Where's the man Newton?"

"He said he needed to keep going. He killed the one and the other one shot and wounded him. Then Mr. Newton shot and wounded the other one and Mary Jane at the same time. The other one ran. Mr. Newton told me to pick up the dead man's rifle and shoot the man running, so I did. He bandaged up Mary Jane and gave me the rifle and left us."

In the telling of it I can't believe it happened. Mary Jane's wounded arm is the only proof.

Pap stares at me. "You shot a man?"

"Mr. Newton told me to shoot if I knew how."

"I should've followed you the minute I knew you were gone. I let your mam talk me out of it, telling me you were able enough, that this Newton was a good man. I never should've allowed it to girls."

He turns downhill, guiding Mary Jane.

I stand still, so tired.

"You light the way," David says holding out the lantern, taking the rifle from me. "I'll guard the rear. You did good."

David is good. Even if I don't want anyone asking me more of what happened, I'm grateful that he took note of what I did.

Lanterns light the back porch as we come through the orchard.

"Sarah!" Pap calls out. "Louise!"

I hang back when he leads Mary Jane up the steps into Mam's arms. He turns and stretches a hand back to me. The warmth of his calloused hand gripping mine, the light of the porch, Mam and Louise rushing Mary Jane into the house. I don't want him to let go.

45

Turning Time Backward

July 1864

Eliza Ann

I AM ALWAYS TIRED and sweaty. Doing my house chores and Mary Jane's, along with hoeing corn, herding geese, and chopping wood, there's been no let up in the work this laying-by time. I don't want to go to the cave ever again. From my place on the porch step, I close my eyes and remember Eli sitting here. I am grateful that his kiss was my first.

Chill bumps raise on my skin whenever I think of the man Hugh's hands and mouth on me, his privates hard against me, what he said about wrapping legs and moaning, what he could have done if Mr. Newton hadn't killed him. I'm glad I didn't tell

Pap that part. I didn't tell Jane either. I wish I could forget it, wish I could forget everything from that first hideout to the men at the cave, wish the War had never happened, and know all this wishing for the foolishness it is.

Nothing has been the same since my brothers went to fight. Nothing will be again. I did one thing, at great cost, helping a man with his way home. And, I shot a man.

Willy trots behind Charlotte in the garden carrying a small basket of thinned beans, tossing them over the fence to the chickens. It's the noisiest event of a hot and humid day. Tomatoes swell from thick vines, collard greens spread, and lavender spikes above the fence. For now, the garden and Willy at play are enough.

The Halfords' carriage turns into the lane.

"There's been a Yankee raid," Harriet shouts, jumping down before Mr. Halford has a chance to help her.

She hurries up to the porch with her satchel. Mr. Halford hands his wife down from the carriage.

"They hit Ben Jordan's gang near Jasper," he says. "Wounded him, killed and wounded some of his men. They burned some of his backers' houses. Jordan and most of them got away. The whole Yankee Army could be following."

"And then we'll whip those Yankees for certain," Harriett says.

"Sweetheart," Pap says. "Do you see anyone here strong enough to take on the Yankee Army?"

Harriet looks around at us—the twins walking out to the back porch, Mary Jane's bandaged arm in a sling, me hunkered up, arms around my knees, Charlotte leading Willy out of the garden, David hitching his bad leg down the steps.

"Not presently."

316

"The last news has General Johnston backed up at the Chattahoochee and Sherman's Army aimed at Atlanta," Mr. Halford says.

"They'll take it too," David says.

"They will not," Harriett says. "Our brave soldiers will defend Atlanta to the end."

I drop my head into my hands. David told me how it was in Kentucky, once an army started retreating instead of standing to fight. The Militia has been called up to defend Atlanta. I know the situation is desperate if those boys are needed. Their experience is no more than stealing their neighbors' crops and livestock. If it's General Johnston backed up, Ananias and Eli must be there too, in the way of Sherman's Army.

"I hoped we could take our minds off the War, so I brought poems," Harriet said, pulling a book from her satchel.

I think there are two conversations going on, not connected.

The Halfords seem to accept the story of Mary Jane's injury, that she has fallen on the rocks in the branch, probably broken the bone. No one outside the family knows the real reason. Only Lucy looked close enough, asking why she was so heavily bandaged for a broken bone. I suspect Mam told her.

The twins come out to the porch in clean shirts, hair slicked wet.

"You two look like you're going to Meeting," I say.

"It's Lafe's doing," Luke says.

Lafe blushes and stares at his feet. Before I can say anything else, Mary Jane cocks her head toward Harriet.

"Let's read," Harriet says.

She sits down on the porch step, pats the place beside her, and leafs through the pages of the book. Lafe sits down next to her. I stretch out my legs and close my eyes.

"I'd forgotten about this one. It's sad, but it makes me think of my mother," Harriet says. "*Backward, turn backward, O Time, in your flight, Make me a child again, just for to-night!*"

I listen to Harriet's clear voice. I don't see how she can keep reading about a mother who is dead, her child wishing for her to come back and rock her to sleep. Tears seep from my closed eyes. I'd give anything to turn time backward.

46

Honor Bound

Ananias

THE STREETS AND depots are filled with townspeople and their slaves joining the hordes of refugees fleeing Atlanta. We have a furlough for Howell, passes to Pickens County, and Howell's back pay. Making it to the line of wagons for hire leaves both of us exhausted. I use some of his money to pay for a ride to the Georgia Rail Road Depot for trains east. At the depot, I find a bench for him and buy tickets to Stone Mountain.

Pushed around by the crowd, two young ladies wearing fancy dresses with hoop skirts, lace gloves, and hats struggle with satchels and baskets. They look like sisters. What if Eliza Ann and Mary Jane were caught up like this? They wouldn't be wearing hoopskirts and lace gloves.

"Do you need help?" I ask, tipping my hat to them.

"We have tickets for a private car," the older one says. "We try to move forward but no one will give way."

"If you'll walk with my brother and keep him from getting knocked over and losing his canes, I'll help you find it."

The train arrives, and the battle begins. I have never seen females fight and scratch so, shoving others aside to get to their cars. The ladies walk close behind Howell, shielding him from the crush. I walk in front. My uniform and rifle help clear the path. When we find their car, I plan to ask if we can get in too. Howell needs better than a backless bench in a box car.

I don't have to ask. They invite us. When the train starts moving they open their dinner basket. In all the effort of getting Howell around, I've forgotten about food. He glares at me.

"Some traveler you are. Take us into a mess of people and don't have any provisions. David would have done it better."

Before I can defend myself, the younger one says, "We'll share. There's plenty."

"That's kindly of you," Howell says. "This here brother is the one who thinks everything good comes out of a book. Can't eat that."

My forehead burns like it does when I'm about to lose my temper. I glare back at Howell sitting there eating a ham biscuit. I have accepted one too.

"David would have had the sense to leave you in Atlanta to find your own way," I say. "I could have dumped you there and gone back to my Regiment."

"Oh, don't take it so hard. You gonna cry about it?"

"We'll see who's crying by the end of this trip," I answer. "You're the one can't walk more than a few steps without whining."

He looks me up and down.

"So being in the fighting put a little more fight in you?"

"You have no idea what I did all that time you were safe in hospitals, those ladies you brag about feeding you jellies and strawberries, bringing flowers."

"Well I'm most happy for these ladies," he says, turning a smile on them. "This is most likely the best food I'll have until I get home."

I am also happy for these ladies. With Howell turning on the charm, it takes his attention away from my failings.

"It might be the only food you'll have until you get home," I say.

***

The Georgia Militia is meeting departing passengers at Stone Mountain, asking for paperwork, inspecting the cars carrying the wounded.

"What are you doing here?" I ask Jimmy Chastain.

"We were called up to Atlanta and sent here to catch deserters. There's Militia companies checking every station between Decatur and Augusta. Where are your papers?"

I hand them over.

"You're a lucky man, going home," Jimmy says.

"I'll be going back to my Regiment once I get him home."

Once started, lying becomes easier.

"You better," Elias Bowen says, walking up. "There's Home Guards out on the roads. They don't check for papers."

"Lucky for you, being in the Militia."

"Our pap bought it. You know that. Watch yourselves. Take care."

I can't believe this Bowen brother cares about my well-being. I look up at the granite mountain glittering above the town, shoulder Howell's haversack and blanket as well as my own, and lead Howell, hobbling with his canes.

The fine hotels are full of refugees. Every place that lets rooms to travelers is full. I find space in a church. All the benches are taken by women and children.

"I'd rather sleep on the floor," Howell says. "Don't have to worry about falling off it."

I spread our blankets above the steps to the altar, making it easier for Howell to sit, then lie down.

"You think someone'll get on us, using the altar like this?" he asks.

"The Reverend Childs would invite us to. We'll have to start walking from here, you know."

"Just let me rest, before I have to think about it."

His eyes are closed, his jaw clenched.

"How much money do I have left?" he asks.

"Enough for provisions."

I haven't told him that I have money too.

"Can we hire another ride?"

"It'd take most of your money. Provisions are bound to be dear in this place."

When the ladies departed the train at Decatur, they gave us little cakes and plums. I'm used to short rations and plan to give most of these to him.

While he rests, I walk the town, asking about roads north. Townspeople bring food to the church. Howell spends the time talking with the mothers and their children, telling them how much he misses his own. In constant pain, he complains how hard it is to sleep, how the pain stabs down his legs and up his back.

I wet my neckerchief and place it on his bare back, thinking the brief coolness might help. The red scar stretches along his backbone.

"That feels good enough," he says. "But you're no nurse, and it doesn't take away the pain."

***

The road is flat. After less than a mile of slow going, Howell is pale and sweating, his face twisted in the same pained expression as David's on our way home from Mobile. But David had only one bad leg, two men to help him, and endured with a wink and a smile. Lawrenceville is sixteen miles away, the same distance as from the farm to Jasper. That road is mostly uphill, and I have walked it in a day. So has Howell.

I stop at every log and stone I can find for him to sit and rest. At each farmhouse, I ask for water and food, a place to sleep. Some let us sleep in barns, others turn us away. They ask why I am not in the fighting. Having to explain so often that Howell is my wounded brother unable to walk by himself, as anyone can see, I believe my own family would treat people better.

A farmer stops his wagon. His white blond hair, steady blue eyes, and thin smile remind me of Pap.

"I'm going past Lawrenceville," he says. "How far are you going?"

"Pickens County, northeast of the Etowah. Home."

Howell struggles to climb into the wagon bed while the farmer and I pull and shove him from above and below. I sit on the seat with the farmer. He too asks why I'm here and we talk of what I am doing, where I left my Regiment.

"You think he'll make it?" he asks, nodding back at Howell.

"I'm doing my best seeing he does."

"Word is General Johnston has fallen back to Atlanta. The Yankees are following. There's a home in Lawrenceville for invalid soldiers. They'd take your brother in. You'd have to go a long way around to get back to your regiment."

"As much as I would like to be rid of him, I am honor bound to carry him home."

He drives through Lawrenceville and stops where his road turns off.

"I thank you for helping us. What can I pay you for the ride?"

"I'd say you're already paying a high price. Only a brother would do this."

***

We pass slaves working cotton fields, chopping with hoes in the hot sun. They don't look up. At this slow pace I have time to think, about Genny and what we will do together, about where Howell and I will sleep and what we will eat, about the slaves, bought and sold. Do they know they've been emancipated? In Atlanta I heard that slaves in north Georgia are taking their freedom, like they did in Mississippi.

"I can't keep going," Howell says.

"Ever?" I ask.

"Just for a while. Can you find me a bed?"

I pull him to the shade of an oak beside a cotton field and hand him the canteen. I ask for help from the closest slave working in the field. She looks at me in fear, shakes her head, and points to a plantation house in the distance. I leave Howell and walk to the house. It has two stories, with paned windows and painted weatherboarding. There are outbuildings—a barn, blacksmith shop, kitchen house, and slave quarters. The woman of the house shows me a room at the end of the roofed front porch.

"It's our travelers' room," she says. "You're welcome to it."

The bed is small and the blanket thin, but there's a hook for clothes, a stand with water pitcher and wash basin, and room for me to sleep on the floor. I leave my rifle and accoutrements, return for Howell, and carry him on my back.

47

Close to Home

August 1864

Ananias

IN ORRSVILLE I learn that the Yankees have burned Stone Mountain and Lawrenceville. We bivouac off the road before approaching the ferry crossing. I light a small fire to bake the sweet potatoes I stole, creeping into a garden in the dark of a new moon, digging with my knife at what I could feel.

"This the best you can do?" Howell complains.

"About what?"

"We've had better food and lodging."

"There's no money for it."

"Seems my money went for everything. What did you put in?"

He is lying on his back beside the fire. It's the only way he can get comfortable when he's hurting.

"You just now paying attention to what we've spent?" I ask. "There's two ferries to go, both take money. I have enough for one."

"Where'd you get money? Holding out on me?"

"Holding out on you? I've held you up for two months. I've carried you, dragged you, begged and stolen for you. I saved my back pay for this. How else am I supposed to get you home?"

I am tired, of Howell, the road, being the nurse. He is not as entertaining as David, as companionable as Tom, or as funny as the twins. He is Howell, the biggest, meanest brother. No let up to the goading, never a good word.

"And now you think you're a saint?" Howell sneers across the fire at me.

I throw the potatoes aside, stand up, and kick the fire to pieces. Kick my rifle and my haversack. Kick Howell's. Pull my foot back to kick Howell himself. He throws his arms up over his face.

"Don't. Please."

My vision is blurred, I'm gasping for breath. Howell is pitiful, choking up, tears leaking down his cheeks.

"Want to beg me to quit?" I shout. "Like you made me do when I was too little to fight? Cry baby, schoolboy, run to Mam, want to be any of that?"

"Why did you bother to come for me?"

"You gave them my name. I lied for you. My friends forged my furlough and pass. I'm a deserter. Who else was going to do it for you? Tom? I'll bet you ran before he even had a chance."

"I told you the truth about that."

"There isn't hardly anyone left alive who can say otherwise."

"You weren't there."

"Not there? I heard every bullet, every man around me fall. Missed every one who did. One who was tougher than you. All you ever knew was to bully a little boy. And the brother you were supposed to watch over never came home."

"You think I want you to see me like this? I'd rather it be anybody but you."

"And now it's not enough. Why don't you ever let up?"

"Because you had everything I didn't. Them loving to tell the story of your naming, like it was a miracle. So proud of you in school, the little ones following you around like you were the Pied Piper. I picked on you because you were easy, trying to hold that little red-headed temper, never telling a lie to get out of trouble. And now I have to feel beholden to you."

So he's jealous. This is something new. It doesn't make a difference in how I feel, looking down at him.

"You're so pitiful I can hardly bring myself to hate you."

I wrap myself in my blanket and lie down away from the scattered coals. I will get this over with, get my life, Genny.

48

Home

Ananias

WE PASS THE dark Chastain farm and turn onto the road home. I could stop and rouse the Monroes, but we're so close. The waxing moon lights the road. I half-drag, half-carry Howell, one arm around his waist, holding his canes in my other hand. I traded my rifle for tickets on the last ferry. He is not always conscious, feet dragging in the dust, head lolling against my shoulder. I rest where there is a place to let him down that makes it easier to stand him up again. We're not a mile away.

Down the lane, no geese awake to raise the alarm. I lower Howell to the dirt, open the gate, and pull him to the porch and up the steps. No one rouses from the house. No one is expecting us.

He passes out. I am not going to wake the house. It's enough to be here. I lie down next to him to keep him from rolling off the porch.

***

Louise's cry awakens me and the rest of the house. She crouches beside Howell. Pap comes out barefoot and blinking, white hair uncombed and wild. He's pulled his trousers over his sleep shirt and grabbed the musket.

"You that happy to see me, Pap?" Howell drawls. "You going to shoot me?"

Pap kneels and holds Howell's face between his hands.

"You," he whispers.

Mam next, one hand on Howell's cheek, the other on his forehead. The girls stumble downstairs in night shifts and loose hair, the twins sleepy-eyed, David in the passage.

I gather myself, hoping no one will ask about the how of it just yet, but Eliza Ann and David settle next to me.

"You did this?" David asks.

"It's too long to tell," I answer. "If I never see Atlanta again it'll be too soon. Him too."

"Finally had it?"

"He's lucky I didn't shoot him."

"Do you have to go back? Was Eli with you?" Eliza Ann asks.

"I'll tell you all about that later."

I want to sleep, let it all fall away. My sisters are turning to me, everyone in tears. The whole family together. Except Tom. And Lydia. In a buzz, everyone turns to fix a meal, hear Howell's story, tend to him.

"I need some sleep," I say.

Eliza Ann is listening.

"Go on upstairs," she says. "I'll bring you a basin and towel. You want anything to eat?"

"I want to be left alone."

"I'll see to that."

I want to be shed of the responsibility and presence of Howell. Be in the room I grew up in. Someone has kept my shelf of treasures dusted and tidy. Probably Eliza Ann. She carries in the basin and towel, soap, a cup of water. I wash away the sweat and dust of the road and crawl into bed.

"I told the twins to stay away. Everyone else is taken up with Howell," she says and leaves.

⁂

Doves call in the trees. A skillet lid clanks. The twins clomp out the passage. I must have slept all day and night, into this morning. I need to see Genny. I roll over and startle at the sight of the small boy staring at me over the edge of the bed.

"You my Unko Annanice?"

"I am. Whose boy are you?"

"Dabid's."

I let Willy lead me by the hand downstairs. Everyone stays at the table and watches me eat biscuits, buttermilk, and blackberries.

They look thin and tired, their clothes worn and faded, Eliza Ann unusually quiet, Mary Jane's arm in a sling.

"Seems like things changed in a short time," I say.

Eliza Ann looks over to Pap.

"We've had our share," Pap says, and starts the telling.

Jimmy Chastain and Elias Bowen hadn't said anything about the Militia raiding the farm. I knew the password plan for deserters but didn't think there'd be that many. Unionist Home Guards, Ben Jordan's gang of bushwhackers, all new. And the incident at the cave. I watch Eliza Ann, her expression wary. There's more to it that Pap doesn't know.

"So you've had your war too," I say.

"I don't think it compares," Eliza Ann says. "I wish it was all over."

"We'll talk about it," I say.

Her face turns white, then red. It's worse than I thought.

"We'll rest today," Pap says. "I will sit on the porch with my boys and thank the Lord for their safe return."

"I need one more batch of berries," Louise says as she begins dinner preparations. "I want a cobbler for the boys. Mary Jane, Eliza Ann, you keep these two from eating more than they pick."

She smiles at the twins, her hands stained. Crocks of blackberry jam sealed with beeswax stand in a row on the food safe.

"I want to hear how they made it home," Eliza Ann says.

"There'll be time for that," Pap says. "Go on and get the berries. I promise it's the hardest work you'll do today."

"What about Callie?" she asks.

Howell is in bed in David's room, Charlotte and Rebecca fussing over him as if he got home all by himself.

"The twins can go for her after dinner," Pap replies.

"I'll be going to Genny," I say.

"After dinner. Stay for now and let your mam look at you. You'll have the rest of your life with Genny. I hope there's no more talk of you returning to the War."

"I'd have to fight my way through the whole of Sherman's Army."

I do not want to wait, but Mam is so happy, and I don't have the strength to argue with Pap. I am tired to my bones, my mind in a fog. Staying is a small thing to do for them, just for the morning. I'll walk to the Wilders after dinner.

49

Blood in the Clay

Eliza Ann

NOTHING MOVES IN the heat. I pick the last berries from the last bush between the branch and the road. Mary Jane and the twins sit on the bank, feet in the water. I join them, rinse my hands, too tired to start a water fight, tempted by how good it would feel. Full baskets beside them, the twins' lips are purple with berry juice.

The hoof beats of galloping horses break the stillness.

"Sounds like the Georgia Militia," Luke says.

"They're off defending Atlanta," Lafe says.

"Yankees?" I ask.

"Or Home Guard," Luke replies. "Let's look."

He pulls his feet from the water and ducks through the bushes toward the road. I cup my hands into the water for a drink and follow him. The dust cloud rises first, then come the horsemen.

"Are they Yankees?" I whisper, as if they're close enough to hear me.

"They're in uniforms," Luke whispers back. "But they don't match."

"They aren't Yankees," Lafe whispers.

"How do you know?" I ask.

"David said Jordan's Gang wears parts of Yankee uniforms to flush out the Unionists."

The horsemen stop at the lane and turn into it.

"Let's get to the edge of the field," Luke says. "They won't see us."

He sneaks through the bushes to the fence and climbs into the branches of a hickory.

"They're at the gate," he says from his vantage point.

He motions to the tree trunk below him, and Lafe moves to it. He motions and points to the next tree. I help Mary Jane creep to it.

I peek around the tree. The horsemen milling at the closed gate raise more dust. Pap stands at the front of the porch holding the musket, Ananias and David beside him.

One man, his left arm in a sling, points at the gate and shouts, "If you raise that musket we'll kill all of you, tear up the house, and set fire to the fields. Now, open this gate!"

Pap sets the musket down. He turns and says something to Ananias who steps off the porch, walks through the yard, and opens the gate.

The horsemen ride through. Some dismount and split up. Two go to the barn and come out carrying reins, leading Shad with a rope around his neck. Two others grab up chickens. One takes out his pistol and aims it at General Cornwallis, again resisting collection. He shoots the rooster.

"They're doing the same as the Militia," I whisper to Mary Jane. "That's all we need. We don't have hardly any chickens left."

"They're taking Ananias," Luke whispers. "And David."

A man holds Ananias by the arms from the back. Another pulls David down the steps. They use the reins to bind the boys' hands in front and pull them to the horses. The men remount and ride through the gate. One leads Shad, two pull at Ananias and David. I don't want to watch but can't turn away.

"We aren't deserters," Ananias hollers. "We have furlough papers."

My breath catches. What we've feared since Vicksburg.

Ananias runs to keep up with the horse ahead of him. David hitches along in his stiff-legged way, slowing the horse and rider leading him. He is grimacing, lips pressed tight. His curly hair shines gold in the sun. His shirt is wet with sweat.

The man holding David's rein yanks on it. My body jerks as if it's me being yanked. David falls to his knees. The horseman drags him in the dust. The leader stops at the top of the lane and turns. He points at David and says, "If he can't keep up, shoot him!"

I can't believe what I heard. The man who shot General Cornwallis steadies his pistol and aims it at David. The shot cracks. Blood flies from the back of David's head. Too shocked to move, I see but can't hear the leader say something else to the man. He dismounts, walks up to David lying in the lane, and sticks a finger in the bullet hole in David's forehead.

"He's dead, Ben, sure enough," he calls out and goes back to his horse.

Ben. Ben Jordan. How can my mind still work with David dead in the lane?

Ananias is tripping on his feet, looking back at David. The man who leads Ananias turns my way to yank him along. He's the man I shot running from the cave.

I slump against the tree, Mary Jane in a heap beside me. Shrieks rise from the house. I raise my head. The dust cloud recedes west.

Any ability I have for reasoning is gone. I stagger to the lane, somehow climb over the fence, and kneel next to David, not knowing what to do with my hands, where to stop the bleeding. Blood pools beneath his head, turning the dust to clay. His body is twisted and still, blue eyes open. The bullet hole in his forehead oozes blood. Hands on my shoulders raise me up and away.

"We'll do this," Pap says.

Mam kneels in the dust, turns David, cradles his head in her lap, and wails, her head against David's, his blood on her face, her silver hair. There is only one thing I can think to do.

I run down the lane past my bent and sobbing sisters, pick up Pap's musket on the porch, pull the cap, and rush into the house. I grab the cartridge bag and cap pouch, sling them over my shoulder. I run back up the lane. Mam and Pap, bent over David, give no notice of me. Luke is heaving up blackberries. Lafe stares, collapsed against the tree. Mary Jane has her head bent into her lap.

"Come!" I grab Luke by the shirtsleeve. "Help me!"

"I can't," he groans and upchucks again. "I can't. I'm scared they'll kill us all."

"You have to! It's Ananias."

I turn to Lafe. Blackberry vomit stains his shirt front, and his eyes move wildly from Luke to me. He shakes his head as if trying to forget what he has seen and pushes himself away from the tree.

"I'll do it," he says.

He stumbles behind me in the road. I look down at my feet, scuffing in the thick dust. How do they keep moving forward? I shift the musket to my shoulder, my mind clearing. I will talk them into letting him go. Then I think of the man Hugh, dead at the cave. These men could act the same as him. And the other one, part of the Gang, he'll know me. I'll have to reckon how to go about it. Hide in ambush. Bushwhack them.

Moody Simpson stands in the crossroads, looking west.

I run up to him. "Did you see them? Is it Jordan's Gang? They took Ananias. You have to help us find him."

"I saw them, a bunch on horseback, one of them leading Ananias on foot. I had my cart off the road. They didn't see me. You can't catch up with them. You don't want to."

I turn away from him and walk up the Federal Road. I would hear horses if they were close by. In the shade of the oaks nothing moves.

50

Bushwhacked

Ananias

PAP IS ON his knees on the porch, Mam stands in the entry to the passage, hands against her heart. The rein jerks me away from the grip of their eyes. I try to keep my feet under me, like double-timing into battle, staying balanced on the run.

A shot. I turn again. David has fallen. I know he's dead. For all their uniforms and pistols, Ben Jordan's Home Guards is nothing but a gang of bushwhackers.

At the crossroads they turn onto the Federal Road. To the right, up past the Meeting House, is Wilders' lane. Genny. Does she know I'm home? I catch a glimpse of Moody Simpson's face in the bushes off the side of the road.

They stop at Fourth Creek where the white oak spreads its limbs over the road. I look up into the leafy branches. This tree has witnessed my travels—to Jasper with Pap, signing up in Calhoun, rejoining the Regiment at Dalton. It has always been a resting place.

"What are we going to do with him, Ben?" the man leading me asks.

"I won't waste a horse on him. We'll water here and keep moving. Hit the rest of these farms another day."

"Do I let him drink?"

"If it'll keep him moving."

The man leans down and nudges me. I kneel on the bank and dip my face into the water, roiled by horses. With my hands tied behind me I have nothing to support myself in the lowering and raising. The water cools my dry throat, drips down my chin and onto my shirt. A yank on the rein pulls me back to the road. I trot behind the horse, feeling the pull of the hill as it starts up. I can't help but slow down. The rider leading me falls behind the others. They stop and look back.

"If he can't keep up, we won't take him farther," Jordan says. "We need to get past Jasper."

"You want me to shoot him?" the man who killed David asks.

"We'll give this one a different justice. Let his neighbors and kin see what happens to Unionists and deserters," Jordan answers, riding up to me. "We heard your family was helping deserters run to the hills. Probably the same who killed one of my men up at a cave."

There is no hint of humanity on Jordan's face. No possibility of understanding or mercy.

"I was there with Hugh," the man leading me says. "There was two girls with the deserter, a tall one and a short one. He took after the tall one, horny as anything, trying to screw her. She was a cherry all right. Took his attention away. The deserter picked up his rifle and shot Hugh dead. I saw that. Then I shot at the deserter. I know I hit him. He got off another shot. Hit me and the short girl at the same time. I ran downhill through the rocks. Someone shot and grazed my shoulder."

I try to think of anything to say except those girls were my sisters.

"I knew a Hugh Owens at Camp McDonald," I say. "We were in the same mess. He went absent when they gave us our bounty pay. Never saw him again."

"That was Hugh."

So now I know what Eliza Ann did not tell. I wish she'd been able to kill this one so full of talk. But if I can keep the talk going maybe someone will turn onto the road and put a stop to this. Surely Moody will have gone for the Monroes.

"Who told you it was our family?" I ask. "There's a lot of Unionists in this county."

"A boy told us there was a hideout and livestock at the Covington farm," Jordan answers. "Told us how to find it, tucked down that lane. I didn't know we'd catch two of you."

What neighborhood boy would do this? The Honeycutts aren't that mean-spirited. The Chastains aren't that young. That leaves a Bowen. Not Kize or Moses. Luther.

"David wasn't hiding out. He was wounded at Vicksburg and couldn't march."

"You're able-bodied enough."

"I had a furlough to carry my other brother home from the hospital. He was wounded at Vicksburg too. We made it, night before last."

"That'll be one more to catch next time. Deserters give aid to the Yankees, like the ones came up here and attacked us." He shifts his arm in the sling. "Now we'll give you Yankee lovers a lesson in who runs things."

"My brothers and I fought on the Confederate side. Why aren't you in the fighting to save Atlanta? Looks to me like you're taking advantage to stay out of it."

If I'm going to die it won't be without a say. Where is everyone? Anyone who can help?

"I'm commissioned to do this."

"In whose name?"

"That won't matter to you." Jordan turns to his men. "This man is a deserter and a traitor to the cause. We'll take him back to that oak and leave his body for crow-bait." He looks down at me. "In time, no one will remember your name or that you died here."

The man from the cave pulls me back down the road and across the creek to the oak. He dismounts and takes a rope from behind his saddle. *Not hanging.* I'd rather be shot trying to run away. The rein is slack. I pull against it and turn. A boot presses against my back.

"Forget about running," a voice says. "We'll catch you and hang you anyway."

I watch, as if outside my own body, the man tying a noose. The loop flops over my head, the rope rough against my neck, tightening.

"Get up on the mule."

Someone has led Shad up behind me and unties my hands. I turn to grab him. The boot against my back again.

"Get on the mule."

I climb onto Shad, steady beneath me. I can't die like this, on a mule Tom trained. I kick at Shad to get him going. Too many horses in the way. The noose pulls at my neck. Pain hammers the back of my head. I howl out. Liquid, my own blood, drips down my neck. The man reties my hands behind my back and pulls the noose tight. I gag. The rope whaps against a branch.

I'm going to die. Accused of desertion. At the hands of proud Confederate cowards riding around the countryside stealing and murdering. What if Genny finds me like this?

"Hurry it up, before somebody comes along," Jordan says.

The man pulls out his pistol, holds it next to Shad's head, and fires.

Shad startles, bucks, and runs from under me. My legs kick at air. The noose pulls against my windpipe, my head jerks, tilts, I can't breathe. The weight of my body pulls at my neck and jaw. I twist and kick, anything to stop the rope crushing my throat. Hoof beats, horses galloping away.

Air, please, air. Genny.

51

Mine To Do

Eliza Ann

A COMMOTION OF CROWS circles and settles. I see him. Head bent forward, hands tied behind his back, bare feet dangling.

I raise the musket, set a cap, and shoot at the crows. I reload and shoot again. I'll shoot every crow out of the sky.

Lafe's hand on my arm.

"You can't shoot them all. It won't save him."

"I will, I will."

I push his hand away and grab into the bag for another cartridge. I know Ananias is dead, know I can't save him, but I will kill every crow that tries to use his body for food. Wheels creak, a horse. I aim again where the crows have been, now all flown away. A hand comes down on the musket.

"Stop." Moody's voice. "I will help you."

My whole body is trembling.

"Let's get him down," Moody says. "Climb into the tree, Lafe. Cut the rope. Use this."

Lafe, face wet with tears, climbs around the tree and crawls out onto the branch. He saws at the rope with Moody's knife.

"You stand beneath and help lower him," Moody says to me. "Take his legs."

Frozen inside, I do what Moody tells me, hold Ananias's knees, feel his weight begin to descend, take the weight of him against me, move my arms until I have him cradled, one arm beneath his knees, one under his back.

"I have him," I say and sink to the ground.

"You can loosen the rope," Moody says.

I tug at the knot.

"I can't."

Lafe cuts it open.

I look into Ananias's blue eyes.

Moody kneels beside me and, with his one hand, closes them. He pushes Ananias's tongue back into his mouth, presses his lips closed, straightens his head.

"I want to clean him first," I say.

"There's a bucket in my cart. I'll take care of this," Moody says.

"It's mine to do," I answer.

I don't want anyone else to see him so. I hold the back of his head with one hand and smooth his face with the other. His hair is soaked with blood and sweat, his shirt wet with it, his pants fouled. His feet are bloody and purple-black, his neck bruised and rope-burned.

I sit holding him, until my body begins to sway, rocking him in my arms as if soothing a child. I lay my cheek to his chest. His heart is not beating. I know it will not beat again, but I want to stay this way, as if I can make it beat by listening for it.

A wail starts low in my body and rises until my throat is raw. It presses up to the place behind my eyes, and my head fills with it. The air in my lungs moves out my throat, and I cannot let any more out or take any in. I want to lose my sense, not take another breath in a world where my brothers can be murdered in such disregard. My chest heaves. My breath catches and returns. I move his body to the ground and sit next to him, with him, watching his face, his hands, pale and waxy.

"I have water," Lafe says and sets the bucket down.

I take off my soiled apron and rip away the clean parts. I kneel beside Ananias and wipe the blood from his handsome face, the back of his head and neck. I unbutton his shirt and trousers, take from his shirt pocket a small silk bag holding something hard and put it in my skirt pocket. Lafe helps me pull off his trousers and drawers. I pour water over his lower body and legs, dip my apron rags in the bucket, and wipe him clean, as best I can. Do the same with his chest and back.

Moody goes to his cart and returns with a blanket. We wrap Ananias in it. I comb his shaggy red hair with my fingers. Lafe lifts him by the shoulders. I lift his legs, and we carry him to the cart.

***

The gate hangs open. Moody drives his cart to the porch steps. The farm is silent except for sawing and hammering from the barn. Pap. Making David's casket.

"We need to see David first," I say and walk up the porch steps.

I don't want to be the one to tell Pap. I don't want to tell Mam either, but it's falling to me and I will do it.

Louise sits on the hearth stones with a poker in her hand, staring at the space where the fire has died out. Rebecca sobs into her apron. Sitting on the stairs, Charlotte and Mary Jane cling to each other, weeping. At the near side of the table, Mam is washing David's body, her blouse and apron red with his blood.

"It's the men who'd wash a man's body," she says, without looking up. "We don't have enough men left to us."

"We found Ananias," I say.

She looks up.

"Is he here?"

"In Moody's cart."

She leans her head on David's body, shoulders heaving. I go to her, put my arms around her, and rest my cheek on her hair, where David's blood has dried.

"Let me help," I say.

I don't know how, worn out from what I've already done, but I'll do anything to comfort Mam. Coming this far, doing for Ananias, this is no time to quit.

"Bring him in," Mam says.

Lafe and I lift Ananias's blanket-wrapped body from the cart and carry him into the house. My sisters stare at the procession of Ananias sagging between Lafe and me, Moody behind us.

"Next to David?" I ask.

Mam nods.

We lay him on the other side of the table. Mam turns from David and touches the rope-burn on Ananias's neck. Tears drip from her crumpled face. She places her hand along the bruising.

"They did this to him? How could they do this to my boy? My beautiful red-headed boy." She buries her face in his shoulder and wails. "Where?"

"Fourth Creek," I answer, my face wet with tears, my voice hoarse.

"Who found him? Who cut him down?"

"Me and Lafe. Moody helped."

"I have to finish David, I can't leave him not ready."

She binds David's forehead with a length of cloth, covering the bullet hole. She combs his curly hair over the binding, rests her hands on his shoulders, looks into his face, and kisses his forehead.

In the silence, Moody shuffles his feet and clears his throat.

"I'll step out to the barn," he says.

"Thank you, Moody," Mam says.

She moves to the other side of the table and pulls the blanket away from Ananias.

"You did this too?" she asks me.

"I did, I didn't know, didn't know what …"

I can't talk, remembering what I have done. What will answer for the actions I took without thinking?

"You did right. Do you want to finish it?"

I nod. I had washed and dried Lydia's body until we reclaimed her as the person we loved. Mam stands beside me as I dip and wring the cloth, washing the rest of his dying from my brother's body. But not the death. When it comes time to turn him, Lafe steps to the table.

"I'd do that," he says. "Since it's a man's work."

I hand him the rag. He wipes Ananias's head and neck, his back, and the long reach of his legs. We roll his body again.

"You girls need to pick up and do," Howell's deep voice booms from the door. "Help your mam. Look who I have." He holds Willy by the hand. "I heard him chucking acorns at the privy when I was in it. About scared the crap out of me. One of you needs to take charge of him."

My sisters look up with blank expressions. Howell looks over at the table.

"No," he says dropping Willy's hand. He limps to the table and places his hands on either side of Ananias, leans down to look at his face. "No. I never took the chance," his voice chokes. He lays his head on Ananias's chest. "Never thanked him. Never gave him his due." He looks up, eyes wet, face twisted. "I need to go home to Callie."

I don't know which way to turn. Mam, now Howell, the girls, all broken down. I lift Willy into a hug, hold the sturdy little body close, smooth his hair, wishing I could be as unaware of what happened. I need to ask Howell about the bag in Ananias's pocket. If he can't tell me, no one can.

"He told me," Howell says when I show him the bag and the bullet that was in it. "When he came for me in Newnan. Genny made the bag for him. The first skirmish after he went back, the bullet hit a rock behind him and bounced into his lap. He said it was the one that didn't kill him, how it made him lucky. I'm ashamed how I made fun of him for thinking so."

Footsteps heavy in the passage, Moody leads Pap and Luke in the door. Seeing the bodies on the table, Luke collapses in the doorway. Pap's hand gropes ahead. He clutches the table edge, leans over Ananias.

"I should've shot that worthless bushwhacker," he says, his voice so low I can hardly hear him. "I should've shot the one who killed David, shot the one leading Ananias away."

"He was the one who ran from the cave," I say.

Pap groans and falls against the table, arms across Ananias's body, sobbing into it.

Lafe squats next to Luke, holding him. Pap does not speak again. Lafe and I look at each other, the only ones besides Mam able to respond and do. Mam leads Pap away to their sleeping room. Moody offers to take Howell home in his cart. And my sisters finally come to life, holding each other, keening over the corpses of their brothers.

As light leaves the day, Lafe and I move the boys' bodies to the back sleeping room, so recently occupied by the liveliness of David and Willy. We take up the work of the house, the others joining in as they can, cleaning the table, sweeping the cold hearth, replenishing water and wood, lighting a fire, bathing and feeding Willy. No one else can eat.

When the tasks are finished, we sit together into the night with David and Ananias, their wounds hidden under bindings.

Grief open on our faces, hands still, voices silent or sobbing, until Mary Jane, so quiet and unwilling to put herself first, with a voice that never fails, starts singing the hymns of grief and hope.

"*Oh God, our help in ages past, Our hope for years to come, Our shelter from the stormy blast, And our eternal home.*"

As we always have at work, in fun, in sorrow, we sing. Our voices join with hers, in unison, the joy of harmony gone.

My tears start with *"Time, like an ever-rolling stream, Bears all its sons away; They fly, forgotten, as a dream Dies at the op'ning day."*

I let them roll down my face and look at what is left of my family. My parents grown old, my sisters unmarried, the twins not yet men, and Willy. This is what the War has done to us, and it isn't over.

If this is what Secession gains, I will hold it against those who support it, the powerful, greedy men who started a war to accomplish it, the rich men willing to let so many die to keep their plantations, their slaves, and their money. That murders like this can come of it. I want them to lose everything, never to be regained. Harriett, the Buchanans if they ever come back, no matter how good and kindly they are to admit the wrong of it. How will we ever heal from this?

And yet we sing on.

"Savior, like a shepherd lead us, much we need Thy tender care…"

"My faith looks up to thee…Bid darkness turn to day, Wipe sorrow's tears away…"

If singing can heal, we will. But I will never forgive.

52

A Shining Mark

Eliza Ann

JANE IS HERE at first light. She drops a bundle of quilt sheeting on a chair and lays a bag of roses at the foot of the bed where the boys' bodies lie.

"I picked every rose," she says. "This is all I have left of sheeting, but it'll do for shrouds. I brought dinner fixings. I hope it's enough."

She sets a sack of pole beans and a plucked chicken on the table.

"The rest of mine will come tomorrow. It doesn't look like you've eaten a thing. I'll stir up some bread. Boys! Start me a fire!"

Lucy arrives alone. She goes to Mam first, and they break down together.

"Genny?" I squeak it out, not wanting to ask, knowing Genny's sorrow will forever be a piece of ours.

"Heartbroken. I gave her laudanum so she can sleep."

Lucy keeps moving, settles Mam in her rocker, straightens the room. She goes to the garden and picks tomatoes and cucumbers, tells Mary Jane to keep track of Willy, prompts Charlotte to gather her own roses.

Jane starts beans to boiling, chops chicken parts, stirs bread batter, and keeps up a one-sided conversation with Louise. I hold lengths of sheeting in place while Rebecca stitches it into shrouds.

Jane and Lucy, the constant stars of heaven, go to anyone when strength fails.

Moody comes in the afternoon. He helps the twins feed and water the cows and Abe. The Monroes take over milking and churning, round up the chickens scattered in the woods, and herd the geese. Pap sets to making another coffin.

The rest of the Wilders arrive. Genny, eyes swollen, face red, walks head-down into Mam's arms.

"I told him I'd watch for him," she sobs. "I thought it would be when the War was over."

"He wanted to come to you first thing," Mam says. "We were so needy to have him home, we said it could wait til after dinner. We were so wrong."

I walk Genny into the room and stand beside her until she raises up from Ananias. I hold her while she weeps, my grief and hers, halves of the same whole.

"Moody told us what you did for him," she says.

"He had something for you."

I hand her the bag and bullet.

"Howell told me about this. The bullet bounced over Ananias's head. He saved it to show you how lucky he was."

She fingers the bag. "I made this for him, he said it held hope." She clenches her fingers around the bullet. "We were lucky. Lucky in love."

***

My brothers are surrounded day and night by voices, candlelight, the scent of roses. Friends care for us and feed us, keep the household going, and mourn with us. Each visitor brings the ways in which the boys are remembered.

Listening to them helps me know what I loved about my brothers. David dancing, his high harmony, laughing and teasing, bringing Lydia to us, devoting his days and nights to Willy. Ananias bringing food from the woods, taking charge of us, including Tom in everything he did. I remember his soft drawl reading aloud, his love of what he learned from books, his willingness for me to learn with him.

Harriet comes, trying to hold me to her small body, murmuring, "When my parents died I thought I would too, of grief."

I move away from her. I can't forgive her for being a slave-holding Confederate, believing in an evil thing.

***

We bury David next to Lydia, then Ananias next to David. Ropes creak against wood as Luke and Lafe strain with Alex

Graham, Jacob Wilder, Mr. Monroe, and Mr. Halford, lowering the coffins into the red earth.

The change is in Howell. He stands off to the side with Callie, eyes closed tight, face wet, shoulders slumped, hardly aware of his little boys clinging to his legs, his girls holding his hands.

On the one leg left to him, the Reverend Jefferson Childs stands between the graves, leaning on crutches. His preaching has inspired and entertained our family for as long as I can remember. He moved here from North Carolina with the Covingtons, Grahams, and Wilders, baptized us all in the Campbellite faith, went off to war with Howell and Tom, calling himself the fighting preacher. He knows us well enough to console us while grieving himself.

"This is not the season, the time, or the purpose under heaven for these boys to die," he begins the service. "It is hard for us to understand why they were murdered at the hands of cowards. As it is written in The Book of Psalms, *But the Lord is my defence; and my God is the rock of my refuge. And he shall bring upon them their own iniquity, and shall cut them off in their own wickedness; yea, the Lord our God shall cut them off.* And in Romans, *Dearly beloved, avenge not yourselves, but rather give place unto wrath: for it is written, Vengeance is mine; I will repay, saith the Lord.*"

I have considered vengeance, and now Reverend Childs is telling me it's not mine to do. But how can God have allowed this to happen? I remember asking this when Lydia died.

"For that, only He can know the time and the season," Reverend Childs says.

I do not believe that can be the answer.

"It is said that *death loves a shining mark*," he continues. "In their shining lives, serving in war, providing for home and family, David and Ananias will no longer be touched by greed, envy, or violence. They have turned to the light of heaven and reside with the angels. David is reunited with Lydia. Ananias is at peace. *I will both lay me down in peace, and sleep: for thou, Lord, only makest me dwell in safety.*"

Safety. I almost snort in disbelief. What safety can there be in a place where trust and neighborliness have been destroyed? I turn to Reverend Childs, not daring to ask it. He looks back at me in sympathy. His twangy drawl, so reassuring in times before the War, carries on.

"Our light is in our love of our Heavenly Father. We take solace in having David and Ananias not lost to us forever on the field of battle. It remains for us to live in the grace of God, remember the shining lives of these beloved sons and brothers, and keep their memories alive for David's son. *He healeth the broken in heart, and bindeth up their wounds. He telleth the number of the stars; he calleth them all by their names. Great is our Lord, and of great power: his understanding is infinite.*"

The men take up shovels. Dirt clods thud onto the casket lids until they are covered, and dirt falls softly onto dirt. Pap pounds oak markers into the mounds.

I remember sunlight turning David's hair golden before his blood soaked into the hot dust of the lane. I remember holding Ananias in the cool shade of the dark-leafed oak that held him in death. Above my sobs I hear those of Mam and Pap, my brothers, sisters, friends and wonder how God's infinite understanding can heal our broken hearts.

53

Salt

October–November, 1864

Eliza Ann

I HEAR HORSES IN the lane. Without looking to see who it is, I grab Pap's musket and go out to the porch. I set the cap and aim at the lead man. It's the Sheriff. Pap said I should do this the next time men ride down our lane. *Aim for the leader.* Pap walks out of the barn with the rifle I carried from the cave.

"There's no need for weapons, Mr. Covington."

"Sheriff, the last time men rode onto my farm, they murdered my sons."

"That was Ben Jordan's gang."

"You come to tell me something I don't already know?"

"Come to tell you it won't go unavenged. We're out to give Jordan back some of his own. Make him beg for a truce."

"The Lord will see to his punishment," Pap says.

"We marked the place where Ananias died. A remembrance of injustice done."

"Revenge has nothing to do with justice," Pap says.

"All the same, we thought you'd want to join us."

"The only *us* I am joined to is this family. You're no better than Jordan if you do the same as him. I told the last ones who came asking, I won't join any group out chasing around the county making war within a war."

"They say he took your boys because you're Unionist."

"He took my boys because they were here. I'm nothing but a tired old farmer who lost three sons to a war I never asked for."

"These boys might want to avenge the deaths." The Sheriff looks to the twins.

"I'll hunt down the man who talks them into it," Pap says and turns to the twins. "You tempted by it?"

Lafe looks at Luke before answering.

"We've seen enough, Pap."

"Does your girl really know how to shoot that musket?" the Sheriff asks.

"Better than the boys."

I lower the rifle. I don't want to shoot anybody.

***

I pull my cloak tight and look up at the sky. A waning sliver of moon tilts above the horizon. One by one, the stars come out.

I've always liked that way of saying it, as if stars are hiding before allowing themselves to be seen. Orion appears, the hunter still chasing after the Seven Sisters, the Pleiades, that wonderful word.

I glance away to fix their position, then look on the slant to see the cluster of visible sisters. Ananias told me how to do that, told me how the old Cherokee called them Pigs In Heaven. That was when I was younger in every way, before I learned that my own strength would be more than household chores, or knew my place among sisters to be counted on, before I believed in my own sense. *It's time for you to know what you can do.* He told me that too.

I believed it was the mysteriously beautiful things that were hidden so, like the seventh sister, before I knew of the destructive forces that can't be seen—greed, rumors, ignorance, lies.

"You'll freeze to death out here," Mary Jane says from behind me.

"Not to death."

"Come back to the fire. Mam says it's time to plan out hog-killing."

"What are we going to do for salt?"

"Pap has an idea."

He paces in front of the fire, waiting for us.

"We're going to dig it out," he says.

"There's no salt in the ground around here," Lafe says.

"It's right under our own smokehouse."

***

The twins shovel dirt from the smokehouse floor into the wash kettle.

"How far do we dig?" Luke asks.

"Until I don't taste it in the dirt," Pap answers, dipping a finger into it.

The smokehouse has been in the same place. It takes the twins all morning, Pap insisting that every square inch of possible salt be shoveled up. He pours water into a tub of salty earth and lets it boil.

When it cools and the dirt settles, he dips a cup into the cloudy water.

"It's weak," he says. "But there's enough to salt hams and side-meat. We'll do it one hog at a time. And hope for better next year."

I doubt next year can be better. Hog-killing with less people to do it, fewer hogs, dirty brine for salt, the War still going on.

The only hope I have is for Genny and her red-headed baby girl. Last week I went for her lying-in, held her and sang to her until the baby came, this tiny one early and quickly. A mother with no husband, a baby with no father except part of his name, Ana. I reckon they'll make their way, like we have with Willy. There isn't much cause for hope, but I do for the little ones. I still believe that love matters.

54

Bones

November 14-15, 1864, The Cave

Eliza Ann

WITH THE FULL moon, November has turned sunny and warm.

"We need to go to the cave," Pap announces. "Settle what happened there. Reclaim it from the evil haint."

Chill bumps raise on my arms.

"I don't. Do you?" I ask Mary Jane.

"No," she answers.

"That's reason enough," Pap says. "It should be a place to remember the best of Ananias, rid of the coward who led him to

367

his death. You'll want to go there again, take Willy and Ana into the woods."

"The twins could do that," I say. "What if men are there?"

I want to think up any and every reason for not going back to the place where terrible things happened, before the worst things happened. It's bad enough walking up the lane, passing the crossroads on the way to Meeting.

"We'll go armed," Pap answers.

"To stay the night?"

"You always did before. It'll take the fear out of it."

"I'd have to think on that."

And I do, all night, Mary Jane restless beside me.

"What if he starts asking about things?" Mary Jane whispers.

"I'll think of something," I answer.

***

We set out carrying quilts and food baskets. Mary Jane's arm has healed, but her elbow won't straighten. Lafe carries the rifle, Luke the small spider. Pap takes the lead with his musket. It doesn't take long for him to get lost. I have been paying attention, not wanting to correct him.

"Don't know why I took the lead when I don't know the way," he says.

The twins and Mary Jane turn to me. I look up at the sky, at the sassafras and hickory trees around us, the spaces between them where chestnuts start.

"We can go back down a ways and turn before we go back up," I say.

"Lead on," he says.

In the last part of the climb, he straggles, winded. I slow the pace. Close to the cave, we come upon scattered human bones and gray rags. I stop and will not walk past the bones, feeling like a mule, stubborn in the face of danger.

"I thought Mr. Newton would clear him away," I say. "Why didn't he?"

Luke comes out of the cave. "There's a man's bones in here too."

"Gather them up," Pap says. "We'll bury them."

Lafe starts on the bones in the rocks. Luke on the ones in the cave.

"I found these too," Luke says. He holds up a hat pinned on the side and a blood-stained, yellow neckerchief.

I sink to my knees.

"Those were Mr. Newton's. How could he leave them?"

"I'm not surprised he'd hide a fatal wound from you," Pap says.

"He never made it home," I cry out. "His family won't know where he is. Just like Tom."

I can't stop crying. Mary Jane puts an arm around me, and I cry harder. She starts crying, and Pap put his arms around us.

"Hush now. You'll make yourselves sick. We'll mark Newton's remains and get word to his people."

I bury my face in my hands.

"I don't want to be here. I don't want to remember."

"You've seen worse than this."

And against everything I thought I wanted, I tell him the rest.

"You've been holding onto it the whole time? You too?" he asks Mary Jane.

"She told me to take the attention for being wounded," Mary Jane says. "And not tell about the rest because it was shameful. She didn't want anyone to know."

He keeps ahold of us.

"The boys will clear the bones away, and you will rest until your minds clear. What that man did was shameful, but you did nothing to bring it on. You have to believe me in this. We can't let this place be remembered for murderers and rapists."

Hugging us close to his sides, he leads us to the cave. The twins have cleared the man Hugh's bones to the edge of the woods and Mr. Newton's from the cave.

Luke starts a fire. Lafe warms cornbread and slices of pork in the spider. I try to eat but it tastes too dry to choke down. In the dying firelight, I sit wrapped in a quilt near the cave's entrance staring at where the mountain tilts down and the country beyond spreads to the south. Pap sits between me and Mary Jane, his arms always around us.

The southern sky turns orange and yellow in the clear night. Great columns of fire and smoke blossom and billow, thick and high.

"That's something big," Lafe says.

Pap peers south. "The biggest thing in that direction is Atlanta."

I shudder. Where is Eli in all this? Pap hugs me closer not knowing the cause of my shivering.

"There's so much more to this world than what we have here," he says. "Men do evil every day. We have to live beyond it."

55

Lone Heart

Eliza Ann

I T'S BAREFOOT TIME again, and I am alone in my place on the porch steps, hulling wild strawberries in the humid afternoon. It takes concentration to keep the tiny berries intact and will-power not to eat them all. The scent of Charlotte's roses fills the air. Some things change, some do not.

The lives of animals go on as if the War never happened. Cassiopeia's piglets are kicking up dust in the pen, and June is bellowing for her calf. Chicks totter in the yard. A young rooster struts among the hens. No one has given him a name.

Goslings wobble behind their parents parading up the lane. The barn cats are hunting mice in the corncrib.

I eat a few berries. This spring has been unlike all others. Lee's surrender to Grant, the assassination of President Lincoln, Johnston's surrender to Sherman, the capture of President Davis, and slaves turned to freedom. The surrendered soldiers are the sons and brothers of other families. We have no one left to die. Anyone who doubts that the War is lost is not in touch with reality.

It took Howell to open Harriett's eyes and mind and make her quit carrying on about the cause lost.

"We rightfully lost it," he said. "Wasn't anything honorable about fighting to keep slavery. It's no sacred cause to keep, and it didn't make heroes out of those who survived. All they want is to love their kin, work their land, and forget the War. Like me. If I could change anything, I'd never have gone in the first place and, in the last place, never have given Ananias's name to bring me home. He deserved better in a brother. Tom did too. I'll have that to make up for my whole life."

Harriet kept quiet after that.

I've taken up reading the Shakespeare book I found in Ananias's haversack, rereading the passages he marked with a pencil, knowing they are important if he marked a book.

But we in it shall be remembered—We few, we happy few, we band of brothers; For he today that sheds his blood with me Shall be my brother.

The worst is death, and death will have his day.

Sorrow breaks seasons and reposing hours, Makes the night morning, and the noontide night.

Some of it is hard going, not only the words but the way of telling the story. I've never seen a play. I read out loud to make more sense of them. I find the words Jeremiah recited, taking his turn with the part of King Henry and try speaking them as forcefully as he did. Willy, fighting sleep, is my captive audience.

I want to know why this was important to Ananias.

***

Alone or in pairs, weaponless, dressed in the remnants of uniforms, barefoot soldiers are coming home from Virginia, North Carolina, Alabama, wherever their last battles left them. Unlike deserters, they walk the roads in plain sight, parole papers in their pockets, no passwords. In gratitude for a meal and a place to sleep, they share Yankee rations given to them at surrender. The beef and milk in tins are strange to my taste. Their packets of coffee, sugar, and salt are wonders.

Levi McFarlin returned to Mary Jane, coming down the lane bearded and bone thin, without his horse. She had not heard from him in four years, and now they will be married at laying-by. I expect the Bowen brothers to show up for Rebecca and Charlotte. We've had no word from Ananias's friend Posey, no news of Eli.

Louise and I will be the last left to take care of Willy, Mam and Pap. She and Rebecca set up the old barn loom in the back sleeping room. What Lydia would have to say about learning to weave makes me smile. It's not something I want to take on. I finally learned how to turn the heel of a sock. But it's Willy getting into the loom and pulling threads that causes Rebecca to fuss so much she doesn't notice as many of my shortcomings.

Our working fields have shrunk to those closest to the house, the far fields grown over in weeds. Pap worries how we will make enough of a crop to pay taxes. Lafe, grown as tall as Ananias, has been helping Howell finish his plowing and planting. According to Callie, he walks to Halford's Mill every evening.

Harriet came to visit and sat with me on the porch.

"I'm sorry it came to this," she said. "I believed what my parents taught me and kept believing it to keep them alive in my heart. I did not bother with truth. I wanted to live the way we lived together. My own grief kept me from seeing the War for what it was. Wrong."

I don't know if I've forgiven her, but I take her at her word. If I lose all of my sisters to their husbands' families, at least Lafe might bring one home. The thought of her going without her petticoats and hoop, pushing up her sleeves and scrubbing floors makes me smile.

***

"First jack deals," I say, flipping the cards face up.

Over the winter, the twins taught us how to play euchre, David's game. And Eli's. We've taken it up on warm evenings, sitting on the porch steps. Mary Jane gets the first jack.

"Queen of diamonds," she says, turning up the trump card.

I sort my hand, both black bowers, two more spades, one heart. The cards are so worn I've colored in the clubs and spades with black ink and outlined the hearts and diamonds with the red-oak. I use that to practice writing, so as not to waste the black.

374

Letters and words flow across paper with the pen-nib. I have a new copy book for use as a diary, a gift from Harriet. At first I felt silly, writing down what happens in a day. Not much. But sometimes I write what I've been thinking, or what I remember of a poem. Some days it helps just to write down the date and day, as if by doing so, my life is something to note.

"I pass," I say.

"Pick it up," Rebecca says. "I can give a little help to my partner."

"That's good because I don't want to go it alone," Mary Jane says and exchanges a card in her hand for the queen.

I stop thinking about the game, my turn, or the cards in my hand. *I don't want to go it alone.* Eli's words from Christmas a year and a half ago. He went back to the Army alone. Ananias went to his death alone. Except for those taken prisoner and not yet paroled, most of the men who survived the War are home. No one wants to go it alone.

"Eliza Ann, your lead," Rebecca says. "You day-dreaming or playing cards?"

I play the ten of spades. Rebecca follows suit with the king, Charlotte the nine.

"That helps," Mary Jane says, dropping the king of clubs and sliding the trick to Rebecca. "What else can you give me?"

Rebecca plays the ace of diamonds taking Charlotte's king. I have no trump, the ten of hearts my only red card. We play what we have until Rebecca lays out her ace of clubs.

"Two points for us." Mary Jane says, slapping down the queen and both red bowers. "Your hand was that bad?"

"Just like my future," I say. "Mostly black with a small lone heart."

"You don't have a lone heart," Charlotte says. "What about Eli?"

Before I can think about the consequences, I retort, "What about the Bowen brothers?"

Charlotte's face turns white.

"That's mean," Rebecca snaps. "Even though we haven't heard, they could still come home. If that's the way you're going to be, you can go it alone yourself."

She gathers up the cards and goes into the house.

I twist my fingers into my apron. "I'm sorry, Char. I thought I was done blurting out stupid thoughts."

"It just took me back a bit," Charlotte says. "Don't feel bad on my account. It doesn't bother me like it does her. I never had feelings for Joe like she did for Ike. She just kindly dragged me into it, maybe thinking if there were two of us it'd make a better argument to Pap. Joe was always with Ike so I went along. They'll all be coming home. And if they don't, well, I don't know, I guess we can't ever be like we were. I don't know what I want but it isn't Joe. And I'm sorry what I said about Eli. I just saw how he looked at you and thought you had feelings for him too."

"It's all right, Char." I gather my legs in and stand up. "We'll still be family. Now if I can just get Rebecca to forgive me. Again."

56

Covington Hang

Eliza Ann

I HATE THE MEN who took my brothers, tied them with reins, and murdered them. The county's Grand Jury has found *true bills for murder and robbery* against Ben Jordan and his gang. None of the cases have come to trial. Some were dismissed because the acts supposedly were authorized. No one will say who did that. Other cases linger because the defendants have never been caught. Ben Jordan is rumored to have gone west.

Hideouts have come down from the hills and rejoined their families. The Home Guards disbanded. It does not matter as much who believed what before the War. The missing men and boys who did the planting and plowing are dead. Those who did come home have no time or desire for vengeance. Refugees returning from the south and east tell of the devastation left by Sherman's Army. None of the atrocities and destruction that his army committed on the people of Georgia happened in Pickens County. Here we fought each other.

***

Pap comes home from Jasper with news of the last case dismissed against gang members from other counties. I leave the house and go to work on the wood pile. The afternoon sun glares in the yard.

"Whatever made me so proud," I mutter, hot-faced and sweating, hacking at a length of wood. "Bone jarring, blistering work. No one cares how neat I stack it. No one cares about anything I do. Stupid grand jury lets murderers go free. No justice."

I whack another split away from a chunk.

"Come sit with me."

Mam is sitting on the top step of the back porch. Her hair shines silver in the sunlight. I wedge the axe into the chopping block and sit below her. She puts her hand on my head. Her hand smoothing my hair is the oldest sensation I know. I wish I was grown up enough, changed enough, to not need like a child that loving stroke. I am well on my way to nineteen.

"Are you expecting revenge against the ones who took our boys?" she asks.

"No. I understand what Pap meant about that on our part. I want justice."

"David and Ananias are not at war anymore," Mam says.

"They're dead." I say.

"We can't change that. But we can keep them alive in our memory."

"How can I remember anything but how they died?"

I can see David falling bloody in the lane, Ananias hanging from the oak, the crows on him. *I'll note you in my book of memory.* He'd marked that too.

"Remember who they were," she says.

"They were murdered. Their murderers are not at war anymore either."

"War makes no distinction between just and unjust or the quality of death."

"What's left if there's no difference between justice and injustice?"

"There's a difference. War doesn't answer that. What's left is the mercy and grace of your own life."

"Hoeing corn, chopping wood, watching my sisters get married?"

"Take up your studies again."

"Lot of good that'll do me. They'll never start another school. I'd be too old anyway."

"If you can do no better in your own reckoning, think of what Ananias wanted, for himself as well as for you."

"He wanted to marry Genny."

"And be a teacher. You could study for that. I know you've been reading that book of his. You have a good mind. He turned to you when he couldn't reckon something out, counted on you to remember the things you learned together. *Neglect not the gift that is in thee.* If you dwell on what those men did, you will give them a place in your heart forever. Do you want that?"

"I want David and Ananias alive, with Lydia and Genny and their babies, on their own farms. I want Tom home. I want our family to never have changed."

Mam's hand rests on my hair. "We all do. But, *shall we receive good at the hand of God, and shall we not receive evil?*"

"If I am being tested like Job, I'm failing. Evil never came upon us until the War. Even the Bowens waited for that before they started on us. I don't see why we should accept what happened to the boys, and I don't know how to fight it."

Everyone suspects the Bowens of pointing the Jordan Gang in the direction of Unionist farms. That did not keep Elias and Frank from dying in the fighting at Atlanta or Ike and Joe not returning from the Army of Tennessee. The War brought suffering to the Bowens. Mrs. Bowen died, some say of grief, others say of overwork. The twin girls ran away along with Kize and the wives of the oldest boys. It leaves Ansell Bowen with half of his sons and no women to work his household.

"I know how you've grown in understanding," Mam says. "And I have the same hope for you as I did before. How could I want your life to be one of bitterness and anger? Would you have us beat our plowshares into swords again?"

"I'd have fire devour their pastures and flames burn their trees. I'd have the earth quake and the heavens tremble, the sun and moon go dark, and the stars stop shining. What if I'm not a good enough person, not strong enough?"

"You're good enough. I raised you. When you question your strength, remember how much you've learned, how you brought Mary Jane home and helped her heal, never minding what happened to you. Remember what you did for Ananias when he could no longer do for himself."

"You heard what they're calling that place?"

"I have."

"Is that how he'll be remembered?"

"No amount of storytelling will change what happened to him."

"It sickens me."

"Who told you?"

"Thad. He heard two boys in the road, one telling the other he'd better watch out for the hainted tree at Covington Hang. The way the boy told it, Jordan's gang killed 'that Covington boy' because they were rounding up deserters and he hadn't gone to the War. Thad tried to set them straight. What if people start believing Ananias didn't go?"

"We can't stop people from telling a story in the way they will. It's how they choose to remember. Some will remember it as an injustice done, and that by itself is a just way."

Willy comes out and sits next to Mam. She hugs him.

"Ask Aunt Eliza Ann to tell you a story," she says and goes into the house.

"Aunt Wizann, tell me a stowy."

He cuddles up against me, and I put my arm around him.

"What kind of story would you like to hear?"

"About a papa and his boy."

"Once upon a time," I begin. "There was a papa who loved his little boy more than anything in the whole world. The little boy had a big family that loved him too. Every day."

It doesn't take much to put Willy to sleep. I wish Eli would come, the Bowen brothers, anyone who would bring love.

57

Decision

June 1865

Eliza Ann

THE GEESE ARE at it. Charlotte and I look up from weeding and thinning the garden. A tall and raggedy, barefoot soldier stands at the top of the lane. He's shed his uniform jacket in the heat. His shirt sleeves do not come down to his wrists. He takes something from his pocket and places it in the dirt.

"What's he doing?" Charlotte asks.

"Leaving a rock," I say, dropping the basket of greens and walking through the gate.

"Do we know who he is?"

I start running up the lane. Without turning my head, I call out the answer as much to the man in the lane as to my sister in the garden.

"Eli."

I run into his arms. His face is gaunt, hazel eyes questioning, but his lips are firm on mine, his arms around me in a way that tells he won't let go. I kiss him back. His lips move to my face, his tears wet my skin. He kisses my eyes and nose, cheeks, neck until I am breathless and pull away even though I don't want him to stop. Tilting his head back, he looks me down and up.

"You still keeping the company of geese?" he asks.

"One. In my sewing basket."

"Is your family going to tease us for this?"

"I don't care."

"Where's Ananias? We knew he couldn't get back to us at Atlanta. The Yankees were everywhere."

I don't have time to take it in that he is here for me, before having to tell him about my brothers.

***

The whole family thinks they know why he's here. I have no peace and no answers. He hasn't asked me to marry him.

I take him into the orchard where I've spent so many evenings alone, reading and daydreaming, hoping he would come back. If we are alone together, we can talk. I am prepared to say yes.

He stands facing me and takes my hands.

"There's something you need to know before we go on with this."

What bad thing could he have done to make him say this? I believe he came back because he wants to marry me. I want to marry him. He has no other place to go. What else do I need to know?

"You don't love me?" I ask.

"I do. I want to marry you. I want you to marry me."

"Then that settles it. We will and we'll live here and farm."

"No."

"No, what?"

"I can't stay here."

"Then we'll find our own farm. Some families are leaving for the West, willing to sell."

The Grahams are going to Kansas. The Graham farm would be almost like living at home.

"I'm going west too. Montana Territory. I want you with me."

I take in a breath. It sticks in my throat. Where is Montana Territory? How far from Georgia? How can I leave what is left of my family? Abandon them? It would make me what Ananias had not wanted to be, a deserter. But I don't want Eli to go anywhere without me.

"There's land," he said. "Gold fields. Men talk about it as a place where it won't matter what side a man fought on. I can't stay here where what we fought for was so wrong, and I don't want to live with Yankees running the place. They'd have killed us all if we hadn't surrendered. I want to forget the War. That's what you need to know before you agree to marry me. Can you do that?"

I don't know, and I don't know how to say so. He pulls me into his arms.

"I have waited for this. I can wait longer. Think on it. Talk to your mam and pap. Would you marry me if I wasn't going west?"

385

"Yes." It's all I can manage to say.

He leads me by the hand to the back porch.

"I fell in love with you before I saw you. The way Ananias talked about you, about the whole family. If you don't go with me, I'll leave soon. Now I'll go on to the Wilders until you can decide."

***

I need to be alone, to think. I go into Louise's room, the one she's given up so many times, for David and Lydia, Lydia alone, David and Willy, the barn loom. Louise would give up anything for the family. I sit on the bed where Lydia birthed Willy and died, David slept with Willy, Howell was taken when Ananias carried him home, bodies laid out for visitation in death. My memories don't help me. Every tree in the forest, every row of crops, every visit with the Wilders, everything good and bad in my life comes back to my lost brothers. A new place would have no memories. It could be a new start, with Eli, because of love.

I slip into Mam and Pap's room when I hear them getting ready for bed.

"You're worrying something over," Mam says. "Where is Eli?"

"He went to the Wilders. He wants me to marry him."

"Why is he not here then? Did you tell him no?"

"There's something else he wants besides marrying me."

"Of course he does," Pap says. "The two of you can take over the farm."

I drop onto the stool by Mam's rocker, put my head in my hands, and cry.

"What's wrong with that?" Pap asks.

"He doesn't want to stay here. He wants me to go to Montana Territory with him. He wants to start over."

Pap pulls me to standing, into the circle of their arms.

"How can I leave you and Willy?" I ask. "How can I leave their graves?"

"A woman goes with her husband," Mam says. "Do you love him?"

"I do. But if I go you'll feel about me the way you did about the boys going to war."

"How could I ever do that again to one of my own? We were all wrong in every way," Pap says. "This is your chance for your own life. There's only harder work ahead of us in Georgia."

"I'm still the first one you can do without?"

"No. You've proved yourself over and over. We never thought a youngest girl would make such a difference. But this is your decision. You're strong and smart. You know what's in you."

58

Wedding

Eliza Ann

I WAKE UP NEXT to Mary Jane. By the end of this day, she will be married to Levi, and I will be married to Eli.

"It's the last morning we'll wake together," I say.

We've shared this bed since the twins were born, greeted each other every morning, whispered most nights before going to sleep. She knows my secrets and loves me anyway. We've been best sisters since we were little girls, and now we'll never live in the same house again. Tears slide from my eyes. For someone who never cried over much, now I cry over anything, everything.

"Don't cry," Mary Jane says. "We'll both have good lives."

"But when Eli takes me west I might never see you again."

"We'll make the best of the time we have. Why cry on your wedding day? It'll make your eyes red."

She's right. I wipe my eyes and slide out of bed. Willy and the twins are fussing in the boys' room, probably bothering Eli. Living in the same house with him before being married is not what brides and grooms usually do, but Pap and Mam want him here.

The few chances we have to talk come after supper when we go to the orchard. Sitting with him in the quiet of an evening convinces me that I will be happy talking with him for the rest of my life.

***

I have spent the morning going through the house, nervously fingering every detail of food and flowers until I tip over a jar of lavender. Charlotte steers me upstairs where I submit to Rebecca fixing my hair, then Mary Jane's, in chignons. For this moment we are true sisters.

The wedding guests begin arriving. Wilders, Grahams, Howell's family, Halfords, Monroes, Chastains, Honeycutts, still neighbors and friends despite losses and differences. The guests of the McFarlins, most of them Secessionists, seem happy for the occasion. Carriages, wagons, carts, horses, and mules fill the lane and yard between house and barn. Mam oversees it all, welcoming each arrival.

A week ago, Jane came with bolts of cotton cloth for dresses, telling how Mrs. Halford insisted on providing them. I haven't had a new dress since the first year of the War. It's pale blue with red and yellow berries on stems of dark blue leaves. Mary Jane's is navy with rows of white and red budded stems. I like the way the sleeves bell out a little, how the skirt falls in crisp folds. It swishes when I walk, and I sway, just to listen to it, like I did when I was a little girl.

Out the window, the yard is in an uproar. Men congregate at the barn door where Pap and the twins are in hiding from the fuss in the house. Moody has shown up with jugs of whiskey, two small ones as gifts for the brides and grooms and two large ones "to make the festivities more festive," as he tells it.

Mary Jane and I go downstairs to help.

"You will not work on this day," Louise says, hustling us into Mam's room.

Genny is watching over the babies laid on the bed, her own, Tabitha's and Callie's. I stand at the window. I'll never have another wedding day and want to see all of it. Women carry dishes of food to plank tables set up in the yard. Children swarm everywhere. Cynthia Graham organizes the little girls into waving brush branches over the table to keep flies off the food. The twins gather up Willy and the little boys and shoo them into the back yard. Reverend Childs has taken Charlotte aside and is saying something that makes her put her hand on his arm and laugh.

When the last of the food is on the tables, Louise places a cloth over it and sends the brush-waving little girls to a corner of the porch steps where they settle down to watch the wedding. The porch is decorated with jars of every blue, white, lavender, yellow, and pink flower Charlotte could pick from her garden. The talk and laughter from the barn grows more raucous as the men trade stories and pass Moody's whiskey.

Alone, Eli half-sits at the edge of the first porch step, one knee resting on the ground, wearing the new shirt Rebecca made for him.

"I know you can sew better now, but let me do this one last thing for you," she'd said.

I want to go out to him, but my sisters are unyielding. Brides are to stay inside until the guests assemble. The last to arrive are Levi with his parents and sisters in two carriages, his brothers following on horseback. Mam leads them into the house and consults with Reverend Childs.

The time has come for me to walk out and join Eli. The bouquet of yellow roses shakes in my hands. Eli takes my hand in his. The Reverend Childs clears his throat and begins the ceremony.

I don't hear a word of it, looking into Eli's eyes, accepting his kiss.

***

The day has gone by in joy, the food eaten, everyone drinking a little or a lot of whiskey. We have accepted our neighbors' gifts—split oak baskets, packets of seeds, the things people can spare. Pap has made blanket chests. The Halfords gave us Bibles, and from Harriet, pressed-glass jelly dishes.

Levi's carriage pulls up to the porch. Laughing and crying, Mary Jane and I hug as if we will never let go. Then he leads her down the steps and helps her into the carriage. It pulls away, and I wave good-bye to the sister who shared every trouble and happiness.

Eli and I are the last left standing on the porch. I have been sleepless about what will happen next. Mam has convinced me that what happened at the cave has no bearing on my life with Eli. But for this, I have gone to Jane.

"I know we'll sleep in the same bed. I know about kissing and hugging. I don't know about the rest. Do you take your clothes off?"

"Of course you do. But then you'll put on your night shift. After that, I think it's up to the two of you. It was for us. If you follow what your heart wants, what your body wants. Remember that he loves you, and you love him, and nothing bad can come from loving. Between two who care for each other, it feels good."

I'm not sure what all that means but hold onto his hand tightly as we walk to the back sleeping room, now ours. My sisters have made up the bed with the star-pattern quilt I finally finished, with Mary Jane's help. They have moved my things into the room. Rag doll, brush, and sewing basket. Diary, Reader, Ananias's Shakespeare. My clothes and bonnets hang from the hooks. My night shift laid out on the bed next to Eli's night shirt. A candle glows on the light-stand.

"I'll go out and let you take care of your clothes," he says.

I hang the new dress on a hook, put on my night shift, brush out my hair, and sit on the edge of the bed. He comes into the room, his eyes warm and smiling.

"We won't need the light," he says.

He takes up his night shirt and blows out the candle.

I can hear him changing his clothes in the dark. He sits next to me and lifts my hair away from my back.

"It's like silk," he says and puts his other hand on my knee.

I'm about to come undone, skin alert, legs and arms twitchy, breathing shallow. He moves his hand to my neck and turns my face to his kiss, presses me back against the bed, and lifts my legs onto it. I don't have to remember what Jane told me.

Sleepless again, but now because I am warm, my skin still tingling from his touch. He is asleep, breathing, next to me. My thoughts drift from this place where I have always lived, seldom left and never far, to what will come, a life on the change. There is no path.

Characters

COVINGTON FAMILY

Pap, Richard Covington
Mam, Sarah Covington
Louise, oldest daughter
Howell, oldest son
    Callie, his wife
    Emily, Lily, Samuel, Daniel,
    their children
David
    Lydia, his wife
    Willy, their son
Rebecca
Charlotte
Ananias
Tom (Thomas)
Mary Jane
Eliza Ann, youngest daughter
Luke (Lucien) and Lafe (Lafayette), twins

NEIGHBORS AND FRIENDS

Wilder, Lucy, a widow and midwife
    Jacob, her son
    Tabitha, his wife
        Gabe, Matthew, Joshua,
        Hannah, their children
    Genny, her daughter
    Noah, her son

Graham, Jane and her husband, Alex
    Alfred, Cynthia, Carrie, their children

Monroe, Zacharias and his wife
    Thaddeus, their oldest son, and three
    younger sons

Halford, Mr., the miller, his wife, Marian
    Harriett, their adopted daughter

Bowen, Ansell and his wife
    Their sons: Benson, Caleb, Elias
    (militia officer), Frank (militia officer),
    George (tanner), Harmon (black-
    smith) Ike (soldier) Joe (soldier), Kize,
    Luther, Moses, Violet and Verbena
    (twin daughters)

Buchanan, Warren, storekeeper and his
wife, Lilia

Chadwick, their son, soldier in the 23d Georgia infantry
Jeremiah, their son

Moody Simpson, distiller
Jefferson Childs, Campbellite itinerant minister
James Chastain, county militia captain
Levi McFarlin, sweetheart of Mary Jane Covington

GEORGIA INFANTRY BRIGADE
General Seth Barton
General Carter Stevenson

40TH GEORGIA INFANTRY REGIMENT
Colonel Abda Johnson
Major Raleigh Camp
Lt. Colonel Young

Company D
Captain Young, promoted to Lt. Colonel
Captain Hall
First Sergeant Williams

The Mess
Ananias Covington
David Covington
Eli Rutledge
Posey Huff
Rufus McDowell
Lewis Knell
Hugh Owens

Other Mess members: Burnett,
Dempsey, Jerome Green, Ira Cobb

52nd Regiment, Company I
Howell Covington, Tom Covington,
Jefferson Childs, Moody Simpson

43rd Regiment, Company C
Jacob Wilder, Alex Graham,
Ike Bowen, Joe Bowen

Other General Officers: Kirby Smith,
Braxton Bragg, Joseph Johnston,
"Old Straight" Stewart

Ben Jordan, leader of bushwhacker gang

Acknowledgements

My husband Bill endured many hours of my distraction, traveled with me to Georgia, drove me to re-enactments, and took me seriously. He read several versions of the story, gave me good advice, never questioned how much I was spending on books and photocopies, and insisted that I have a book to show for it all.

In memory of my friends Sharon Boardway, Dee Merrell, Jeff Holder, and Donna Sisson who, without having read a word of it, believed that I would write a good story, and my cousin Edward Meeks who was a Covington, read the manuscript, and loved the characters.

With special thanks to Virginia Covington Dial, my first cousin twice removed, who gave me the family's version of the story and took me to a Covington family reunion.

My fellow writers who had faith in me before I did: Wendy Tyree and Jenny Alexander, my first listeners

Mary Robson, Sally McNall, and Debbie Miller, forever writing friends.

Judith Barrington & Ruth Gundle for *The Flight of the Mind;* Karen Joy Fowler for her workshop on historical fiction at Haystack, Cannon Beach; Michael Olson who read an early draft and questioned the right stuff; Karen Fisher who edited and coached me through many drafts, turning it into more; Cathy Smith for her final reading and support of the characters; Lea Page, always ready and willing to help; Tami Haaland for insisting, in the end, that I self-publish to have a real book; Anne Depue, my agent, for her story suggestions and for always trying; Pacific Northwest Writers Association; Rock Creek Writers; Cheri Lasota for format and cover; Craig Lancaster for making it happen.

Members of the Generals Barton & Stovall History & Heritage Association: Mike Griggs and Gary Goodson for answering every question and coming up with more details to consider; Kay Borden and Bob & Randy Lotridge for their kindness to the only Yankee in the group; the guys on the bus for including me, answering my military questions seriously, and sharing their jokes and recipes for brains and eggs.

Professor Robert S. Davis for his correspondence, oral history interview, and discussion of the "complicated fairy tale about the Civil War and the Confederate States of America having nothing to do with slavery"; Reverend

Charles O. Walker for the map and his articles about Pickens County; the Confederate re-enactors at the Battle of Port Gamble, June 26, 2006 and the School of the Battalion and Battle of Marblemount, April 29, 2006; Atlanta History Center; Vicksburg National Park; Cumberland Gap National Historical Park; Perryville Battlefield State Historic Site; Public libraries in Pickens, Cherokee, and Dawson counties, Georgia.

Family members who cheered me on: Emily Hilderman, Kristen Carder, Jeanette Shultz, Annie & Rick Meeks. And my sisters, Ruth Lohela and Joyce Herod.

Old friends who honored the story and kept listening: Marita Holder, Ann Flaharty & Jay Holder, Jill Holder & Dana Dugall, Barb Stoll, Suzanne Matsen, Ward & Anne Marie Carson, Sally & Carl Yanagawa

New friends who kept me going: Jodie Moore, Kerri Wolfson, Cathie Osmun, Jim & Marybeth Woodcock, Bob Nickoloff, Gwen Williams, Annie McNamara, Polly Richter, Judith Gregory, Hope Smith

Covington Hang is Lee Cooper's first novel. She is a published poet and has worked as a writer, editor, and oral historian. She and her husband Bill, after living in many places around the country, reside in Red Lodge, Montana. She is a member of Rock Creek Writers.

Covington Hang is the coming of age and going to war story of a sister and brother in northern Georgia during the Civil War. It is a portrait of a family, their neighbors, conflicting politics, and the men who reluctantly served in the Confederate Army of Tennessee.

In the spring of 1861, Ananias Covington, at age eighteen, is trying to be his own man. Against the beliefs of their Unionist father, he and his brothers enlist in the Georgia Infantry Brigade to avoid conscription. A competent soldier, he questions the South's cause and conduct of the War. He wants most to go home, continue his education, and marry his sweetheart. When he deserts to carry home his wounded brother, he faces a different war within the War.

His sister, Eliza Ann, is fourteen, the youngest daughter in their large family. Her war is at home on the farm, working the fields, defending herself from home guards and jealous neighbors, and learning more of life, war, death, and grief than she wants to know. When two of her brothers are murdered by Confederate bushwhackers, she finds the strength and courage to care for their bodies, help her family when they need her most, and take a chance on her own love.